AF479495

THE RAPTOR'S GRASP

FREYA SMALLWOOD

TEKLA

Always first to Rita

Contents

Principal and Recurring Characters

LISETTE HOUSEMAN, lit lecturer at El Al U.; her husband ALLAN, oceanography professor

GERALD MACKEY, driver of a car Lisette encountered near the beach

DR. OMAR GEORGE BRADLEY ("OGY" = OH gee), brain surgeon, neuroscientist, med school professor, and widower of SYLVIA BROWNELL; their adult children, ANTHEA and CAELAN

DAN GRISWOLD, Anthea Bradley's maybe-fiancé

WILEY CHROMSTAD, city councilman and Ogy's neighbor on Avenida Placida

DETECTIVE TOR ABELOVE of the Santa Christina P.D.'s Homicide Division; his wife, LINDA and children CLEMATIS (Clemma, Clemmie), ANDREW AND TIMOTHY

HIRAM ADLER, Provost of El Al U.; his wife PRICILLA and son WOLF

BABBY BLENHEIM and LIONEL FRIEDLANDISHER; both deceased. Ogy's former neighbor to west and her husband

TED FRIEDLAND, software designer, now Ogy's next-door neighbor

INGRID BECKER, archaeological anthropologist, widow of MATTHIAS, resident at Casa Bunya Retirement Home

MRS. PARK, the Bradleys' cleaning dominatrix

JON DOERR, U.S. Navy oceanographer and member of the Santa Christina Diving Club

CRIS HARBISON, graduate of El Albergue U.'s Institute of Oceanography

RON SEAGRAVE, astrophysicist at El Al U.; his wife, GLORIA and daughter, LYNLEIGH; Ogy's neighbors two doors east.

CLAIRE FIELDS, administrative assistant at the oceanography school

REBECCA SAVAGE, chairwoman of the oceanography school

GINGER GUARDIAN, elementary school teacher; her son PETER, with Down syndrome

MARJORIE KIMURA and nurseryman HIROSHI KIMURA, Linda Abelove's parents

ARTIE VACCARI, homeless waiter who frequents El Albergue's beach area

DETECTIVE CHUCK LIANOPOULOS and OFFICERS ALVARO LOPEZ, BRUNO BELKNAP and BETTINA SMITHERS; also CAPTAIN TONY MARCOS, all from the SCPD's Homicide Division

THE REVEREND JIM MANNERING, Allan Houseman's minister

CHIEF BILL MARGOLIES of the Santa Christina Police Department

ROCCO, restaurant Volpe di Sera's original but still debonair barkeeper

ESTHER AND MANNY COLEMAN, Ogy's next-door neighbors

LITTLE PIGGY, proprietress-chef of This Little Piggy's porkery

MASTER HWAN, owner-instructor at Seoul Dojang; his students JANE, MARA and NADINE

NICOLA HARBISON, Cris's mother

ELINOR BURNS, Allan Houseman's half-sister

GLADYS APTED, manager of Casa Bunya Retirement Home

PEACHES, the Housemans' orange tabby; GHAZI, Ogy's Rhodesian ridgeback; CONTRAIL, Tor's Irish wolfhound; and LEILIA, Ted's Abyssinian cat

THE
RAPTOR'S
GRASP

ONE

THE SCARF STRANGLER

It took months — years? To admit there was a chance. Had she caused a death?

After her Tuesday run Lisette Houseman strolled to the corner of Avenida del Sol and Strand Road as a Lincoln MKZ with open windows lurched to a halt, rocking at the STOP sign. Music too close and loud mixed with the voices of rowdy teens in the car made her glance across the street to the beach area's Homeless Guy, reading on his bench outside the taco shop.

As she approached the curb, a young girl raised herself to lean out the car's back window and fling the contents of a soda cup into her face.

Momentarily blinded, Lisette gasped and heard a burst of female laughter, then saw ice pellets cascading down her sweatshirt.

The girl who had doused her wore a scarf that hung outside the window. Thinking, *Wait! Why — ?* Lisette's palm touched knotted silk.

But immediate revulsion at that personal contact caused her to draw back as someone shrieked, *"Put the window up!"*

While she fled across Strand Road, the Lincoln lurched left.

Later she would wish she had looked back at Mr. Homeless Guy perusing a free real estate magazine of luxury estates, but while wiping her eyes on a sleeve she had forgotten him.

The next afternoon El Albergue's Wednesday weekly *Strand Piper* reported that the girl who threw root beer at her was dead. Santa Christina Police were searching for the "girl" who yanked her scarf while the car drove away and — according to the *Piper's* report — the back window going up asphyxiated her.

Lisette was stunned. *That was untrue! AND LUDICROUS.* Surely a rising car window lacked sufficient force to do that? Besides, she had touched the scarf for scarcely a second.

At fault was the driver who threw the window up while somebody's head was thrust outside it!

But clearly the vehicle's occupants must have colluded in their account.

All afternoon Tuesday she'd been in an anxious dark mood. The ugly incident was so upsetting she couldn't tell Allan about it. After last year's argument about the university's policy of student evaluations, she had not wanted to revisit the subject of malicious young adults.

Then Wednesday after dinner he exclaimed, "Lise, read this story about some stupid beast who strangled a kid in a car here…!"

Terrified, Lisette tried to recollect exactly what had happened. Now she worried —

The leisurely homeless smoker on a bench across Strand Road might have been watching the incident over his magazine. But, if so — how much did he observe?

Did he see her hand scarcely brush the scarf?

Did he read her sweatshirt?

In southern California, it proclaimed "HAVERFORD, PA."

She memorized the name of the driver — "Gerald Mackey" — quoted as saying he would "find that girl who killed my sister."

Lisette was thankful she looked younger than her age.

On Thursday she had her hair cut short and bleached blonde.

"What happened to you, who did that!"

Just arrived home, Allan turned from the front door and flung up his right arm in horror, knocking the shade off the floor lamp.

"If you hate it I can change it back. Next month."

Forlornly he pleaded, "Where's all your beautiful hair…?"

As the proud scientist drooped, his left hand released their mail. Envelopes and circulars fell slapping the Mexican tiles like mock applause. A science journal bonked the head of the cat coming to greet him, causing her to leap with a snarl onto the magazine rack.

"Oh, Peaches!"

When Allan extended a hand in apology, the rack toppled with a crash. Not consoled, the indignant cat bounded yowling from the room.

In the little Spanish house they had made so cozy together, suddenly Lisette's legs weakened with a sense of collapsing toward a chasm. If his "stupid beast" wife was somehow identified, the renowned oceanographer would feel disgraced. Unlike her ruined hair, which could grow back, Allan's love for her would be forever bleached away by caustic scandal.

Two days after the story in the *Strand Piper* — an eternity — the *Santa Christina Sentinel* printed new facts about Tuesday's fatal accident. Usually a truck belonging to Strand Kayak Shop was parked outside it. Evidently when her brother swerved around the corner, Miss Mackey's rigidly wedged head had struck the truck's sideview mirror, mounted on a long arm. The police pathologist who discovered contusions on her skull and throat declared that, even at just twenty miles per hour, the force of that collision had fatally fractured her hyoid bone.

This news absolved the "girl" who "yanked" the scarf!

… But not if people believed she'd held the scarf and trapped a young teen's head.

Lisette stopped running on the Strand. If obliged to enter the beach area, she watched nervously for the Homeless Guy; but apparently the accident's potential witness had disappeared. Still she suffered chronic fear of the male driver who had threatened her — in the newspaper! If he was violent, didn't that mean — if he ever found her, *he must act with stealth?*

Although friends' joking references to the Strand's new local legend of a "scarf strangler" tormented her, she did not dare bring up the exculpatory report of that accident's bludgeoning truck mirror. Over two years of silence, a vivid visual memory of her encounter with the Lincoln still affirmed her innocence.

… Until one day, a damning new thought occurred — *might her own brief touch have caused a critical second's hesitation in the girl's intent to pull her head inside the car?*

Now when she infrequently ventured onto Strand Road, Lisette felt secret shame. Wrongful public perception kept eroding her old self-knowledge, while Gerald's uncontested falsehood seeped its taint beneath her skin. Even when waking in pre-dawn hours, often in bed she sensed inner spoilage — a contaminating guilt that she vehemently disbelieved but struggled alone to defy.

TUESDAY AFTER THE FIRST

MONDAY

For Dr. "Ogy" (O.G.) Bradley, at home with his daughter and her maybe-fiancé on election night, Tuesday evening's highlight — he thought — was a phone call from a neighbor winning an astonishing margin in his run for a city council seat.

"Funny," mused Councilman-elect Chromstad. "In the Marines nothing scary ever happened. Then —"

"Victory's assured, Wiley. Detective Abelove will be pleased too, seeing you so publicly vindicated. Enjoy your party —"

But Wiley couldn't stop effusing thanks for Ogy's recent role in clearing him of a homicide charge. Such sincere praise caused sympathetic Dr. Bradley to forget his soufflé in the oven. He managed to salvage the rigidly over-baked dessert by serving its crusted top covered with the softer interior as a sort of sauce. After the presidential race was called early, Anthea slipped from the room. Her father and her fiancé watched further coverage accompanied by Ghazi, the Rhodesian ridgeback fidgeting with his pumpkin jingle toy beside the fire.

Looking bereft, Dan thanked Dr. Bradley again for the crunchy persimmon concoction.

"Agh, I made cardboard of it," scoffed Ogy. "Next time you come — soon, persimmon season doesn't last long — I promise you a proper one you won't need a knife to eat. With sauce, I skipped that speckled vanilla ooze Anthea loves so much because poor Wiley's been beyond anxious —"

But Ogy ceased disparaging the soufflé when he noticed Dan's eyes were swimming — had he made her neglected fiancé think that Anthea loved him less than vanilla sauce?

Scarcely three years had passed since O.G. Bradley lost his wife. He remained in mourning. Now, watching vulnerable Dan Griswold try to conceal misery, a frightening new concept pressed his heart: *losing Anthea.* The idea of losing such an exciting woman was unimaginable. With his own presumptuous words ringing in his ears, *Next time you come* — he remembered that this sweet man remained insecure in her affection.

A bolt of pity forcing Ogy to his feet only compounded the awkwardness of the moment. Searching to justify his abrupt move, he recognized an envelope on a nearby table.

Microbiologist Dan was computer-savvy. That newly arrived party invitation might divert him.

"This affair at the Provost's will be interesting." Ogy's grin predicted high amusement. "When the university was founded, the administration offered senior faculty the option of building a home on university land, some of it waterfront — near the oceanography school.

"Here's the invitation, for Saturday after Thanksgiving. This house belongs to Hiram Adler now. If you didn't know, he used to be White House Economics Advisor."

"Hope he has ideas for nudging up employment."

"This place they bought? — Top of the bluff over the Strand, forever sea view. But many people wouldn't want that house."

"How weird does a house have to be, to put you off owning the view?"

"Oh, it's a fine house, but the lot is downright fearsome. The backyard, it just — plunges away. Nobody with children would consider it."

"You can install a *fence?*"

"Dan. Kids climb fences. Think — a tall fence would cover the view, and a low one is gym equipment. The Adlers wanted to install a glass screen like people do on decks, as windbreaks. Only nobody wanted the job, working even a few feet from the edge. Cliffs are unstable. Chunks fall down sometimes."

"Guess I don't want that job either."

"One of the contractors told Priscilla, 'Ma'am, if we did install it for you, who would you get to clean the other side of the glass?"

He handed Dan a computer-printed page decorated with pale dollar signs. "*In Support of the U.S. Economy,*" it began, "*Spend all you can on Black Friday.*"

Below that, "*THEN COME CELEBRATE BLACK SATURDAY!*"

The time and the address of the Adlers' home were provided next. Under them was an added stipulation: *"Attire: BLACK. Anyone wearing* RED *turned away at the door."*

The invitation was personally signed by Priscilla Adler. At the bottom of the page appeared the hint, *"Don't you really want a new car?"*

When the news show commentators deferred to an analyst with electoral vote maps, Dan interrupted the tally.

"Is something happening?"

"You mean… besides that we've just elected a new president?"

"You and I are left alone here. Are we supposed to be having a heart-to-heart or something? Because I wasn't informed, if we are."

"Why would we do that?"

"It wouldn't have been my idea. But Anthea's disappeared."

"Oh, she always floats away to work a bit, you must know. How she gets ahead."

"While I get nowhere," sighed the researcher.

"Bosh. You have post-docs pouring out of your ears."

"But not money. *I* wouldn't consider me an attractive suitor."

"It's a bad job market for highly trained scientists now. Still, if you're doing the work you love, consider yourself lucky."

Even to himself, Ogy's assurance sounded pompous.

"I complain too much. I'm driving her away," mourned Dan, glancing toward the den.

"Trust me, Thea's tending to something important. Besides —" Trying a different tack, he lamented, "You're aware that my own son with a top-notch degree appears to be doing nothing whatsoever. Just built himself a crude shed in New England and… contemplates injustice, I suppose. I know Thea sends him money — enough to hold off frostbite, anyway."

"Sorry to keep bringing myself up. You've got worries too."

"Yes, and I make her bear the brunt of them, damn me."

"Damn both of us. Only — *is she hinting for me to leave?*"

The normally tactful scientist sounded so wantonly needy that Dr. Bradley reached for the wine bottle.

But then the study door opened, and with a laptop folded under her arm hospital director Anthea Bradley did return — dazed, and strangely halting.

Witnessing that young spirit apparently shut down, Ogy's mind balked, unwilling to believe such languor in his bold brave girl.

When Dan observed Anthea's father suddenly transfixed by dread, he swiveled on the sofa to confront some ambush.

Thea might have been sleepwalking — except that her blank face suggested consciousness… somewhere.

Both men loved her, but were alarmed in different ways. Her physician father's first reaction was reflexively to seek a medical reason for her shocked look. Too young to consider mortal dangers, her lover became more convinced she would revoke their wobbly engagement.

"*Daddy…?*"

Her whimper sounded so unlike competent, implacable Anthea that Ogy and Dan both jumped up. Clearly she was trying not to cry.

Ghazi on his rug before the fireplace unfolded upwards too.

"There's a photo of the house — *this* house. — On the internet…. And… one of Mom's bronze statue — of Caelan….

"*…DADDY?*"

Baffled and afraid, Ogy rushed to hold her as she wept.

The laptop pressed against her ribs, his daughter threw an arm around his neck.

"The people of New Hampshire? *They've just elected Cael to Congress!*"

"WHAT? No. No."

"Yes! Yes, it's true! I was just looking over the hospital accounts, half-watching the TV. 'Caelan Bradley' zipped by…. I thought I must have misread it, but —"

"No. They couldn't. *He lives in a chicken coop!* He still doesn't have a job, does he?"

"Sounds like he has one *now.*" Dan Griswold did not disguise his envy.

"You've seen that 'fort' he built out back? That heap? He lives in an eyesore like that, with some hodgepodge roof?"

"But that's *why*, Daddy. New Hampshire voters like Cael's chicken coop house. He's not materialistic." She dabbed an orange witch paper napkin at her tears.

"Everybody's scared." Dan sounded defensive. "We've got a recession in the works."

"He doesn't even own a phone!"

"No. But his campaign office seemed to have several. It sounded really busy there. I called — and spoke to a thrilled old lady."

"What did she…?"

"Those photos I saw posted online… were to discredit him. They backfired. He's lived there for quite a long time. So simply. As an environmentalist. They *like him.* Cael… has a following."

Her father started to laugh. He laughed so hard he had to sit down.

"This lady said — it wasn't even his idea to run. They had to talk him into it."

Ogy dragged himself upright again. "Champagne, obviously," he chortled, heading for the kitchen.

Anthea slipped into Dan's arms and kissed his cheek.

"Danny," she whispered, "I've never told this to anyone, but Dad's old friend Ingrid from their archaeology days — sometimes she calls him 'Zeus.' After the champagne, please make your excuses, okay?"

Dan took the paper napkin to sweep its broomstick over her wet cheeks.

"Poor Daddy…. He has to be thinking about our mother now."

With an arm around her, Dan brushed sun-streaked hair back from Persian eyes with the luster of dark plums ripening to brown.

"While she was dying Mom fretted so much and cried so long, about my poor brother. And now I'm worried…. With this? Caelan a *congressman*?"

When she shook her head the privacy curtain of hair fell across her face again.

"Our big tough 'Zeus' may just dissolve."

THREE

PARLAY

The Sunday after election day was two weeks shy of five months since the heart attack Dr. Bradley suffered while preventing a murder. When email arrived with a reminder of his diving club's next meeting, without consulting his cardiologist he decided to attempt a deep dive. But as the *Urchin* headed out to sea he was disappointed that his friend Detective Abelove was not aboard. Very likely, Tor was teaching his volunteer surfing class for barrio kids — those lesson dates were dictated by tides. Not many minutes into the brief journey offshore Ogy was approached by Jon Doerr, an oceanographer whom he had first met on his last excursion, in June.

"O.G. Bradley! Great to have you back," called Jon, still fastening his dive suit.

"Grateful not to be forgotten, Jon."

"Ah. Touchy subject. I'm losing memory even faster than hair," carped the totally bald Navy scientist. "But seeing you now reminds me of one thing I forgot. I was trying to recall the name of a grad student I met — at your oceanography school. 'Cris' something. 'Madison' — 'Harrison'? No. Why this constant mental whispering of 'arbitrage'…?"

Sympathetic brain surgeon Bradley nodded. "Probably it's on your 'down' elevator right now," he diagnosed.

"Talented kid. Serious athlete too. He was supposed to go to Woods Hole —"

"I know most ocean sciences faculty, but don't have contact with their students."

"Wait — the point is, this terrific kid was excited he'd landed a place on a Pacific research voyage. But something happened. I heard half a rumor he got sick — then nothing."

"'Harbison!' Ha. Thanks, Ogy, it wafted in with you. Cris Harbison. Promising scientist. And a gymnast.

"This was… two and a half, maybe three years ago now? I've wondered what became of him. The big guy in charge was Allan Houseman —"

"Allan I do know, but not well. Basically we were guests at the same dinner party once. Although that was memorable, I know them more by campus reputation."

"How 'memorable'?"

"It was just… unfortunate. More about Lisette than him. She's a popular lecturer."

"What field?"

"History of the novel, I think."

"Way more diverting than organic chemistry. You're being evasive."

"What was uncomfortable this particular evening was — while she lectured us about how uncaring *'all these elites'* are, meaning us — everybody at the table except possibly Allan was aware that the man she was staring at so accusingly is a surgeon who founded a clinic for the poor downtown, where he donates two days a week of his highly valuable time."

Instead of sitting below with the other members, they had been standing at the *Urchin*'s rail. As the engine quit the rest of the group began to assemble on deck.

Jon shook his head. "Immersion hour."

Ogy and his dive partner agreed that they would not go very deep or remain down very long. But despite his extended absence from the realm of sea life, swimming about in the partial gloom did not prompt his usual almost religious elation. Typically, the lumpy underwater terrain of Christina's Shelf would entertain him with the whimsical suggestion that its valleys were enlarged convolutions of the human brain he researched. But today the beguiling submerged scene appeared paradoxically arid, parched of inspiration.

Last Tuesday evening he had promptly sent a telegram of congratulations to his son's congressional campaign office. Caelan did not respond. Yesterday over lunch Anthea pointed out, "He must have received lots of mail. I'd guess he's not even aware of ours."

Seeing her father so despondent, she added, "Clearly he's busy, and probably not even home now. In his *shed*? Unlikely. — No, don't look at me like that! We're not in some secret correspondence. I'm as ignorant and neglected as you."

Unable to recall when he'd last seen Cael, down here the person Ogy particularly missed was his fellow diver Detective Abelove, with whom he shared no real ties. He felt a forlorn sense of disconnect. — And now, gossip's remorse. He kept recalling his wife, ever the artist, as she gazed in admiration across a table at Lisette Houseman, whose lyric face in turn was cocked in poignant concern for invalid Mrs. Bradley.

Back on board, the other divers just nodded and descended out of the November gusts. Although Dr. Bradley had been in the newspapers for solving one murder and foiling another, apparently the physician and Navy scientist had more routine topics to discuss.

Alone again in brusque muffling wind at the rail, Ogy resumed, "You called Houseman 'the big guy,' What's the 'big' part?"

"Allan wrote a book. One. But it made a splash early in his career. And the way he's distinguished himself since has been the diligence with which he's parlayed it into remarkable prominence and prestige."

"You're not a fan."

"Initially. It was a very good book. *Sinks and Sediments of the Pacific Plate.* But his later efforts have been much more as a politician than a researcher. Broadcasts his name everywhere. Brings in money. To his own pocket, I mean."

"From where?"

"Hah. Strange places, Ogy."

"Two and a half years ago my wife was fighting — losing — to cancer."

"Sorry. I didn't know."

"If there was any talk of this 'Cris' you like? I wasn't around campus much then."

"Forget it. Not important."

But after the *Urchin*'s return to their downtown pier, the oceanographer caught up with Dr. Bradley on the path to the parking lot, calling, "Ogy! Hold on."

When Ogy turned back, Jon was shaking his head.

"I didn't express well what's bugging me. About Harbison? What I was told by people at your school is — Cris just completely disappeared. He'd had friends, a girlfriend — but suddenly —"

"That does sound strange."

"More like, unheard of. Popular students, particularly scholars with a future? They don't vanish without anybody's even hearing shreds of rumor. Just — shrugs."

Turning toward his car, Jon waved apologetically. "Not my student, though. I know, none of my business."

"Still."

FOUR

EVALUATIONS

The Housemans' bungalow on Calle Canciones del Mar was just four short blocks from the ocean. Lisette loved the assertive way marine air coursed through its kitchen and bedroom. In bed they felt rocked by the cradle song of the sea. Their living room's broad arched window surveyed a walled front garden. With its small black-trunked eucalyptus weeping tiny coral blossoms, the enclosure's ferns and hanging fuchsias provided a picture so serene that they had arranged their desks back to back beside the window's antique leaded panes. Often its center decoration of a red tinted glass swag was inspected by hummingbirds. Both academics enjoyed working together at home, with soft music playing, and coffee or wine.

But on the evening before Thanksgiving, while Lisette was happily reading her students' short essays about D. H. Lawrence's tortoise poem, Allan started to curse under his breath.

Finally he muttered, "Damn you brats. *I know who you are…!"*

After the university instituted a policy of class evaluations by undergraduates, Allan's attitude toward them had gradually turned acrimonious. During the first year responses on the forms were straightforward. But soon students' criticisms became more aggressively *ad hominem.* When her husband became annoyed by some sneering critiques, Lisette argued that the bad manners of a mean-spirited few did not discredit the usefulness of reviews by those who performed them scrupulously.

"We shouldn't take childish jabs personally," she soothed. "Readers disregard them."

"You wouldn't say that if somebody described *you* as 'the runt in a litter of ferrets,'" growled her husband.

To soothe him, she had helped him match the anonymous evaluation forms by handwriting with his students' exams, thus identifying them all. Allan was shocked to discover that one friendly, even sycophantic young man had written quite nasty comments.

"Do NOT lower his grade," she warned. "Then you'd be as spiteful as he is."

"Don't watch," he mumbled.

But tonight, sipping juice from the season's early blood oranges on Thanksgiving Eve, she was amazed to see him slam the box of exams onto the floor, then stand and stomp on it.

"Three of them!" he exclaimed. "They come skateboarding in for the second midterm in their hoodies pulled over their big long hair

— and I pay no notice. But on two short essay questions, I've got three identical answers! *Identical!* They're cheating somehow — I wonder if there aren't earbuds hidden in all that messy hair, with recorded crib sheets?"

"You're sure?"

"Hell, yes. And if I say anything to the little crooks, I'll get skewered in the *evaluation.*

"This nonsense confers power they can't handle. It fosters sadism," he harangued.

"Oh, I can't believe the evaluations *created* sadism — NO, Peaches!"

Lisette hustled around the desks to retrieve the crunched cardboard box of midterms stamped with a shoe print from under the cat's inquisitive nose. *"Not your litter box!"*

"We're corrupting mildly rebellious undergraduates into nihilists, and this topsy-turvy system of students-grade-professors undermines an ages-old institution. Instead of building up their professional reputations, now untenured people curry favor with the kids. *Telling jokes!* I may start teaching just graduate classes —"

"Oh. Allan —" She turned back. "Can you tell me? What happened to Cris Harbison?"

"Cris. Why do you ask?"

"That med school surgeon we met once — his wife was the sculptress — he stopped me outside the library and asked about him."

"I'm not sure where he is. He hurt his foot — or leg, was it, during that biomass study off the Pitcairns. And flew home. Cris was headed for Woods Hole — but if he's still there after this long, I couldn't say."

"You're not there to amuse the kids," she conceded. "But an angry display would generate negative stories in the student paper."

"I'll tell you what won't help my popularity, Lise. If we go to the Adlers' party Saturday and you start patronizing your betters in that way you tend to do —"

Allan dogged her as she carried his carton of stomped tests to the laundry room.

"My betters?"

"Yes. Where celebrated people like the Adlers are concerned? Speaking of pretensions, I can't believe you've sent off another of these donations without consulting me." He plugged in the iron for her. "There is a budget, and although it may seem crass, the payment on the Mercedes comes before some African tuberculosis fund."

"It was only a hundred dollars."

"A hundred is a lot of money. I sympathize, but you can send ten or twenty like everybody else."

"What do I have in black that you'd like me to wear to the party?"

"That Audrey Hepburn outfit like in *Sabrina.* Simple and you look fabulous in it."

"If I'm 'fabulous' in my teaching pants."

"Lise, I'm sorry. That's so good of you." With a kiss on the back of her head, he removed the bottom exams from the box to return to his desk as she began ironing shoe imprints from the crimped top pages.

Lisette had experienced a scare today. Since tomorrow was Thanksgiving, the Strand was far more crowded than usual. Visiting relatives were sent out to entertain themselves on the beach while serious cooking was attended. She wore her old "HAVERFORD" sweatshirt and risked walking on the beach. But on Strand Road outside Burger Basement she had been aghast to see her homeless witness!

On his bench again, the smoking vagrant did not award her even a glance.

That disregard alone spooked Mrs. Houseman.

Routinely, when passing male strangers she attracted notice longer than a glance.

FIVE

BEND THE CULTURE

Apart from financing their house and the children's education, Ogy and Sylvia had never spent much money. He bought his clothes at Sears because he could park close. She had often sewn her outfits because she admired the artistry of textiles. Their ordinary furniture was scarcely noticeable among family heirloom carpets and art works either created by Sylvia or collected during the elder Bradleys' archaeology tours in the Middle East.

But a strange catalysis occurred when exuberance over their son's election to Congress collided with the Adlers' party invitation whispering, *Don't you really want a new car?*

Unconscionably large for drives to campus, Ogy's sedan had been intended for eventually touring the USA with Sylvia. Now he admitted to himself that honestly he did want a new car — partly as a suggestive example to so many El Albergue residents driving gas-guzzling elevated performance vehicles; but overwhelmingly, in solidarity with the new ecology-minded representative of New Hampshire —

— And as an act of thanksgiving.

To entertain his astrophysicist neighbor Ron Seagrave, Ogy invited him along to a dealership where he signed away an insane amount of cash on a just-introduced lithium-ion battery pack roadster — black, to drive to tomorrow's Black Saturday fete.

The physicist was thrilled. As a hobbyist, Ron had designed a small windmill called the MiniWind Booster Boy for supplemental backyard power generation.

"Ted thinks his uncle Lionel underestimated the problems of selling Booster Boy in Uzbekistan, or wherever," sighed Professor Seagrave.

Ogy's new neighbor Ted Friedland had recently acquired half ownership of Ron's device, originally purchased by his aunt's entrepreneurial husband.

"Uzbekistan? Why there?"

"Lionel said, even people who live in caves with no electricity at all want to watch TV. But Ted says, in remote places you'd have trouble distributing the Boy. If we ever sell the company, maybe I'll start driving one of these. Great move, Ogy. Bend the culture."

Two weeks ago when Ogy invited Ted Friedland to accompany him and network for his tech firm at the Adlers' party, the young software designer had declined. He was spending lots of time with an attractive divorced schoolteacher and her son. But on Friday Ted called to say that the lady was unable to keep their date. He asked if he might still come to Provost Adler's party.

Ogy was delighted. On Saturday he drove the two hundred yards to Ted's house and was rewarded with whoops of ecstasy when Ted saw the innovative Tesla roadster in his driveway.

"WHAT HAVE YOU DONE, YOU MANIAC?" he crowed.

"We're arriving in black. Want to try it out?"

While a rapturous Ted drove the exotic roadster, Ogy explained how back in the 'sixties the new university had allowed senior faculty to build homes on university land.

"Pampering the privileged?"

"Maybe overly. Some people made egocentric design choices — like a big windowless ballet studio with mirrored walls. This family throwing the party has one of those oddities, but it's a quite attractive feature. There's a stage in the family room. Not big enough for a production of *West Side Story*. But adequate for a piano teacher who wanted her students to experience playing on a stage during recitals."

"Could convert to a nice reading room? Media room?"

"The Adlers are second owners, but I think they've maintained the intended use for it. Their son is atypical, not easy to describe —"

"Why should he be?"

"My son's not. Yours won't be. But their boy is certainly a musician and — with those parents? — Heaven knows what besides."

SIX

I KNOW WHO YOU ARE!

Lisette was not looking forward to the Adlers' party. Not if Allan was disposed to find fault with everything she said. But soon his mood should improve — a lot. As a member of The Lecture Notes, performing tonight, he had added a new black blazer to his wardrobe. The four men in their musical group included a pianist who could double on bass viol, plus three vocalists. Tonight the theme of the Notes' program of course was money. Their first number would be Barrett Strong's 1959 hit "Money (That's What I Want!)" featuring Allan's biologist friend Louis Lerner. Allan was soloist in the second, "Money Changes Everything." Since his tenor voice was distinctly sweet, its natural pathos created an unusual rendition. They would conclude with "Money Can't Buy Me Love," expecting other guests to sing along with the Beatles hit.

As they left home for the very short drive, Lisette opened her purse to retrieve sunglasses and discovered a small packet of cookies. They had been a holiday gift from a student. She knew the girl was fond of her. Opening the baggie, she sampled a cooky.

"What are you *doing*?" scolded her husband. "Don't eat junk now. You'll crumb up your lipstick."

"Yummy…!" she chirped, taking a second one. "I'm not offering you any."

Lisette did not tell him she had heard that the Adlers, her *betters,* often served sushi at their parties. She did not intend to apologize for not wanting to eat sushi.

"There's going to be *sushi*," he protested as she crunched. "It's great, you'll love it."

"I don't want sushi."

"Fine, Lise. Be a little Pittsburgh provincial forever."

Above all, she did not want to tell Allan she was afraid of eating raw seafood because she thought she might be pregnant. That wasn't in his budget.

By the time the Housemans had parked and hurried back to the Adlers' address it was almost twenty minutes after the stated starting time for the Black Saturday party. They rang the bell and were waiting on the porch when somebody else walked up.

Surprising them, this newcomer made both Allan and Lise wonder if he was at the wrong house. Clearly he was very young, in his twenties.

"Hi," he nodded without looking at them. The Housemans did the same. All three stared at the door. But there was no way Allan and Lisette could miss the fact that the new arrival was wearing a very bright red T-shirt — when their invitations had expressly forbidden red clothing. Not only that, this red shirt was covered with dozens of letter "X"s drawn with black marker — huge "X"s, tiny ones and every size in between.

Priscilla Adler opened the door with a broad smile already lighting her face. She and Hiram were both still exhilarated because just minutes earlier totally plain Ogy Bradley had arrived in a one-day-old, state-of-the-art, zero-emissions pricey vehicle — a *black* one, purchased to attend their rally for the U.S. economy!

But when she saw the negative-looking "X"-covered red shirt, Priscilla's euphoric grin suddenly twisted and her eyes narrowed with suspicion.

"Madam, good evening," unrolled the young man's unctuous baritone. *"My presence is urgently required here."*

Mrs. Adler was not about to allow any dubious rule-breaking whippersnapper to outdo her in formality. She drew herself up to her full four feet eleven inches and raised her nose into the air, as if it might bestow an extra inch of loft.

"Wait," she commanded her challenger. "While I confer."

Then, turning to the Housemans, "You two," she waved, "Proceed."

Once past Priscilla, Allan immediately plunged into the crowd in search of his singing group. Lisette lingered near the entry hall to see what would happen.

Almost immediately the great macro thinker and advisor to presidents appeared with his vigorous mowing charge to confront a troublemaker. But when he saw the young guest on his doorstep Hiram Adler nearly swallowed his cigar.

Sometimes when Provost Adler chomped on a cheroot, brown juice would slide from the corner of his mouth. People who had known him a long while claimed that was why he maintained a short thick beard — to sop it up. Now he removed the cigar and wiped his mouth with a sleeve that already bore streaks.

"I KNOW WHO YOU ARE…!" he bellowed. "Come on in here."

Carrying the cigar with one hand and grasping the upper arm of his guest in the "X"ed-up red shirt with the other, he strode back into his crowded family room. Ready with a baby grand piano and microphone, the small stage looming ahead awaited performers.

"EVERYBODY? SOME RESPECTFUL SILENCE, PLEASE! …Thank you."

Priscilla scooted past to remove the cigar from his hand.

"For the non-economists in the room — allow me to introduce — *The Multiplier.*"

The few economists could be recognized by their applause for a young colleague's "multiplication" shirt.

"My wife's theme for this party was that we should celebrate the movement of American retailers into the territory of profits during this weekend's historically high-volume sales.

"— Our particular thanks, Dr. Bradley.

"But make no mistake, we're facing crisis. What the Keynesian Multiplier here reminds us is — to avert recession the government too must act. As a nation we must go *into the red —"*

Lisette petted the elderly Newfoundland who sat obligingly rolling her head to be caressed. Although she did not attempt to follow what Hiram Adler was saying, her eyes filled at the dog's nuzzling welcome and the importance of this economic moment.

So what if Allan got cranky when he felt crossed? They did love each other.

"It's not even personal, not really, if he puts me down sometimes," she recognized. *"I'm his comfort zone. I'm lucky to be here. These are wonderful people, I enjoy them all.*

"If I left Allan, some other woman would have my life."

She was feeling very happy, watching other scholars crowd around to congratulate that daring assistant professor who was already the hero of the evening, when someone approached her with a tray of hors' d'oeuvres that were not sushi.

After he extended the tray towards her with a polite but almost knowing smile, after she reached to accept a tiny quiche — Lisette realized that this server in a black jacket and bow tie was her long dreaded witness.

Not only had the Strand's Homeless Guy returned. He might even recognize her.

SEVEN

PRELUDES

Lisette returned the waiter's near-smile, hoping that in different clothing she did not remind him of the catastrophe he had witnessed from Strand Road's fish taco shop more than two years ago.

Fortunately the doorbell rang again, and since she had not moved into the expansive family room she was present when Allan's departmental assistant Claire Fields walked in.

At first she was a little surprised that a secretary had been invited to what appeared a convocation of luminaries; but then she recalled that Claire was a member of a service committee chaired by Priscilla Adler. Probably she was Priscilla's guest.

They greeted one another warmly. Lisette was awed by Claire, who used to perform with seals and whales at the water show on Christina Bay. After a co-worker was injured by a whale, though, her parents had pressured her to find an office job.

"I hope I haven't missed Allan's trio," she fretted.

"No. Ask somebody to explain to you about that guy in the red shirt. I didn't get the gist, but it was good theater."

A different server, a young and athletic-looking Black man, extended a tray of mulled wine in mugs. Lisette declined, thinking that later she would search for a non-alcoholic beverage.

After a half hour's circuit of the room to greet other guests, she found Allan in a close clot of mostly men, most of whom she did not know. The pianist/bassist Josh was there with the third trio member, new to The Lecture Notes. She had never heard him sing. All held mugs of the hot spiced wine, which they seemed to have forgotten as they crowded more closely together. On the stage behind them, the Adlers' son began playing Gershwin's *Three Preludes for Piano*.

Trying to maintain their conversation in a polite whisper, the circle of men with a few women kept constricting into a tighter but constantly shifting group. Lisette found it impossible to hear anything except the piano. Although friendly with these women staffers at the ocean school, she knew she was wearing a pasted-on smile for the benefit of Rebecca Savage, the Institute's senior oceanographer. Probably Rebecca guessed that Allan's wife only pretended to understand what they were discussing. From so many steaming mugs of glögg, the penetrating scent of cloves created a sweet fug trapped by bodies all leaning in.

Finally the Ocean Sciences' chairwoman lowered her face toward Lisette and whispered, "Don't be offended if Claire has to leave. Today is her mother's birthday."

Then just a few minutes into Wolf Adler's performance, an unfamiliar woman came to warn, "These Gershwin pieces are short and there are just three. You're next, better get ready."

Allen rolled his head in an "Oh, *great!*" gesture. But Rebecca was speaking, so he waited for her to finish before shoving his warm mug towards his wife.

"Hold that, won't be long," he said.

As people began to applaud Wolf's performance and Allan's group left the room, the press of the black-clad throng was pushing Lisette toward the adjacent room's tables laid out with sushi. She scrutinized the jewel-like rolls in pastel colors and could think only of salmonella.

"Allan will begin his solo soon," she assured herself. "Nobody will be offended if you just stand aside and listen."

Allan Houseman had a fine voice, and some of the audience were doubly entertained to observe his chic wife watching him. Long accustomed to delivering lectures, Lisette was surprised to feel so self-conscious at having become a spectacle during his solo. She felt as trapped as an insect on a pin. At least the mug was a prop, *something to do with your hands.* To present a more relaxed picture she kept swallowing warm sips, trying to look as if she enjoyed the glögg. But all she could think of was that homeless quiche server.

He had looked as if he was trying to remember where he had seen her before.

Her impulse was to turn and flee — but if her witness was watching, running now would only remind him of seeing her do exactly that on the day when somebody died on Strand Road.

What she needed to do was to hide from him. It shouldn't be hard, with everyone wearing black. Later she could try to keep the back of her anonymous black sweater toward him.

Then she realized how to avoid sushi and make the busy waiter quickly forget her, too —

When they get to "Money Can't Buy Me Love," just sneak outside for a few minutes and eat the rest of Andrea's good cookies.

Dr. Bradley had been circulating with Ted Friedland, making introductions. As he hoped, Hiram Adler showed interest in Ted's innovative restaurant guide app, once he understood that it was useful for sidewalk research during business trips to Wichita or St. Paul as well as in destination cities like Zurich or Madrid. Ogy and Ted got separated when a group of older ladies snagged Ted, wondering why they had never seen him before. A while later when they crossed paths again Ogy stopped him to remark, "Did you notice? One of the waiters is our local Homeless Guy who hangs out along the Strand. You've seen him."

"You don't mean — that Mediterranean-looking older one?"

"Yeah, this caterer hires his help from the homeless shelter."

"Bu — *but that's absolutely ridiculous!"* blustered Ted, striding off with two mugs of glögg for his pair of elderly female captors.

The university's dowagers had immediately been intrigued by the male ingenue who so incongruously walked in with preternatural O.G. Bradley. Amused, Ogy wondered how long it would take Ted to extricate himself.

Santa Christina's disadvantageous longitude in the Pacific Time Zone means that, even in high summer, the sun sets earlier than seems "fair" to residents from more northern latitudes. Although the hour was not late, a waxing crescent moon made this night a stunning dark background to the stars. There was still plenty of wood stacked beside the fireplace. Competing Monopoly games, London and New York, threatened to drag out toward morning. Guests had the options of

Italian decaf, or of Limoncello or Chambord. Obligingly, teen-aged Wolf Adler had produced a book of carols and would accompany anyone who wished to sing.

There was no reason to go home. And although the crowd in the spacious house appeared thinned, that was mostly because some guests had slipped outdoors to sip their coffee within the safe confines of the patio, marveling at the uninterrupted firmament above the sea.

When the doorbell rang again after nine o'clock, Priscilla could not imagine which of her invitees had not yet arrived. She was totally astonished, almost frightened, to discover four uniformed policemen on her front porch.

"Good evening, ma'am," said the one in front. "Are you having a party here tonight?"

"Yes, but we certainly aren't making any noise. Who —"

"Ma'am — I'm very sorry, but — are you missing anybody?"

"Miss....?"

"Maybe you should sit down, ma'am. I'm sorry, but — we have a body. On the rocks. Below your home."

The Adlers' Black Saturday observance shared a quality of all such successful gatherings — their leisurely affair had slipped the bounds of time. When that timelessness of music, conversation and Monopoly was disrupted by police intrusion, mentioning a death, the guests, although not drinking heavily, were at first uncertain. That dangerous dark space outside where some calamity had happened now seemed foreign. Many had not ventured out to see the Adlers' fabled 'eagle's nest' backyard.

Indoors the fire still crackled so hypnotically. Properties on "Piccadilly" and "Park Place" remained unsold.

But men in uniform were present now. Tugged from perplexity, soon everyone agreed — much earlier, they all had seen the slender woman who looked like a dancer; but no guest saw her leave the house. Even her husband with the lovely tenor voice had no idea why she would.

OLD FOREBODING

Years ago Tor Abelove heard the phrase "marriage of true minds" and promptly forgot it. His wife was a full-time mother and he was a homicide detective. Not much mental commonality there. Before joining the force he had been an internationally famed surfer. Linda was a competent surfer, but that was the extent of their shared interests. The marriage was unashamedly founded on passion. Equally, he realized, his attachment to his children was a matter of adoration, not of some sitcom "friendship." Because the practical concerns of their lives were separate, they seldom quarreled. But three weeks ago on election night, when they'd intended to watch local returns, they had floundered into a quarrel with potential for repercussions.

The previous day was Linda's birthday. As a gift, Tor enrolled her in a martial arts class. That did not bring smiles from either his in-laws or his wife. When she still looked somber the next evening, the likelihood that she and her mother had spent hours on the phone made him miserable. He knew, he *knew* a flower arranging class would suit her better than any martial art.

"It's not a case of buying you what I want myself! It was because I think you need it plus I think you would enjoy it. You need more stamina. It's a strain taking care of them all day."

"Speaking of which, I'd better go change Timmy for the night."

Perched on Linda's small boudoir chair beside the door Tor waited, churning with remorse, anger and hopelessness. Wondering if he really wanted Linda to glimpse his own mental landscape. Unsure that enrolling her had even been worth displeasing her mother, whom he liked. But Marjorie didn't comprehend his cop's view of the world either.

When Linda returned he tried to explain, "The class is a full body workout, it would make you feel good like you haven't in a long time."

"Don't tell me how I feel."

"Fine, then you tell me. How do you feel?"

"Like you don't find me attractive anymore."

"*What?*"

"I don't look good enough to interest you unless I get as firm as you are —"

"OH, I have something to prove here?" All Tor's Russian features were large, but now his steppe's-width grin revealed a phalanx of strong teeth. "Great! Hop in the bed, Linda."

"— Or at least as firm as that woman at the dojang you talk about. Joyce."

"Joyce? Perfect. She's exactly how I want you to be. But not 'cause Mini-Piston is something so attractive. Only because she is a *killer!* She's not much bigger than you, but I've sparred with her and *she can take me down.* Us guys talk — if anybody ever messes with Joyce, he is a dead man. We're all fans, her agility is amazing —"

"Do you hear what you're saying! You want to make me a KILLER —?"

Linda was sobbing, and Tor felt wretched that he had done this to her. He rolled with her onto the bed, holding her, guessing how hurt she must feel — and he understood that she did not, could not comprehend the fears he tried never to talk about.

"Why did you marry me, Tor? Why were you willing to have three children, if we — if my ordinary life isn't what you value and I disappoint you so much?"

"No, no, you don't! It's hard — maybe it's impossible to understand. But you and them — you're all I ever wanted. Exactly that is why I did it — "

"It's not fair, not *right* to expect a person to change so much."

" — Because I can't protect you always. Not every minute —"

"I don't want to be 'a killer.' I don't want to fight at all, even for *fun —?"*

Then Linda's very strong, always confident husband pled in a despairing squeal unimaginable from him, *"Help me, baby, please? Just try to understand... my life? The things I see each day — while I'm thinking about you? Who are so unprepared —"*

"I know you see bad things. But you can't ask me to change instead of the world changing. Darling — please don't want to make me a killer.... *I don't want to —"*

Tor pulled her very close and whispered, *"Oh, yes. You would want to!*

"Linda, listen to me — you are so beautiful. Your children are so beautiful! But if anyone ever grabbed Clemmie — *you would do anything. You would disable him. You would kill. To keep her.*

"It would help me…. To know you could handle it…."

"What has this job done to you…?"

Five months ago, Tor's friend Dr. Bradley had observed that Tor was "nothing if not controlled." Now the detective reasserted that control. Until he could speak calmly he stroked Linda's long hair. It seemed to respond, its fine sinew flexing to caress his fingers with erotic warmth.

"If it matters to you — even with all the years I've got in? I could give up the force. I don't want to. I don't say this easy. But I'd think about it. For you. But you've got to be clear — even if I worked in a bank — and I bet they'd be thrilled to get an ex-cop — even if I went back to giving surfing lessons, it wouldn't change anything. What I know now, about the world outside this house."

"Dr. Bradley's house — it had good karma too."

"She — was special. But, if I *was* working someplace else? The difference would be, then I would not be armed. And I couldn't call for backup. In this exact same ugly world."

While Linda wept quietly she held him reassuringly close.

Finally he did relax more.

"Honestly, I thought the class would be fun for you. It's just exercise. Not fighting."

"I'll go," she murmured. "I'll forget the 'killer' part. Think of it as exercise class."

"All very good manners there. Courtesy's essential, or you get kicked out of the dojo. Even your dad would approve of the place."

"I'll try not to embarrass him and you, getting kicked out."

"Just a workout with a partner. Not intimate. A lot like square dancing."

"Oh, I can picture you at *that.*" She sighed, "Other people get a sweater… earrings."

"That's another thing. I catch on that Marjorie expects me to buy you good clothes."

"I wasn't hinting for earrings."

"It's just — one, I don't know how to. Where I'd look for something you'd like. But, two — I don't know where you'd wear what I bought. I guess we could try going luxe for dinner. But usually you want to take the kids along. Maybe I should get you a season ticket to the opera? But you know I couldn't go with you, too likely I'm working."

"That's sweet. After Timmy's bigger, I'll go to the opera. Alone, I don't mind."

"Your mom's proud of you, wants to see you in classy outfits. The way I feel is, buy yourself something good. Up to five hundred, you don't have to ask me first, okay? The only… reluctance I have is, buy it if *you* want it. Not because somebody wants it for you."

"*Put your ring on,*" she whispered.

Detective Abelove slid off the bed and went to check the baby. Timmy was asleep, his one permitted daily bottle empty. Andy and Clemmie were sleeping too. When he returned to their room, his wife was under the covers, smiling now. He opened the bureau drawer and put on the wedding ring he was no longer willing to wear in front of criminals.

~ ~ ~

Notified about a suspicious accident at Hiram Adler's cliffside home, Tor remembered that recent election night, when with the door bolted and weapons near, the delicate satin length of Linda in his arms had felt absolutely protected.

Long before arriving at Bay Street to view the deceased woman, he lost November fourth's cozy feeling that he had found a simple way to make his family more secure.

The department was not yet certain this death was a crime. But the old foreboding had returned.

No woman was ever really safe.

Not lovely Lisette Houseman.

Not even Linda Abelove.

NINE

BLACK SATURDAY

Eventually released by the Santa Christina police, Dr. Bradley made the short drive to his next-door neighbor's home in silence. Tonight had been the maiden outing of his new car — more prophetically than he could have imagined, a black one.

When they turned onto Avenida Placida Ted said, "Instead of just dropping me off, Ogy, I'd appreciate it if you'd come in for a drink."

"I'd appreciate it too."

The little antique Spanish castle Ted had recently moved into was designed with beautiful detail. As they walked in, its dramatic architecture was immediately upstaged by snivels of neglect from

Babby Blenheim's loquacious Abyssinian cat, Leilia, whom Ted had inherited.

"You've put her leg warmers on her!" exclaimed Ogy, scarcely able to believe that this young man with such large hands had managed to maneuver the independent-minded cat into all four of the rose-colored stockings Babby had fashioned for her from a pair of woolen gloves.

"Yeah, well, laugh at me. I won't let you see my arms for a week or two. But she's a skinny little thing. Aunt Babby thought the house was too cold for an equatorial cat, and I admit I prefer keeping it near sixty degrees. So I owe her. Bought a sweater, too."

Ogy could not help noticing that the only change in Babby's living room during the few months since Ted Friedland had moved in was the addition of a climbing tower for Leilia.

"Come have a look in Uncle Nel's wine cellar — unless you'd rather have a whiskey?"

"No, wine sounds right. A disaster like this demands thought. Not oblivion."

"Yep."

With his cane Ogy followed his friend's nephew to the former coat closet, which Lionel had converted for his wine collection after marrying Babby. When he saw the array of premium bottles, he was tempted to demur and advise Ted not to race through these vintages recklessly.

But not only had Ted found a very good job with a Santa Christina tech firm, he was also inheriting a substantial amount of money. He could replenish this cellar without a thought.

The creator of an international online guide to fine restaurants opened the French burgundy his new neighbor selected, then offered the solemn toast, *"Mrs.* and Mr. Houseman."

For a time they sat quietly. The circumstances of his aunt Babby's death had been deeply disturbing for Ted, and Ogy did not question that the sensitive young man must still be struggling with that.

Finally Ted said, "Those people tonight — all new to me. Thanks, Doc, for taking me. Mr. Adler — he seems really a sharp man. But, first impressions? I was turned off by this guy Houseman. Thought, 'Well, don't want to buddy up with that one.' And then? Four hours later? The poor man is sitting there crying. My heart is bleeding for him. And I'm thinking… *What a goddamned jerk I am. I don't know him. I'm writing him off…?*"

"And he sure does sing like an angel," sighed Ogy. "I have to say — I've got about the same confession as you. But worse. Your quick judgment at least was private. Not mine.

"It was about *her*. I cringe to say — I disparaged her to a friend. Once at a dinner she annoyed some people, preaching — there's my interpretation, see — asserting that the well-to-do don't care about the poor. This evening I've been thinking, 'Why couldn't I interpret that situation as — *she just wanted to talk about what's important to her?'*

"Because that's all she was doing. Instead I reacted churlishly. To a good woman who might be a suicide. — I wonder if she was an investor? Maybe… just lost their savings…? In an economic mess Adler's trying to get us all to take seriously…."

Ted nodded, stroking Leilia on his shoulder.

"This… concentrates the mind."

"Oh yes."

"I was thinking of calling you anyway. With my dad gone. And Uncle Lionel."

"Anytime, Ted. Always happy to talk with you."

"Stupid question —"

"Nothing you say is stupid."

"If you don't mind me asking. After this sad scene tonight. How many women have you been in love with?"

"Three."

"Wow. No thinking time."

"Nope."

"Insights?"

"First time — sensational woman, the best. But completely inappropriate. Then —"

"Wait! How, 'inappropriate'?"

"Married, to my father's best friend. Eighteen years older than me. I was sixteen."

"Aw, cripes."

"Second one: very attractive. Except that I wanted to change everything about her."

"And third, Mrs. Bradley?"

"Perfection."

"Because… I've been trying to figure out if I've been in love lots of times — or never. I used to think, lots of times. But something's happened that's — entirely different."

"How?"

"I never…. I always… used to think in terms of what a man wants. Marriage concept? The sex and friendship package."

"Sure."

"Somebody you can really *like*. But what's happened — I never even thought of it before." Ted drew a deep breath and looked almost scared. "I want to have children with her."

"Bingo."

"You get it? I never thought about that. But now — it has to be Ginger."

"None better!" Ogy raised his glass. "I toast your good taste. She's incomparable."

"You think —?"

"Enormous admiration for her. Never met a better mother."

"But… do you think —"

"You're worried by Peter's Down syndrome?"

"Should I be?"

"There's always a risk, for anyone. But it's a small one. In your place, with *that* woman? I'd jump at the chance. But — you didn't look online?"

"'Course I did. Doesn't mean I trust 'online.'"

Ted refilled their glasses, thoughtful.

"So, tonight? What happened there, Ogy?"

Dr. Bradley shook his head.

"She had everything to live for. Financially secure — even if divorced, they don't have children. Very pretty woman, too. But mainly? She was widely liked within the university. We have these student evaluations, and Lisette's were stellar."

Ted nodded, solemn-eyed for the alluring lady who died tonight.

Ogy had already witnessed the video game designer's natural tenderness with the Down syndrome boy of elementary school teacher Mrs. Guardian. Now he was thinking that any woman who saw how Ted had managed to put Leila's leg warmers on her would be praying to have this man parent her children.

TEN

LIFE-AND-DEATH AGENCY

Finally the police were gone. Dull Dina scuffed into the kitchen where Wolf's mother slumped crying over the counter, surrounded by dozens of clean mugs needing to be shelved.

Dull Dina recited, "Anything I can do?"

"No, it can all wait until tomorrow, go to bed," wept Priscilla.

Wolf Adler did not believe his mother needed her assistant to live in. He suspected that what she craved was more female presence in the household than just the Newfoundland,' Isolde. The lumpen inadequacy of this "assistant" made him even sadder that his little sister did not survive being born. He liked to imagine Lili in the house with them instead of Dina, who smoked in her room and did not love Priscilla the way anyone with even half a brain should.

His mother swept back into the family room, where old Isolde dozed beside the embers. Wolf had brought out the wheelchair when his father admitted he was having another gout attack.

From the chair Hiram was stowing Monopoly pieces into their boxes, while Wolf pondered how much the dog might know. Isolde had greeted many guests tonight, including the one they'd lost.

"When I think!" wailed Priscilla, "I could even be to blame? That youngster at the door in his red shirt, he was so cute! I paid no attention, Hiram — *I don't believe I said a word to Mrs. Houseman.* Not a word, and then I never even saw her again. He was just — so captivating, and I was curious to find out what you'd —"

"Gansi, of course you were. Naturally, and you should have been. That young man went to a lot of trouble. He enriched your party, he was an ornament. I too was enthralled."

"One never imagines a woman with a figure like hers could possibly feel… insignificant, or — not a valued guest. It was in my head to find her, invite her to join my Oceanistas —"

"As you would have — *if she'd been here, Gansi.*"

Priscilla sat slouched on the floor, her cheek on Hiram's knee. Watching his father pat her braided graying hair, Wolf announced, "Guess I'm going to bed. Taking you too, Pop."

Ignoring Hiram's *"Gute nacht,"* he pivoted the wheelchair toward his parents' bedroom, trailed by his mother. The wheels' creaking woke Isolde, who lumbered arthritically behind.

"I could almost blame Ingrid. If only she'd come, she might have stood in for me —"

"'Stand in' is exactly what Ingrid isn't up to. As you know."

"— She would have spotted Lisette. Talked, engaged her —"

"She would learn everything about her for generations back — to when her ancestors climbed down from the trees, crawled up from the sea. But Ingrid doesn't wish to attend such standing-around parties."

"Hiram, can you forgive me? I can't help believing — I could have made a difference."

"Point taken. Okay. My dear, you could have made a difference — *HERE. Tonight.* If the lady was depressed. But not tomorrow night. Not someplace else.

"Such a diminutive person, but you arrogate a life-and-death agency to yourself, Gansi? Even big-headed I never presumed *that* much. Even trying to strong-arm the economy."

"You helped the economy more than you're helping me! *In dieser verfluchten Nacht!"*

Hands flung high, as if at gunpoint, Wolf fled his parents' bedroom.

"What's needed now is for *you* to help *me.* Bring that big coffee carafe, *bitte.* My favorite piss pot." Hiram eased himself onto the bed. "Flames are erupting from my feet."

"You ate up all those pickled mushrooms tonight, didn't you."

"Piss pot —?"

"I can't believe it."

Troubled by their unusually raised voices, Isolde stood alert, gazing from one to the other.

"Mushrooms are at the top of your *gout-verboten* list!"

"PISS *POT!"*

"Pee in your shoes if you must, love…." Priscilla hurried to fetch his coffee carafe urinal, singing to soothe her dog, *"Keine Toilette, nein, nein. Es war nur immer Kaffee in…."*

Humming, Wolf shut himself inside his room. Soon his parents would migrate to all German, abandoning the comparative decorum of their English. He preferred recalling the musical part of tonight's party, that interlude when people casually came onstage to sing Christmas favorites. A few soloists, but small groups who knew harmony too. Hearing the timbre of their unique voices had been an intimate, sensuous sort of pleasure, like sampling chocolates. Accompanying them all had made this evening feel like a sacred time — while what had transpired outdoors was still not dreamed of by anyone inside the festive house… he hoped.

Distressed by thoughts of murder, Wolf went to bed calmed by his most un-Deutsch parental antidote, *Prelude to the Afternoon of a Faun*. The wistfully lilting tune reminded him of Lili, fourteen years old now, maybe small like her mother or robust like her father — but entirely kind, like both her parents.

He wondered if Lili had been down there, on the Strand, to meet Lisette when she fell.

ELEVEN

FIRST STRING

Idling an hour with Ted after their evening at the Adlers' turned tragic enabled Dr. Bradley to return home in a less dispirited mood. Ted was in love with Ginger Guardian, an early-grades teacher whose hair fell in soft mounds like poured caramel. After her divorce from a pugnacious man who regarded their relatively bright Down's child as an affliction, Ginger had been struggling to balance her job, the challenge of a father with Alzheimer's and the needs of the ten-year-old she had diligently raised to a quite high level of function. Last June at the aquarium's Fiesta Ogy had observed with astonishment as Ted noticed Peter and promptly treated him to a long horsy ride on his substantial shoulders.

Clearly brainy, the software designer was also zany. Quietly thoughtful Ginger was conscientious and sensible. As a couple they would complement one another well.

Ogy went to bed with cheerful hopes for that likable pair who were still sharing the cat Babby had named after an orchid. But as soon as the light was out, Lisette's horrible accident overwhelmed him. Lacking power to resist its undertow, he was swept back to the night when his own wife died.

By now Dr. Bradley was able to will himself not to dwell on Sylvia's final hour — at home, in the bed they still often shared. But renewed by this evening's shock, that event felt still fresh. He succumbed anew to its anguish. With her death, the house he had built for her became a consuming void, each aspect of their shared lives tugged from him. Past those moments while he felt her life ebb, he had wandered alone seeking relief in dark room after room.

All were filled with pain.

Waking on Sunday morning sick with grief for several seconds before remembering why, now he reconsidered. Attributing Mrs. Houseman's loss to suicide did not seem credible. Yet he himself had seen Lise standing beside the wall, sipping glögg with a somewhat forced smile while the illustrious oceanographer's melting voice sang — very well.

Then he recalled the question pestering the back of his mind.

The clock read a few minutes after eight.

He decided it was forgivable to call this early.

"Yo."

"Ted. I'm sorry, it's Ogy, but there's something about yesterday I can't understand that feels important. Don't ask me why. It got knocked out of my head by — after."

"Yeah."

"When I mentioned to you that the servers were hired from the homeless shelter — last night I asked the caterer, our own old guy who hangs around here is named 'Artie,' you said —"

"'Artie?' *'Artie'—!?*"

"Yes, he hired them all from St. Rita's, and you said—"

"That is preposterous!"

Ted was awake now. Ogy could picture him sitting up in bed.

"More like, *'Arturo'*? Ogy, that waiter is as good as any I've seen in Rome, Lake Como or Milan. He's first string professional. Couldn't you see?"

"Uh. No…?"

It was Ogy's turn to feel just half awake. He had to remind himself that Ted Friedland had burned through his first inheritance, from his father, just dining out all over the world in service of the restaurant software he'd been working on. That investment clearly had paid off. Since it was perpetually updating and increasingly spanned the globe, Ted's app was far more useful than printed restaurant guides. Atrociously named *allQzeenz* made them almost obsolete.

"You still there?"

"Yes…. Yes."

"Didn't you notice how he maneuvers, this Arturo — ? It's like ballet. While the other two, the scrawny reddish-blond fellow and the muscular Black guy, they were fumbling their trays along with wine shaking in the glasses. They tried, but gave up fast."

Then Ogy realized why he had scarcely noticed "Artie" during the party. The man maintained near-invisibility by moving with consummate grace.

"Thank you, Ted — and for the great burgundy last night. Sorry I woke you up. Well — no, but I apologize."

For a quarter hour he continued to contemplate that curiosity, while Ghazi restlessly paced beside the bed with those eyes that radiated, "So are we going out? Do we have a date?"

Ogy was trying to figure out what to tell the dog when the phone rang. He did not allow himself to look at its display, he felt so certain.

"Know anything?"

"I don't know *what* I know but I learned something. Relevant or just a loose thread, I don't know."

"Ten?"

TWELVE

THE DOG GURU

Although at the end of November the ocean's temperature had dropped, in the small bays enclosing Santa Christina's dog park waves lapping its beaches were not intolerably cold. As was his habit on Sunday mornings, the dog guru slowly waded only a few feet offshore. Today the boxer Punchy trailed gaunt sloughi Khartoum, their blonde owners in fleece jackets and runners' tights grumbling about problem Thanksgiving guests. Pink-rinsed miniature poodle Petitfour trotted along the water line, nudged deeper by the often lascivious water dog SinBad. Already the mysterious ocean stroller's presence had entranced Ghazi and the Abeloves' great white wolfhound, Contrail, who eased into the ocean to join their Sunday coreligionists.

"I enrolled Linda at the dojang," Tor told Ogy. "A birthday lead balloon on my record."

"How come? Did you do it."

"Look at her!" carped her supremely toned husband. "All the defenses she's got are those short fingernails. At least she hasn't quit attending yet."

As always, what impressed Detective Abelove was the dog guru's passivity. Although he would sometimes raise a hand — greeting his canine followers? Suggesting they back off? Mostly he ignored them. Well familiar with the martial arts concept of using an opponent's strength against him, Tor was puzzled by the lack of any discernible dynamic in the guru's relationship with the dogs. Without visible interplay, somehow he subdued his devotees.

"Is it possible you worry too much?"

"*Yes.* Any more complacent-civilian questions?"

"After last night? I surprise myself asking that one."

Now the dachshund Dolores arrived, gingerly stepping into a few inches' depth. But side-stepping pekinese Tango had been trying to keep up with a rambunctious flat-coat retriever, Miss Adventure, who suddenly bounded around him into the water. Missy splashed up a wave that sloshed Dolores' belly.

The dachshund's dedication impressed Tor. Having been taught as a boy to use a sewing machine, he liked to picture Dolores in a custom canine wetsuit.

Each time he resisted approaching the guru and speaking to him, at least to learn his name, the detective congratulated himself. He was powerfully curious about how the man related to humans. If he did.

"So what's this thing you know that may not have relevance to our case?"

Near water, Tor kept his fifteen-month-old son Timothy in a harness. It looked odd, since most of the dogs here were unleashed. But the child was very quick. Beside the attractive grasping sea, his ocean-savvy parents knew better than to try to direct his determined rambles.

Ogy explained that El Albergue's local Homeless Guy had haunted the beach area for many months until he disappeared nearly three years ago. Neighbors mentioned spotting him at an intersection in Almira Heights. The diving club's sociologist had said that some homeless circulated the city, since only a small population in any locale were likely to give handouts.

"An exception is the Strand's Homeless Lady, Gert," he elaborated. "She never wanders from El Al, but she's addled. Artie does not appear to be demented. Yet he was hired from the shelter downtown, even though Ted Friedland insists he's a world-class waiter. Who can — and probably does — work anywhere.

"I know it's not likely related to yesterday's incident. My trouble, Tor, is — what's striking about his behavior is — the *gaps.* Something's odd.

"Why did he hang out so long in El Albergue? Disappear? After a long time he returns, but not to work downtown at Perugia — no, he's hired the one night, at the shelter's pay scale. Never saw him panhandling in the Strand, either. He acts more… the chronic tourist."

"I can't tell you much yet. If Mrs. Houseman jumped? Got tossed? We can't speculate until the autopsy. What we do know: She was last seen during the trio's performance. Her husband never stepped outdoors. By design or great luck Houseman went straight from singing onstage to a chair at one of those Monopoly games, which he left only to grab some food. Apparently oblivious that his wife had disappeared.

"One tangent mystery — we don't have her purse. That's why the autopsy's rushed. This morning."

So their visit to the dog park was partly the detective's way of forcing time to pass until he learned — maybe — whether Lisette Houseman's death was murder.

Tor hauled his boy in like a big fish, removed his harness and lowered him into the stroller.

"No purse? Then I hope there weren't any homeless camped out on that hillside above Adlers' house. They get accused of everything."

"That's being checked right now. The waiters told us a little. One, the jumpy undernourished-looking blond, had no contact with her, but saw her during the singing performance — taking sips of glögg, presumably. The oldest one — your 'Homeless Guy' — is Artie Vaccari. Says she accepted a quiche from him. Spinach.

"But the most interesting witness is the young Black guy. Looks like a fighter, right?"

"Definitely. But — a thoughtful one, I'd guess."

"Point for Dr. Bradley. Yes, indeed. He is one highly dignified evangelist. Wants to have his own ministry someday. He recalls very well that when he extended his tray of mugs to Mrs. Houseman, she backed off. He also offered the opinion, just to be clear, that he was not suggesting she backed away from him because of his race. His strong impression, from the way she looked at it, was that she had some aversion to the glögg he was passing.

"Furthermore — Davy Jones — that's really his name — says that did not surprise him. She was wearing these skinny pants, and he could see she took care of her body."

"But the singing event happened early. And during it she did have a mug."

"Yes. Our only — potential — discrepancy. Maybe she was drinking water."

The day was blustery, with the season's first rain predicted for tonight. But when his phone rang Tor ceased tucking Timmy's blanket around him in the stroller and stepped away.

Politely Dr. Bradley also turned away, bending to resume the task of securing the boy against gusts that were starting to feel moist. He raised the hood of Timmy's sweatshirt and pulled it tighter around his ears before snugly tying the cords under his chin. Timmy was more interested in trying to lick the tongue of Contrail, who was licking him.

Still on the phone, Tor turned and started striding back towards the parking lot. Ogy turned the stroller to follow him.

Tor ended the call saying, "There within the hour." He took over piloting his son's stroller, pushing it with unnecessary force that cut deep tracks in the sand.

"She was pregnant. And poisoned."

"Poisoned? At *Adlers*'? How!"

"Stomach contents: besides the quiche — glögg and some just-consumed cookies definitely not served at the party.

"The medical examiner says — if she got nauseated — started vomiting — she might have thought it was severe morning sickness. But when delirium set in, or blindness?"

"The poor hallucinating woman just… stumbled off the cliff…?"

"Or threw herself off, to end the pain. Cerebral swelling — that must hurt?"

"Oh yes. But — could this have been accidental? What substance —"

"Solanine."

"From *potatoes?*"

"Concentrated toxicity, Doctor. Somebody worked at it."

THIRTEEN

EL ALBERGUE

According to local proponents of no discernible authority, the neighborhood of Santa Christina known as El Albergue del Valoroso derived its name from a sailing ship that foundered and limped into its harbor. A contrarian view is that the "valorous" part of the name refers instead to a renegade priest who escaped Mexico City bishops to seek refuge in Alta California. A surviving oil portrait of Padre Jacobo Baroja lends credence to the claim that such a fugitive civic father tarried in the city's antique Ocaso district. Decades ago, an excellent cast statue of Father Baroja was naturalistically emplaced in chaparral at the summit of Mount Reposo, where he appears to be striding still farther north, beyond his less intrepid inquisitors.

Mount Reposo's largely wild northern slopes terminate in the El Albergue neighborhood served by Avenida Placida. From there the town descends into the flat beach area known as the Strand, before climbing towards farther northern elevations belonging to "El Al" University.

But even in the Strand's nearly sea-level neighborhoods, some residents enjoy a view of Mount Reposo not obstructed by either gray-needled pines or eucalyptus crowns arrayed with scarlet blooms like rose bouquets. During early hours when eastern sun fires the bronze cassock of Baroja's effigy on the mountain's summit, those families greet morning with what realtors call a "padre view," witnesses to his march toward the City of Angels.

Although the Housemans' Spanish bungalow on Calle Canciones del Mar did possess such a sanctifying padre view, today the clergyman opening the gate in the front yard's surrounding stucco wall did not feel particularly blessed by the sight of it. He had entrusted his curate with delivery of today's sermon in order to relieve Allan's sister, who gratefully let him into the house to take over her vigil while Allan slept.

Not a religious believer, Allan Houseman sang in the choir of the Bayside Church of Santa Christina. He enjoyed singing. And he was a hearty believer in exploiting any opportunity for networking among the respectable classes. That benefitted him on the morning after the Black Saturday party. When Detective Lianopoulos arrived with Officer Alvaro Lopez shortly after ten, Houseman's door was answered by a minister prepared not only to support his parishioner, but also to discourage the police from any unseemly suspicions they might harbor toward a man who sang such ethereal hymns.

"I'll try to rouse him, Detectives," nodded the Reverend Mannering. "I believe Dr. Houseman was sedated by a physician last night."

But scarcely had he turned from the door than a tenor voice called out, *"Jim?"* and Allan emerged barefoot in the living room, tying a bathrobe over his BVDs.

When the bereaved man saw the two officers he exclaimed, "I know why you're here!"

Houseman looked pitiful. Not only were yellow flakes of sleep dried at the corners of his eyes and in his lashes; but a dribble of drool had scaled one corner of his mouth, and his cheeks bore salt remnants of dried tears.

"And, so help me, I've thought and thought. My wife would never kill herself."

"Dr. Houseman," Detective Lianopoulos interrupted politely. "May we sit down?"

"'Course, forgive me," waved Allan with a sigh. "But you said last night you hadn't found her purse. *Isn't it obvious?* Somebody was hidden out there, only Lise is lots stronger than she looks —"

"Sir, we're truly sorry for your loss. But I have to tell you — Mrs. Houseman was poisoned. Lethally. As… it happened."

"Wha — no. She never — I don't — never saw…. *How…?"*

That's the question, sir. Present in her stomach were the mulled wine being served and some cookies which your hostess Mrs. Adler insists were not —"

"COOKIES? — Those cookies…? I told her not to eat any, I told —"

"Which cookies do you mean, sir?"

"— But she said she didn't want sushi…."

"What cookies were these?"

"I don't — she had a package — an envelope, ribbon, gift-wrapped…. Her students like her so much, I thought — a little gift…. Nobody ever brought me any cookies."

"Do you know a name?"

"No. No idea. She was so popular, you know —"

Allan's face suddenly registered that his minister was sitting with them.

"Jim! So good of you to come. But I don't think — there's no need for you to —"

Seeing that this tragedy was taking a different direction from the one he'd feared the police might have in mind, the Reverend Mannering stood, nodding at Allan and the officers.

"Later, Allan. Any time you want to talk, I'm there." And he departed.

"The lit department," Allan was thinking aloud. "This fall two classes. Somebody must have seen when —"

As the door closed behind Jim, an orange striped cat leaped to huddle protectively, or protected, on Allan's lap.

Detective Lianopoulos lowered his voice. "Sir. Did you know? Your wife was pregnant. We'll need a sample of your DNA."

Officer Lopez had seen some pretty good actors but, as he would later confide to Officer Smithers, he had never seen anyone turn abruptly white in the way Allan Houseman did, realizing the implication of a DNA test. Despite Lianopoulos's genuinely sympathetic tone, for a moment Alvaro thought Lisette's husband might faint.

While he sat in that weakened state, shaking his head, Chuck followed up.

"Sir, you understand, we have to ask. How were you and Mrs. Houseman getting along?"

The detective's forthright accusing question clearly rallied Dr. Houseman.

"Fine," he declared in a much stronger voice, color returning to his face. "We got along fine. A lot of years now."

"Are you — or have you been involved with another woman? Because we will find out, sir. Have to, now."

"No," replied the oceanographer with increased assertiveness, crossing his legs. "In fact, Detective, I invite you — please, ask around about me. Do," he nodded. "What you'll learn is that I'm considered very ambitious. Which happens to be true."

Then he leaned toward them, in complete control of himself.

"The world I work in is a very small one, gentlemen. One thing I learned early about university culture — there are guys who play around — and among their colleagues it's not really held against them. They still get tenure, if they're good. But among the *wives* —?

"Different story. Wives don't want to invite them.

"As I said, I'm an ambitious guy. I'd like to be a dean. A chancellor or provost, someplace. And, *I've got* — . I had the perfect wife for it. Lisette could smile and talk to, charm anybody. From a bulldog to Hiram Adler."

FOURTEEN

BIBLICAL SIN

On Sundays Ogy usually spent a quiet morning at the lab. Then with a sense of accomplishment he could visit the Casa Bunya assisted living complex to chat with Ingrid Becker in the tiny kitchen her good friend Babby had referred to as "Casbah" Bunya. Ingrid kept an antique carpet draped over her table to make the kitchen resemble a favorite Damascus coffee shop. There she and Ogy often discussed the state of especially the ancient world, which both remembered with indelible fondness.

But today he was far too distressed to contemplate resuming lab work. His own upset over last night's events was compounded by the disturbance he'd sensed in Tor, who internalized police work to excess and was particularly agitated by violence toward women.

Arriving home from the dog park, he was surprised to see the Voyager of Mrs. Park, the cleaning dominatrix, at the curb in front of his house. He had completely forgotten their agreement that she could come this Sunday morning instead of on Friday, when her out-of-town relatives had been visiting.

"NOOOO ROSES!" Mrs. Park's chiding voice resonated over the vacuum cleaner as he came in from the garage.

"*Noooo* rose plants inna house! Not on Mrs. Bradley' floor. No roses onna rosewood! You take outside, right away. I clean up stain you make then."

"But, Mrs. Park — you can see that something — some huge rodent — has gotten into them. A couple are chomped away, just stubs. I don't want to lose these, they're very important."

"You take outside. Buy spray can, repellent. Works all animal. Dry heat no good for rose indoors, no. Is November they need *sleep, moister.* Inna house confuse rose clock. Better out. Quick, Doctor! After I'm come down, finish floor up."

Sylvia had adored Mrs. Park and so frankly did Ogy. He was terrified of displeasing her.

So now instead of settling on the sofa with the Sunday newspaper, he would have to remove his baby rosebushes and call around the hardware shops inquiring for repellent spray.

After replacing the plants on the patio, he refilled Ghazi's water dish and placed a canine treat inside his Chinese puzzle toy. The ridgeback was getting quicker at hitting the mechanism to make the ball release the treat, but rolling it around would still engage him for a few minutes.

Intending to phone the hardware store, he discovered a message from Ingrid. That was unusual.

"I was going to bake us a persimmon cake but didn't, sorry. Priscilla called late last night. Wolf picked me up this morning. To sit and let her talk. Hiram's on wheels again, more gout. Can you come today?"

Because the cosmopolitan Adlers had found her late husband entertaining, Ingrid knew them quite well. She retained a smattering of German and a formidable repertoire of recipes for Matt's favorite pastries. In addition, as the spouse of a famous archaeologist she was well-travelled in parts of the world the Adlers did not know. That impressed them, particularly as her ancient classical haunts one after another were collapsing into war zones. It amused her how Hiram always seemed to forget that her own professional reputation was scarcely inferior to Matt's. But where she had written scholarly papers, Matthias authored popular photo books.

Immediately Ogy called her back.

"I'll tell you what I'd like to do. I'll pick you up in ten minutes. Let's go to the beach, try Burger Basement for lunch."

"'Basement'? You can't excavate those at the beach. They'd fill up with water, no?

"Maybe the novelty of a basement brings the kids in. Chilly and dampish. Anyplace else here is so sunny and dry."

"Omar — we're not kids. What for?"

"It's something we've never done."

"There are lots of things we've never done," she replied tartly.

Which, in view of their near-scandalous distant history, Ogy found hilarious.

"Besides, the Basement's bench is one of the places where our Homeless Guy sits around smoking. I've just learned his name. Soon as I get a chance, I want to try it out."

He was relieved to see that Mrs. Park had somehow made the tiny water spots disappear from the floor beside the patio, and even more gratified to sneak after her to the front door. As soon as she was descending the stone stairs, gleefully he unstraightened the small rug she had just straightened, so that again it lay angled twenty-five degrees from the wall.

Dr. Bradley supposed that when Mrs. Becker saw his brand new roadster in Casa Bunya's driveway she would make some gently snotty remark about old men with boys' toys.

Instead she looked amazed, about to burst into tears.

"Forgive me, Ogy dear..." She grasped his arm. "But — you understand? Matt would have raptures over this! *Electric*? Forget your silly Basement! Let's drive to San Francisco."

"It can't. I've no idea yet where to charge it up."

When they arrived in the Strand's business district, Artie Vaccari was not visible anywhere along the street. But for lunch and a private conversation on a rheumy November Sunday, the restaurant proved a good choice. As they sat with local beers, munching the sampler of differently-flavored fried onion rings, Ingrid unburdened the progress of Priscilla Adler's reactions to last night's tragedy.

"Of course at first it was just shock. I gather she was quite a beautiful woman. They had only met her, maybe a few words —" The emphysema sufferer paused to breathe.

"If that. But even in a big group you noticed her."

"Terrible experience for everyone. Then later last night came the thought — '*Our home*. It's been defiled by violence.' And that's another shock. A different grief."

"Hadn't thought of that. But I suppose we'd all come around to 'not in my backyard.' — I like these orange-flavored onions.*"*

"Nice with the beer.

"Then — suddenly it occurs to her: 'Why here?' Don't people kill themselves at home?"

"Or jump off an impersonal bridge?" he contributed.

"What you certainly do not do is invade a stranger's house… and create — an incident.

"So next Pris wonders…. 'Could there be a reason?'"

"I didn't think of that either. Okay, what reason?"

"She didn't know. Couldn't sleep. — These cider ones are quite nice. — Which is why first thing this morning… she phones. Chairman of the lit department."

Ingrid needed a big breath, gulping down the cider onion. "And that was interesting."

"You have my full attention."

"No I don't. You're eating more than your share. Anyway, the chairman tells Priscilla — Lisette Houseman is popular, but not on a tenure track. Well liked, but her research has been… negligible. So, if she's unhappy — an academic failure, then —"

"Take her own life in the Provost's backyard to punish the administration. But what explains that missing handbag the police rumbled on about? I worried they might badger the waiters."

"Priscilla explains that too. A woman's purse is part of *her*. It's identity. Of course she would jump with it."

"But —"

"Pris says, then somebody found it on the beach. Stole it. Maybe, as payment for calling 911. About the body."

Ogy polished off an arc of onion. Wiped his fingers on the paper napkin.

"What time did Wolf drive you back to Casa?"

"Just past eleven. …Now you're going to tell me. What happened before twelve?"

"Autopsy results. Murder. Poison."

"So…." Ingrid sat back and inhaled deeply. "Priscilla's cogent explanation at least got her through this morning."

"Graphic, isn't it? Our compulsion to 'understand' everything? First biblical sin.

" — By the way, I assume Priscilla didn't know her?"

"Never heard of her. Allan is the big deal."

"Also — she was pregnant."

Even he could hear that he'd spoken with the dropped pitch of stoppage.

"You imply…? With motherhood, she might not care about her job?"

"I don't belittle anyone's career, Ingrid."

"Have I ever — *ever* disparaged any woman for staying home?"

"No. And I know your success had to have come at some personal price."

"We enjoyed owning nothing. Living out of suitcases. But now? I sit in that assisted living — and can't bring myself to sell my house."

"You're doing the right thing. Go back whenever you miss it. Throw a party."

The waiter brought their salads and cod burgers.

"This question of 'Why at the Adlers'?' may or may not be important. But I'll tell you, what bothers me a good deal more is, 'Why Lisette?' Any number of people there would seem far better candidates for elimination. — Including me, with a coveted academic chair. And now we know she didn't even have academic rivals. Surely everyone knew she wouldn't get tenure. In the university's politics, she was a cipher."

He chewed a first bite of the burger. The crispy concoction of ground fish and herbs resembled a crab cake more than a fillet.

"Frankly, I find it incomprehensible. She's the last person you'd think anyone would dislike or fear with anything like violence. Well regarded by students, not a threat to anyone —"

"Ogy, no. You don't know that. You think like… an important person." Ingrid squeezed the little paper cup of remoulade sauce onto her sandwich, pausing for breath. "Murder doesn't generally have cosmic implications, does it? Affecting the course of medical research — for a generation? Deciding — who gets to be president?"

"Usually the motives are banal. Petty. Base personal ones. Her husband doesn't want her. Somebody wants her husband.

"That's all it takes. Your entire marriage you spent purring. But you must know — that's not true for everyone." She sat, onion ring in hand, breathing sadly. "And the pregnancy? It would exacerbate a dangerous situation. Put a deadline on dispatching her. To someone who knew about it."

The emphysema patient rested.

"Why, after fifty years, does it still surprise me that you never languish over sentiment?"

"You say that after Syria, Omar? After Iraq? Through much of it you were a child —"

"Here you sit, visibly moved by the loss of a woman you never even met — but that won't impede your thinking, not a jot."

"— It's true the remains there were so very old. But after so long, living with ritual… wasn't sentiment observed best… at the last?

"When the artifacts were labeled and crated…. With the bones assembled and wrapped? Then — we'd invite all the Arabs… and hold proper rites for the dead."

"I just fished this different onion out from underneath the rest. Could be pomegranate?"

FIFTEEN

OUT OF THE FRAME

Since subtropical El Albergue's houses are not usually insulated, any resident who wasn't deaf knew before Monday morning that although the promised rainfall arrived with force around midnight, it was disappointingly short. Allan Houseman was not even contemplating getting out of bed at seven o'clock when his phone rang. But, remembering it might be police, he did answer it.

"Allan? Scotty DuBois across the street. Sorry to call so early, but — you'd better get dressed and come outside because cops will be here shortly. How do you like your coffee?"

By the time the police cruiser pulled up, Allan had finished a plate of French toast and mug of coffee carried outdoors by Beth DuBois. When Detective Chuck Lianopoulos got out of the car, Allan was sitting on a step of the DuBois' front walk. Staring across the street at his own home, he threw up his hands in bafflement.

Chuck and Alvaro inspected the desecration of the Housemans' privacy wall. During the night someone with a can of black enamel had sprayed "TRAITOR!" to fill twelve feet of the south side of the adobe wall along the sidewalk.

After carefully placing Beth's dishes on her front porch, Allan crossed the street to meet the policemen.

"Don't ask," he shook his head. "I've no idea what it means. Aimed at me? At Lise? I'm clueless."

Officer Lopez inspected the graffiti closely.

"The letters are kind of feathered. I'd guess it was done after the rain stopped. But the stucco was damp."

"I don't really care," the homeowner shrugged. "As soon as you guys let me, I'll have it removed or re-stuccoed, whatever. Not fair to the neighbors. Looks like hell."

Chuck took several photos of the black scrawl.

"Of course you didn't hear anything."

"Doctor gave me 'sleep aids.' Not taking any more, though. Maybe tonight they'll set fire to my house.

"How stupid people are! Somebody's got some huge grudge and can't even make clear what it is?"

~ ~ ~

From the perspective of Bay Street's Murder Room, Saturday night was the unhappiest of times for the commission of a major crime. Sunday's edition of the *Sentinel* had already gone to press.

Normally they could hope for at least some public awareness of the crime, if not news saturation, from Sunday's television coverage. But on this holiday weekend?

Anyone not taking advantage of the pre-Christmas sales was most likely immersed in perpetual football or movies. They had to wait until Monday morning's newspaper alerted the populace to the crime that had occurred at one of El Albergue's most dramatic oceanfront parcels before they could expect any public response.

Thus on Monday, while Detective Lianopoulos photographed graffiti on the Houseman's privacy wall, just a few hundred yards away veteran sanitation worker Stanley Kerchowski was routinely loading up trash bags from the Strand's waste receptacles. Most November weekends did not generate an inordinate amount of trash, but this was Thanksgiving.

When he reached the final container on the south end of the beach, he removed its swinging door cover and noticed something unusual. To one side, below empty beverage cups and paper plates from pizza slices, he saw pastel leather different from a running shoe. Pushing aside the rubbish, he discovered an attractive clutch handbag. It was pale blue, with a closure flap appliquéd with raised pink roses fashioned of glove leather.

This unprecedented find filled Stan with misgivings. When he opened it, he saw that any wallet or I.D. was missing. There was nothing in it but routine female junk.

Deducing that the purse must have been stolen, he wondered if he ought to report it. He had a teen-aged daughter, Sandra, and thought she might like this discarded purse. Not new, it was still in nice condition. Uncertain what to do, he tossed it into his truck, concealed it under his rain jacket and forgot about it.

~ ~ ~

On Floor Three Officer Bettina Smithers announced what sounded like a piece of luck.

"There's a video taken at the party," she called. "Mrs. Adler just thought to mention it."

"Why hasn't anybody else —?" Tor was shocked by the guests' apparent indifference.

"Don't get your hopes up. Probably almost nobody noticed. Their son Wolf's friend took it. It's of just his piano concert. The friend left right after. But he's on his way downtown from school, bringing it for us. Aaron Kaufman, he is."

The Murder group were edgy enough that finally Captain Marcos sent Officer Belknap to Taqueria Bahia across the street for enough tacos to hold them over. Tina Smithers continued phoning the guests, rechecking their testimony with a view to the poisoning. When the Kaufman boy arrived with a copy of the video he'd made for the Adlers but said they could keep, Tony Marcos was so grateful that he sent him home with tacos, chips and salsa.

Everyone gathered around to watch a short film that proved brutally disappointing. Unlike any other party video they had ever seen, in this one the camera did not move, almost at all. Aaron had positioned himself less than twenty feet from the proscenium of the small stage on which Wolf was performing Gershwin's preludes. He scarcely deviated from that perspective, shifting slightly only if someone crossing in front of him stopped long enough to obstruct the camcorder's view. Since the stage was elevated nearly four feet from the floor, the bottom portion of the video showed only the upper bodies of many guests moving or standing between Aaron and the piano.

In particular, there was a thick cluster of mostly men congregated in a tight group about midway between the camera and stage. As Wolf

Adler played, the group continued to tighten. Clearly people were trying to converse without raising their voices to a level that would be rude during the recital. But they were so closely packed together that it was all but impossible to distinguish their separate black clothes or sort through so many quiet voices' white noise.

Not a tall man, Allan Houseman could be glimpsed at one point at the far left of the group. He was in back but leaned out for some reason, enough to be recognized.

"I'm beginning to wonder if Mrs. Adler isn't our murderer," grumbled the Captain. "She's the person who insisted on black costume. Thanks to her, we don't have a chance of figuring out who they are. They just blend."

"Play it again," said Tor. "But mute it this time."

"Aw," jeered the others. "You don't like Gershwin?"

"Messing with my head."

They watched the video a second time. Without audio it did seem easier to concentrate on the assembled figures moving through it. To Tor it felt odd to see Dr. Bradley wander across the screen. Sometimes he visited Ogy at the lab, but he had never previously seen him in his social element.

"Who's that woman in glasses?" asked Alvaro. "It looks like she might be talking to Allan. If he's still in back there."

"Probably Wolf's piano teacher," offered Tina. "When we spoke she mentioned she did talk to Allan one time. — Well, she said, 'the tenor.' Didn't know his name. She warned him their group would be up shortly. Those Gershwin pieces are fairly quick."

Tony was checking photographs. "That's the trio's new singer, walking backstage now."

"You can almost see parts of women's heads back there too, but not enough to make them out," sighed Tina. "And everybody's hands are out of the frame, phooey."

The video ended.

"Need to see it another time."

Abelove's patience could be irritating.

"There's a Warhol movie of the Empire State Building you'd love," grumbled Chuck. "Eight hours of it."

"What's it do?"

"'Do'? Just — *be* the Empire State Building."

"Impossible," groaned Alvaro. "No place you can figure out whose hair is whose."

During this third viewing some of the group drifted away. Smithers, Lopez, and Abelove hunkered in front of the screen. Without any sound, they now realized Wolf was concluding the andante second prelude when the woman in glasses arrived to cue the singing group. Like eavesdropping, it was titillating that they knew she was talking to Allan even if he wasn't visible.

"'You're up next!'" Alvaro filled in, gushing "piano teacher," "'You sexy rock star oceanographer!'"

"The pieces may be short, but this thing still runs a few minutes. Know what, though?" pondered Tina. "We never see Mrs. Houseman pass through."

"There goes that Italian waiter," murmured Alvaro. "It's true, the wine in his glasses doesn't jiggle up and down. It sails."

Then finally Wolf had soundlessly concluded the agitato third prelude. After a moment, he rose from the bench. The video cut off.

"*THERE!*" barked Tor. "Five seconds? Back it, before they start leaving."

Lopez rewound just a bit and restarted.

"Stop! Do you see it?"

"Hint?" pleaded Tina.

"Very back, right in front of the stage. See that one guy passing, young one in a red shirt all crisscrossed?"

"So?"

"So — what's in the middle ground, outlined by red shirt? Ignore his 'X's, they distract. Just emerging from that black pack of bodies? Just snaking out, held high — in black?"

"Sleeve and hand," said Smithers.

"Zoom, Alvaro, *please.*"

"Hand with mug," agreed Alvaro.

"And what else?"

"*Oh,*" reacted Bettina.

Captain Marcos returned.

"What do you have?"

"Lisette Houseman's little Navaho ring."

Everyone pulled away. Alvaro saw that Bruno had eaten most of the chips. He drifted back for guacamole.

"So — all we know?" Tor reviewed. "One, she declines Davy Jones' offer of mulled wine. Caught her shortly after they walked in, he says. Two, the piano teacher comes to warn Allan they're about to go on sooner than they expect. And three, Lisette leaves the group carrying a mug. Presumably… mulled wine."

"*Did — Houseman — Drink — Any?*" Tony weighted the words.

"I doubt anybody asked him." Smithers looked crestfallen. "Captain? I'm afraid — Mr. Houseman never mentioned taking a mug. Nobody thought to ask.…"

"Even if he had one… *if he didn't drink any* — if it's the same mug —" realized Tor, "And *if* the poison was placed in the wine… then we can't know *when.* Or be sure which of them was targeted."

"But — if the solanine was in his mug," Tina gasped softly, "Then he could be —"

"A poisoner who passed it to his own wife? What if he lies, claims they both had one?"

"And he's a great chemist, no?" Tony sighed, "Did that couple have separate mugs."

The desk phone rang and Smithers answered it.

"You know…. The man had a lot to say about how well-liked Lisette was," recalled Chuck. "Perfect camouflage, if he wants to conceal he didn't like her."

"Yes, thank you so very much, sir! Detective Abelove wants to speak to you —"

Officer Smithers handed the phone across her desk.

"Hi, I'm Kerchowski, sanitation department. Had my radio on." Stan sounded stunned. "…Is that purse you want blue with flowers? I have it. It's got no money, no I.D. —"

"Sir! Mr. Kerchowski, those aren't what we're concerned about. It's all the other stuff, the odds and ends we want. I hope you haven't thrown anything away? Please, if you discarded anything, *anything* — find it for us. I hope you haven't eaten anything, *you should not eat even one crumb* from that purse, sir!"

SIXTEEN

WHAT I SAY —

On Monday Inigo Graves of the trusts and estates law firm Fiddler, Fiddler, Graves and Ascott arrived at the firm and began opening two days' mail. During Thanksgiving weekend he and Mrs. Graves had frolicked in Newport Beach. Since his partners still had not appeared at the office, Inigo asked Miranda to make him some coffee, then indulged himself by unfolding the *Santa Christina Sentinel* before eleven o'clock. He'd intended to give the local rag a glance before settling in with his caffeine to read the *Journal*. But what he saw on the *Sentinel*'s front page so stupefied him that he forgot the telephone number of the firm's senior partner. When Miranda reached Josiah

Fiddler at home and Inigo explained his predicament, his mentor agreed to come to the office.

Shortly after one Josiah arrived with Rich Ascott, whom he had summoned to join them.

"My sincere apologies to you both," began Inigo, "But I'm in uncharted waters here. This couple — the Housemans — were among my first clients at the firm when I arrived — what? Seven years ago? They didn't have much money but were astute enough to be planning.

"I can't pretend to actually know them. In particular, I certainly did not get the impression that the wife was an over-dramatic individual. They were both academics. One assumes that sort are rational. But then, two and a half — maybe three years ago? She handed Miranda this letter for me —"

Inigo displayed the still-sealed envelope to Josiah and Rich. In ink the envelope stated:

Mr. Inigo Graves

To be opened in the event of my death

"Well, gentlemen — you can imagine my reaction. My first thought was, 'Her husband must be having a little on the side. Maybe she's inheriting some money, enough to be afraid of him. She's overreacting.'

"But — nothing happened, and I entirely forgot about the letter. Until today.

"I assume you're both aware? The poor woman was murdered Saturday. At the home of Hiram Adler, just about the top official at El Albergue University.

"So again, if you'll forgive me — because a major crime is involved, I thought it best to open Mrs. Houseman's letter before unimpugnable witnesses."

Inigo raised his ivory letter opener to slit the length of the envelope. He unfolded the single sheet inside, displayed it to Josiah and Rich, and then read the holographic letter to them:

Dear Mr. Graves,

Last week I was "involved" in an accident in which somebody died.

I had been running on the Strand and was walking home when a car stopped in the intersection near the mariscos shop. I think there were four noisy people in the car. As I started to cross the street, a very young girl inside it threw her cold drink in my face. She and her friend in the back seat were giggling. I was shocked, and for a few seconds I couldn't see. The girl was wearing a tied scarf which I batted at, maybe saying something like, "Why did you do that?"

I'm certain my hand left her scarf before her friend yelled, "Put the window up!"

I was so upset that all I could think of was to run away. (Allan and I have argued about how nasty young people can be today. I did not tell him about this unpleasant experience.) I took off running before the car turned east onto Strand Road, much too upset to even look back. Only when the El Al paper came out did I learn that the car window coming up had trapped that girl's head.

In the article her brother, Gerald Mackey, blames ME for her death!

What I say — the other girl who screamed, "Put the window up!" and the driver who did so are responsible — as well as that poor girl herself, who hung her head outside a car — to be struck by a truck mirror!

If something happens to me look for Gerald Mackey. I did nothing wrong!

Also — there was a witness, if he was paying any attention. Our old Homeless Guy was sitting reading across the road outside the fish taco shop when this happened. But I don't know him or how reliable he is.

I'm sorry about the girl, but did not cause her death.

Lisette Houseman

The three attorneys, who represented three generations, all sat considering the legal position of each actor in this sad history.

But finally, Josiah Fiddler himself casually concluded, "Our obligation to our client and to justice is cut and dried. Phone Bay Street to inform them it's coming, in her handwriting. Then fax it to the police. Chief Margolies will send someone to claim custody."

SEVENTEEN

DARK SPICE

Those glints of unidentified lighter hair that briefly sparkled through in the Kaufman boy's video kept Detective Abelove fretting — as did the anguished words in an attorney's faxed letter from a woman whose living voice he would never hear. Lisette Houseman was a brunette. If the toxin that caused her death was administered via a hot spiced beverage she drank, *almost* surely it was introduced after the mug came into her husband's or her own hands.

Until this morning Tor had retained the smallest suspicion that the Black Saturday murder might have been random, its perpetrator someone thrilled by the idea of tossing a lethal lightning bolt into such a large group of mostly quite powerful people and waiting, god-like, to see whom he or she had felled — mortifying Hiram or Priscilla Adler in the process.

But the overnight decrial "TRAITOR!" on the Housemans' wall did imply that somebody intended a message to someone.

— Unless those black capitals were a diversion?

He paid particular notice to names on the guest list attached to persons no longer present when the patrolmen arrived at the house. Three were geriatrics unacquainted with the Housemans. The fourth was the piano teacher, who had not known the name of "the tenor" when she spoke to him. But the fifth was a younger woman, Claire Fields, who worked at the oceanography school for Allan and his group, including the female scientist who had also been present — the Institute's chairwoman, Rebecca Savage.

Detective Abelove wanted a good long look at Ms. Fields.

In Tor's estimation, Officer Tina Smithers was a well qualified policewoman — principled, intuitive, and with the sort of passionate intelligence that makes even such gentle personalities courageous when the occasion requires it. The one subject in which she had had trouble at the academy was driving. On highways she lacked the assertive confidence required to drive... say, "reflexively." Consequently Tor often had her accompany him on interviews, and always made her drive. His goal was to make Bettina feel so familiar and confident on every street in Santa Christina that someday, if needed, she could perform with bold competence on the road.

Even after a brief detour to glimpse the Housemans' desecrated wall, they arrived at the Institute before three. At the bottom of a broad flight of stairs, the university's Ocean Sciences Department was fronted by a sheltered rose garden over the sea. Dr. Bradley had mentioned that Hiram Adler, who lived not a quarter mile uphill from it, was in the habit of sitting in the rose garden eating a lunch packed daily by his wife, who sometimes joined him there.

Unlike the recent concrete monoliths of the university's main campus, some buildings of the Oceanographic Institute were still the same frame huts quickly erected during World War II for both war-related ocean research and as a northern warning installation to safeguard the fleet many miles south. That entire complex of dilapidated cottages was inconvenient, uncomfortable and treasured. A directory map led the pair easily to the structure occupied by Houseman's group. Smithers shuddered with sugar lust as they entered to pass a kitchenette containing a small stove with a teapot, coffee percolator, and tray offering frosted slices of what had to be pumpkin bread.

Just beyond the kitchen in an office with three desks they saw a young woman with long fiery hair. She was working at a computer while snacking from a container of black grapes.

Sensing their presence, she turned to demand, "Who are you!"

Tor began to introduce himself and Smithers, but before he could finish she interrupted.

"Dr. Houseman is a very important man and a very busy one. He actually came in this morning for a meeting, but then he left again. He wants to be alone and I don't think he has time for you now."

"We'd like to talk to *you*, Ms. Fields," he suggested quietly, having noted the small name plaque on her desk.

"May we come in?" Tina's hopeful request made their intrusion into that idyllic workspace with a hanging Christmas cactus seem like a royal dispensation.

"It's not 'my' office," Claire allowed. "The others aren't here. Take their chairs."

Placating, Tor pointed out, "You are one of the few guests who knew the Housemans, or at least Allan, with something like daily familiarity. That makes you a more valuable witness than those who were strangers to them."

"I don't see why." Claire's eyes flashed, not mollified. "I wasn't even there very long."

"Do we have this straight? You're a friend of Mrs. Adler?"

More mellow from Tina.

"Hah. Mrs. Adler is a great lady. But my invitation was a kindness. I do some work for her in the school's Oceanistas service club. — Priscilla made up that name. I think she likes how it sounds a little… I don't know… Marxist."

"A 'kindness.' But you didn't stay long." Several feet past the tray of sliced cake, Tor was still aware of breathing dark spice.

"I would have loved to stay. I'm her biggest fan. But Mrs. Adler understood — Saturday was my mother's fiftieth birthday. A big deal, and my parents don't live close to here. In the afternoon I was at the house helping to prepare for *our* party. Then I drove out and stayed as long as I could —"

"So in the time you were there, what contact did you have with the Housemans? Did you get to talk to either of them, at all? With such a large group we're having a hard time reconstructing who was where, when…."

"And the black clothes!" Tina's tossing gesture nearly flung her ballpoint at Tor. "Makes it much harder for people to remember who they saw."

"I saw each of them one time. Coming in, I ran into Lise right away. Just a quick 'hello.' Then later — during the piano — I found Allan. To tell him I had to be back for Mom's birthday dinner. I said I hoped I'd get to hear them sing. With the piano concert, nobody could hear themselves talk."

"You're very protective of your boss. You like working for him?"

"You mean Dr. Houseman? He isn't my 'boss.' I work for all of them, the whole group. And, yes, I'm equally protective of all of them."

"I wish you worked for us." Tor's manifest sincerity surprised both women — one his most diligent subordinate, now fixedly staring at a wartime group photo on the wall.

"When my sister and I were about to look for our first jobs, my father told us, 'Always give your employers more than they expect.' I believe they appreciate it."

"I'm sure they do!" The detective was grinning now. "Tell us about Dr. Houseman. You like him? Get along well?"

Ms. Fields glared at him, then at Tina, then back at him.

"You mean, 'Am I in love with him? And did I *kill his wife*?'"

"No, ma'am. You understand, we don't know the man. We're trying to."

"I said he's an *important* man. I didn't say he was attractive. In the first place, I have one of my own, who I'm engaged to marry."

She opened her desk drawer and rummaged through it briefly before resuming her brittle speech.

"And in the second, of the two of them, *Lisette —*"

Then her face crumbled and tears came.

"— Lisette is the one everyone really likes. But — Allan counts as a friend."

"We are so sorry for your loss, Ms. Fields," cooed Tina. "Everyone says that about Mrs. Houseman."

"You're not wearing a ring."

"No, Detective."

Claire Fields pulled a framed photo from her drawer and slapped it like a gauntlet onto the desk beside Abelove's chair. It was of a young man in military fatigues.

"His name is Patrick. Pat Connell. I like him lots more than Dr. Houseman."

Tor handed the photo to Smithers.

"Handsome," she mooned.

"That photo is in Afghanistan. Patrick doesn't want me to be committed to him — no ring, no date — until he's out of there. Intact."

"Okay." Tor handed back the photo. "Speaks well of both of you. He's a selfless patriot. And he trusts a very attractive woman like you."

"Thank you." She dried her eyes with a tissue.

"You keep Pat's photo in the drawer?" Tor did not sound derisive, only curious, but Claire Fields glared at him again.

"Oh, you're a psychologist as well? I'm paid to *work* here! Not to sit around being tortured by morbid fears all day. But maybe if you had a loved one in *Afghanistan,* being reminded every single second of the danger over there *wouldn't bother you at all —?"*

Amused, the overprotective detective could not help feeling some rapport with her.

"Did we hear" —Tina's face was all admiration — "Before coming to work here you were a performer in one of the water shows? With seals, or —"

"With a whale. Lupe. Until there was an incident. With one of the other women, and Lupe got put down."

"That's a very glamorous job." Tor was beaming again.

"Like being a farm worker. The animals eat and poop and don't cooperate. My dad got scared about the danger. I was ready for a change."

"Does Dr. Savage get along as well with Dr. Houseman as you do?"

"She's never mentioned her opinion of him. She's older. And his superior."

Tor stood and thanked her for her time. When he gestured for Officer Smithers to precede him out the door, Claire cast Tina a smile that seemed mocking.

"Remember. Give him *more* than he expects."

As they mounted the concrete staircase towards the street, Bettina wondered whether she was mistaken to feel insulted.

"Do you think she dyes her hair?" Tor asked. "I know red hair does come in some wild colors. Certainly knows her own mind, that one."

Clearly he approved.

Normally a pleasantly chatty companion, Officer Smithers drove wordlessly out of El Albergue and onto the freeway. She had great respect for Detective Abelove as a dedicated policeman and a friend who tried to help her learn the job. Never before had she had occasion to think about his earlier life as a star of the surfing circuit.

Finally Tor said, "Smithers — what's on your mind."

"Nothing."

"Question was an order."

"Wondering, sir, why you stopped wearing your wedding ring."

"I haven't worn it for a couple of years."

Silence.

"You disapprove, Smithers."

Silence.

"Say it."

"No."

"You're verging on insubordinate."

"I didn't think the question was about the job. Sir."

"You think I was flirting with her."

Silence.

"It's true. I was. I do."

"None of my business, sir."

"*But it is*. Any way we can connect with the witness — make them want to please or offend us, that's a positive. I try to provoke an honest reaction. Once that moment of truth happens, it's hard for them to climb back into lying. At least, it's hard for amateurs."

"Yes, sir."

"If sometimes it's fun? That doesn't make it wrong."

As both lapsed into their own thoughts, Tor reminded himself of a bias never mentioned at the police academy. He had noticed that some men react with resentment or downright hostility to attractive women not sexually available to them. If Linda decided to work someday, he did not want her subjected to such abuse.

And he was long resolved never to be guilty of it himself.

EIGHTEEN

VALENCE OF SORROW

While Ogy Bradley recuperated from his heart attack he recognized that as a physician he was honor-bound to follow his doctor's instructions. He lost a few pounds. He resumed driving to the lab, alternating with the bus. After Thanksgiving weekend, Sunday's brief rainfall had left the air so blissfully moist that on Monday morning he decided to reverse schedule and begin the week on the bus. To reward that virtue he quit work early. When he descended at Strand Road and realized that the sun would not set for almost an hour, he felt like a truant from school — which he was, sort of.

The beach area beckoned, and so did the notion of a short walk followed by an indolent Happy Hour libation.

So instead of proceeding home he turned west, thinking that even if he wasn't capable of trudging on soft sand he could manage a boardwalk stroll. His non-physician daughter had been correct — regular walking did seem to alleviate the pain of his peripheral artery disease.

For the length of time it took to pass the insurance office and the dental building he walked in a seaside surfeit of delicious oxygen, contentedly empty-headed. Then —

There he was.

Despite the fact that Ogy had seen this vagrant so many times before, it seemed wondrous that the Strand's Homeless Guy really was perched there, straddling a bench on the next block.

"Mr. Vaccari," he called when just a few yards from the bench where "Artie" slumped smoking. "Good to see you."

Immediately Vaccari sat up. Turning to his visitor with a tight smile, he declared, "You're the doctor."

"One of them."

"Good to see *you*," parroted the waiter.

"If we walk very slowly," suggested the man with a cane, "And I don't have any choice about that — we could arrive at Volpe di Sera at the beginning of the cocktail hour."

"As I remember — not long ago you raced to the top of Monte Reposo with that cane," challenged the Italian.

Ogy was taken aback — this outsider knew he had apprehended a killer last June! But then he recalled that Artie whiled away hours on his benches, reading anything that came to hand, typically newspapers left in trash bins.

"Agh! You've made me remember it too. Now I really do feel entitled to that drink. Let me buy you a cocktail, won't you? I'd love the company."

Vaccari shook his head.

"Right now I don't smell so good."

"They have an outdoor patio, with lots of sea wind if you choose it. You'll be fine."

"It would be cold." Spoken deferentially.

"Patio has gas heaters. Heat comes free with the drinks."

Mr. Vaccari's acquiescent smile as he stood with a slight bow reminded Ogy of the Italian bocce fans in Casa Bunya's expansive backyard, invariably courteous while not playing.

"I'm O.G. Bradley. Everybody calls me 'Ogy.' Please do."

"Artie."

"Not 'Arturo,' then?"

"Not — at the shelter."

"The reason I ask is that my neighbor who accompanied me to the Adlers' has pretty much traveled the world, eating in fine restaurants — he's written a computerized guide to them. He says your professional skills look top-notch."

"I thank him."

"My friend — Ted — he assumed you have to be Italian-born, to have such style. May I ask where you're from? To tell Ted?"

"Rome."

For a few minutes while they completed their stroll through the old-fashioned beach neighborhood to the waterfront restaurant, Ogy kept Mr. Vaccari talking about how Rome was changing. While they discussed the Italians' perceptions of American politics, he still scrupulously avoided personal references.

Then they were seated on Volpe's patio, partly sheltered from the wind but with a splendid view of sun-saturated clouds over the sea. When the heater beside their table was turned on and the Happy Hour menus presented, Ogy suggested, "Let's eat something. I'm attracted by the grilled scallops salad. Have anything you like. Then, please, do me the favor of selecting a wine for each of us."

Vaccari ordered pumpkin risotto with smoked cheese and a glass of Ribolla Gialla. For his host he chose a Friulano, explaining that its richness would complement the citrus dressing on the shellfish.

Ogy was having a very good time.

"Of all the places you've worked, which do you like the best?"

"Villa d'Este."

"That one I've heard of. One of Ted's favorites. If we were there, looking at the lake — what would you want for dinner?"

The waiter shook his head, but was clearly amused, grinning.

"I would choose… *Costolette Valdostano.* A veal chop, stuffed with mushrooms. Topped with fontina. We had fresh truffles there."

Since Ogy still waited expectantly, he added, "And marsala carrots. My own trick is, you add a splash of sweet marsala to the reduced dry marsala."

"Dessert."

"Fruit. Cheese."

"What a world that one must be! Clearly you've been in the States a long time, your English is very good. I'd think — it would be hard to leave Italy, of all places."

"The usual reasons. Like any immigrant. Hoped I could do better here. I had a job offer in New York."

"That's a difficult place to live. Expensive."

"That. And I wasn't so successful — as I hoped."

"Hard to believe, Artie."

"America is different. Big people. Big straight teeth. All Americans are young."

"By definition?"

"By desire. That man inside, behind the bar?"

"Rocco. You know him?"

"He is the… *type*. They want here. To me he looks Bolognese. I'm Roman, but he's what Americans think Romans look like."

Now Ogy realized that Rocco truly did possess that 'centurion' look. Artie was a smaller man with a much plainer face, despite his elegance of movement.

"So — I go back. I work in Europe. Then return here."

"Is it good memories of Lake Como that bring you to the Strand? The resort ambience?"

"In part."

Their plates arrived, and Ogy ordered another glass for each of them even though Artie had punctiliously saved half of his own for the risotto.

"And I have a relative nearby."

They both tasted their food and nodded in approval.

"And, in a small part — I came back for Mrs. Houseman."

Ogy was flabbergasted.

"You knew her! *Lisette?*"

Artie shrugged. "I'm a waiter. We watch people carefully. And are ignored."

"But — *did she know you*?"

"Of course. Like you knew me. Like everyone here does. Just not by name."

"Then why do you say…?"

"Because of that accident, Doctor Ogy. Almost… three years ago? When the girl was killed by the car window."

"*That* — I had forgotten! The freak hyoid break — !"

"I saw it. She did nothing, she was not to blame. The window started going up after Mrs. Houseman ran off. It was just a — stupid thing. I thought — drugs. Why else would some kid throw her drink at a stranger, just passing? But I didn't know the girl was injured."

"What did you do?"

"Nothing. I thought it was nothing, just — because of marijuana? I was watching Mrs. Houseman, not the car. She looked so scared, upset. She ran away. And I forgot it."

"But then —?"

"Well, I don't watch TV. Sleep on the street sometimes. But a week or so later I read it in the little paper. The girl who threw the drink died. And the ones in the car said —"

"Yes, I remember. Someone outside pulled on her scarf, trapping her head — before the mirror blow caused the fracture. A great pity, of course. But their story, it did sound… dubious. Did you think of coming forward?"

"That I could not do. There was nobody else around — just me. I was sure they'd never find her. For reasons of my own, a month later I was in Berlin."

"But you said — you came back for Lisette…?"

"Just to see her. Maybe, on the street sometime. That she was okay. I did feel bad." Vaccari shook his head, clearly with self-disgust.

"Because I ran out on her, you could say. But the library has computers. Sometimes I'd go look her up. She was still at the university. Maybe a new photo, different hair…."

Now he drained his second glass like a serious drinker.

"So I thought — *she's safe now*. She didn't need my help."

Again Ogy was stunned.

"Oh, Artie. Are you blaming yourself….?"

"*Yeah*. Some. Sure I am. Wouldn't you?"

They watched the sunset, knowing that scarcely a half hour of visibility remained before true nightfall. Together they strolled back to the bus stop. Artie could bus back to the shelter in downtown Santa Christina. Ogy shook the hand of his new friend, with a few inadequate words still hoping to reassure him he wasn't to blame for Lisette's murder.

As he trudged the final block to the intersection, his earlier lighthearted mood vanished.

One thing he felt certain he had learned from observing Artie Vaccari: apart from this present turmoil about Lisette, his restless soul harbored deep sadness.

Passing Casa Bunya on the final quarter mile home, Ogy recalled that Mrs. Becker must be having dinner there now. But even thoughts of his friend's wit and warmth behind the Casa's merrily lit windows could not relieve the familiar, suddenly piercing ache for Sylvia. It plunged to accost him, obsidian wings of night enfolding his shoulders to cloak the raptor's grasp.

Maybe what had long attracted him to Artie Vaccari was the man's valence of sorrow.

NINETEEN

SUSPECT UNIVERSE

Unable to imagine any plausible motive for the brutal killing of a woman who everyone agreed was well-liked, on Sunday the Bay Street murder team had felt inadequate about their uninspired sleuthing. Then on Monday while Abelove and Smithers were out interviewing Claire Fields, and Bruno and Alvaro were meeting the sanitation worker who found a purse, a faxed letter arrived from the Housemans' attorney. After they read it, Detective Lianopoulos kissed the fax.

Everyone in the Murder Room began laughing —

Nobody was clever enough to have guessed the bizarre incident that led to Mrs. Houseman's accusation of a suspect she actually named — "Gerald Mackey"!

What had seemed an impossible case with dozens of potential suspects appeared almost too easy. It was December first. A holiday euphoria seized everyone.

But just as abruptly, Chuck realized, "Was Gerald Mackey — or any other Mackey — anywhere near that party? If the poison was in the wine he must have —"

"Or, no, then the poison would have to have been in the gift cookies, and we still don't know where those came from," Tony backtracked. "Was that 'gift' anonymous…?

"Maybe left in her university mailbox, supposedly from a student?"

"Questions for the husband," dictated the Captain. "Did he drink any glögg himself? Did he pass his cup to her? Based on the video, it sure looks like she walked away with a mug *after* he found out they were about to perform.

"Does Allan know the source of the cookies?

"How did we not ask these basic questions?"

"Herding cats, helter-skelter," sighed Chuck. "Too many people swarming indoors and out, plus the caterers, plus 'helpful' calls from Mrs. Adler? Nobody's had a chance to think in a straight line."

As the mood turned glum Lianopoulos added, "Jarritos for everybody on me, if you don't tell Abelove I kissed the fax."

Soon Belknap and Lopez returned with the purse, jubilantly reporting that it definitely contained cooky crumbs. While Bruno took that new evidence to the lab, Alvaro began researching the accident referred to in the letter.

The autopsy of Sheila Mackey had revealed a skull wound. What's more, nobody in Homicide recalled that after the news story about a grotesque accident, the owner of the Del Sol Kayak Shop had called to report that when washing his truck he was puzzled to find blonde hairs caught in the frame of its sideview mirror.

Gerald's girlfriend, Eve Gollbart, had been in the back seat with Sheila. Eve's brother Robert was in the front passenger's seat. The explanation given in the police report for the fact that Robert instead of Eve was in front with Gerald was that Robert needed the extra leg room. But the detective writing the report had suspected that either Sheila Mackey did not want to sit with Robert Gollbart, or else Gerald had not wanted Robert beside his fifteen-year-old sister.

Alvaro left a message for the reporter who wrote the newspaper story. But since it quoted Gerald as implicitly threatening Lisette, for now he was their principal person of interest. By the time Abelove and Smithers returned from the oceanography school, Lopez had determined that Gerald was a new medical student at Boston University.

"Aha," noted Lianopoulos. "Then he's another possible who could cook up poison."

Alvaro wondered if they shouldn't prioritize interviewing the parents to gauge any hostility harbored there.

"Did they hire someone to track down Mrs. Houseman based on her description?

"Did they speak to — pay — the homeless witness for some tip to her identity?"

But in view of the Thanksgiving holiday, Captain Marcos preferred contacting the Boston police department first, to verify Gerald's whereabouts before alerting his family that he was a suspect in a crime committed a short distance from their home. For all they knew, Gerald Mackey might be here in Christina right now. Or flying back to Boston.

Unfortunately, they hadn't succeeded in locating Houseman.

~ ~ ~

On Tuesday morning Tor phoned Ogy before nine. As soon as he answered, mild background noise alerted the detective that the physician was in the hospital cafeteria.

"Another ratatouille omelet today?" he asked. "Good morning."

"I was just thinking about you. I have news that should be of interest."

"I'll trade you. My news for your info. First — did you hear about the nasty graffiti that appeared on the Housemans' front privacy wall yesterday morning?"

"No."

Tor described the "TRAITOR!" message and invited Omar's reaction.

"No idea. Makes no sense to me."

"Excellent. That's the universal reaction."

"Why, what do you think?"

"My favorite guess? Given that it's so ambiguous as to be worthless, I'd love to think Houseman did it himself, to muddy our waters.

"Second, we have Lisette's purse and — yes, there were some bits of cookies left in a little package. Last night forensics assured us they're clean. The tech said he was hankering to eat them himself. So the poison had to be in the mulled wine. He thought so before, but couldn't be positive because the cookies she'd eaten were pretty well sogged up with glögg."

"That definitely bears thinking about. Certainly narrows your suspect universe."

"And, my third bit's the charmer! Yesterday we heard from the Housemans' attorney. Lisette left a letter identifying herself as the missing accused woman in that weird case of strangulation by car window in the Strand a couple years ago, and Artie Vaccari was a witness to it. Since he's your neighborhood vagrant — have any suggestions where to start looking for him?"

"Huh. Artie came with me to Volpe di Sera yesterday. Told me the whole story, his side of it. About the accident, and about how ever since he's been worried about Lisette —"

"WHAT? You're kidding me —"

"He knew her name. He'd even look her up sometimes on the library's computer, just to be sure she was — 'safe,' he says. Was reassured when he'd see a new photo, different hairdo."

"You're making up this whole soap, right? Spinning it to lead me on."

"He's despondent and feels guilty. Clearly became fond of her, from a distance. Fascinating man, Tor. When I left him he was on his way back to St. Rita's, I believe — "

"Gotcha. No, he was not at the shelter last night. That's where we looked for him."

"I hope he's okay, then. Not enviable to be homeless, and a witness who's maybe a danger to somebody dangerous."

As Tuesday progressed, frustration in the Murder Room turned to consternation. Allan Houseman had not come home on Monday night. Chief Margolies and Tony were debating whether to regard their victim's missing husband as a fugitive and begin a search when late that afternoon Dr. Houseman telephoned Detective Lianopoulos, who had given him his number Monday while inspecting the graffiti.

"Where have you *been,* sir? We've been trying to contact you."

"Sorry about that. I was hiding. And working."

"Where? May I ask?"

"The El Albergue public library, chiefly. In the reference room. Nobody in there."

"Hiding from us?"

"No. From the person who tried to kill me."

"You mean yester —?"

"On Saturday."

"We have things to tell you, sir. And things to ask. Can you come in? To Bay Street now?"

"Detective, there's no place I'd rather be right now than police headquarters. If it weren't for their maybe too public plumbing facilities, I'd be begging one of your rooms with the bars."

TWENTY

SURE LIE

The Homicide team had no disagreement about how to approach this witness. Nothing was to be gained by trying to bully testimony from Dr. Allan Houseman, professor and prominent lecturer. As a speaker, the man was both highly capable and experienced — better than any of them. In addition he seemed a considerable egotist. Whatever he said would not be blundering in the fashion of their average witness. His thesis would not be poorly articulated. At least, they would certainly be surprised if his statement were not well thought out —

For the past day and a half he'd been holed up in the library.

Far from challenging him or attempting any intimidation, then, the plan was to make him as comfortable as possible, fanning his already high confidence. Whether Lisette's husband would prove their collaborator or antagonist remained to be seen. But at this point they thought they would learn more by giving the intelligent and disdainful scientist free rein.

"You say somebody tried to kill you," began Captain Marcos.

"Oh, I think so."

"Tell us. Everything you judge to be important."

Allan sipped from a bottle of water.

"Yesterday after you left my house there was a meeting I really couldn't miss, so I went in for it. Then I go into the office to check my mailbox. One of our department secretaries was in there, Claire. The other two are middle-aged and off visiting kids for the holiday.

Claire was surprised to see me. She looked blue. She'd found out Sunday when Rebecca Savage — she's the senior member of our group — thought to call her. She cried a little.

"We're not close. Not personal friends. But... Claire is pretty fond of Lise, so we wound up talking a couple minutes. About how neither of us could understand this. Nobody had any *reason* to... harm Lise.

"Then... I just needed to get away. So I left, to go home. But on the way? I finally remembered. That older waiter, the blonder one — he had a tray. Mugs of hot wine. I took one. The guys in our Lecture Notes, we stood together, with lots of other people, coming and going. The kid playing Gershwin was pretty good, I thought.

"But, here's the thing. Singing matters to me. In my teens, I wanted to go pro. My dad opposed me. Well, he was right. But if you're going to sing — best be careful what goes down your throat beforehand. Strange things can happen to your voice. So I just held on to that cup, forgot about it. Then some woman came and said the

Gershwin concert was almost over. The last thing I said to Lise —
'Take this, I won't be long.'

"We'd missed a rehearsal and were nervous. I know, our act
wasn't some big deal. But Hiram Adler's been entertained at the
White House. We didn't want to look like idiots, either.

"Our numbers went okay, we thought. And after, that older guy
waiter came by with glasses of white wine. I felt like grabbing two of
those but only took the one.

"Somebody said, 'Want to play London Monopoly?' and I said
'Sure.' Never seen it. Getting through our numbers all right — makes
us want to cut up, small time. Like grown-ups.

"I just can't believe how confused I was, when the cops showed
up at Adlers...."

His voice broke. It sounded like emotion, not vocal distortion
from swallowing water.

"At first it seemed like it had to be someone outside, from that
hillside above the yard? That she'd run into out there. And after you
came by Sunday — I thought, 'Those cookies!'

"Whatever the doctor gave me knocked me out. But yesterday
morning it registered. — How slow can anybody be?

"HEY. That was *my cup.* If the *cup* got poisoned, *it was for me.*

"Lisette died in my place. So I'm doubly angry. And scared."

Whatever crafted fabric of lies the team had expected, so far this
wasn't it.

"Dr. Houseman — can you think of anybody who would want to
harm you?"

"No."

That was the first sure lie. Everyone saw it.

TWENTY-ONE

CREDENCE

After drinking one bottled water Houseman asked to go to the restroom, making Abelove wonder if he wasn't a cocaine user. Be pretty cheeky, though, to snort up in the SCPD's own john.

More important, the obvious lie about whether he had enemies did give credence to the man's claim that he didn't believe his wife was the intended victim. Tor admitted he felt some bias. Houseman was smart, confident he could deceive them. But the natural desire to catch him out was no excuse for refusing to consider that Lisette's death might be a murder gone wrong.

When Allan returned to Homicide's Room 313, Tor realized he now felt on shakier ground. Captain Marcos was opening a can of soda. Next was his lead.

"Something you might clarify for us, sir. You've just told us you can't think of anyone who would want to harm you — right after insisting you and not your wife were a determined killer's intended victim. How do we square that?"

Houseman raised both hands in the ironic *oh-spare-me-this-foolishness* gesture, then quickly thought better of it.

"I draw that conclusion from the facts, Detective. My mug. Therefore, meant for me. And I don't even know how determined this person was, nobody's told me what substance —"

"Determined, sir. The poison was created in a lab. And in view of that determination, and the fact that by your own admission you held the cup in your possession, in a very tight crowd, for at least several minutes — we have to wonder whether you yourself might not have introduced the solanine into the mug you handed to Mrs. Houseman. 'Try it, it's delicious?'"

"Omitting no option, just conceivably it was added *after* I handed her the cup, right?"

"Not really. No, sir. Because Mrs. Houseman walked into the dining room and stood alone against the wall, holding the mug beneath her chin with both hands and sipping from it while she watched you perform in the other room. We now have photographs, and other guests' corroboration of that."

The witness shook his head. But his sigh now sounded more like sorrow than disdain.

"I do understand. You have to consider me. Of course. All I ask is that you think about *motive?* Because I don't have any. Nothing! Yes, there is a life insurance policy — on me. Lisette is beneficiary. No financial benefit to me in her death. In fact, even though she makes less than a third as much as I do, I'll be worse off without her. Those extra thousands made for a much nicer lifestyle, with just the two of us. Trips. Restaurants."

"She was pregnant."

"I didn't know."

He reached a taut hand toward the water bottles. Lopez handed him another.

"Let me be clear about something — even though I told you this before.

"I said — I am ambitious. What that means, at a party? I work the room. Look other people over, figure out which of them's worth talking to. Worth playing Monopoly with. Who would be an asset. A connection I can play some day. A step for climbing.

"This is realism. The business world's no different. I'm being blunt here.

"But that was not my wife. Lisette was very — hell, *too* — sentimental about people. She cooked well. We entertained. The guest list? Mostly dictated by me. Professionals I wanted to know better. The right friendships. But Lise held these romantic views about the university. I don't mean just about her own department, but also about mine. We were a *family,* according to her. So everybody got invited. Top people, but also staff. That meant something to her. And it made her popular with them.

People like our secretary Claire, as I was saying. She came to us from that job working with seals and I know she cares about the ocean and so forth, but she's no scientist. You put her at a dinner table next to Dr. Savage? Let me make this clear — if you can't discuss oceanography, Rebecca doesn't say a word to you.

"But Lisette — was talented, that way. She would draw out the guest. With the older staff she'd ask about kids. Pets. What they're reading. Make people feel they'd made a contribution to the party...."

"You think I could replace that? *Ever?*

"I will not sit here and degrade myself, pleading with you all to believe I loved my wife. But neither will I leave this room without making you understand — it wasn't just that she was pretty. That she had a halfway decent job, at least. And infected students with enthusiasm for old fiction nobody reads any more.

"Even received *cookies…!*

"Lise was an asset to me. I appreciate her… qualities."

"Dr. Houseman, all of us here condole with your loss. Sincerely. These past days we've heard only high praise for Mrs. Houseman."

"Thanks for that." Allan did appear moved.

"But since everyone seems to appreciate *her* qualities — what qualities of your own might make you the intended victim here?"

"But — that's an entirely different matter!

"Look. At this university the med school pulls in the highest salaries. Econ maybe a couple, political science, physics maybe a few more, but ocean sciences do quite well. I'm in the top ten percent salary range at El Albergue, so that's one reason right there. Somebody — plenty of somebodies — would love my job, if it were open. Add to that professional disagreements, jockeying for a position on advisory boards — well, not to exaggerate, but, yeah, I've got my rivals, all right."

"So you're more significant than Mrs. Houseman."

"*Not morally.* Not humanly. I did not suggest that, Detective. Just, I occupy a top slot. Lise did not. She was not an impediment to anyone's high-dollar aspirations."

Politely Tor waited while Allan opened the new water bottle and drank some. He had never previously wondered what Dr. Bradley's salary in the medical school might be. But now he felt more curious about whether the fabled academic community was actually as cut-throat as Allan made it sound. By comparison, he and his police colleagues in this room got along reasonably well — besides being sworn to one another's protection.

"You say you and Ms. Fields are not friends. She said you are friends. Which is it?"

"Oh, *surely* the answer to that one depends on the context of the question! Was Claire in here being interrogated?"

"Because Ms. Fields did not seem the insubstantial person you describe. In fact, she holds up her side of a conversation quite competently."

"Presuming you don't talk about ocean sciences."

"What I can't help noticing is that both of you emphasize that you don't know each other very well. That information is conspicuous, because it's not something we ever asked about.

Yet both of you put it up front. So then I wonder why."

"And what do you conclude?"

"Maybe you know each other very well."

"We don't. She's got some boyfriend."

"Conveniently. In Afghanistan. You corroborate one another. 'Lise was wonderful.' But— if you didn't really like your wife or just prefer somebody younger, Ms. Fields covers for you very well."

"No. Check our phone records. We never even talk."

"You're in the same building, every day."

"I don't — Claire's not that attractive."

"Really? She got hired to perform in a wetsuit in front of thousands of people! I would have watched her, not the whale."

"I like women with hair."

"She has quite stunning red hair."

"That's not — *it's a wig*. Sorry, Claire. She didn't tell me, she told Lisette."

"What happened to her hair, Dr. Houseman?" Officer Smithers sounded dismayed.

"I don't know. Could've been some childhood disease, did Lise say? I forget."

TWENTY-TWO

EVERY DAY, AGAIN

Captain Marcos terminated the interview after Houseman grew abrasive, challenged by Tor to suggest even one person who might have tried to kill him on Saturday.

"Detecting is the police's job!" he snarled.

"We can't investigate 'Anonymous.' Tell us who you suspect. Somebody in Kansas? Right now you're the obvious suspect."

"With no grounds at all, you accuse me just because YOU are so intellectually lazy!"

"We welcome any other ideas," smiled the Captain. "When you decide to share them with us. You're free to go, but we need to know where you can be reached."

"I was at my sister's last night — in the mountains. Guess I'll go back. 'Cause I sure don't feel safe around here."

Bruno led Allan out. His stiff indignation wobbled by nervous exhaustion, Allan already had his phone out to ask his neighbor Beth DuBois to please feed Peaches until Friday.

"Did you notice," deliberated Officer Smithers, "He directed everything to Detective Abelove? Like the rest of us weren't here."

"Abelove's tall and muscle-bound." Captain Marcos looked amused. "He's the mark our terrier most wants to bring down."

"Maybe he really has decided someone's after him?" debated Tor. "He just does not intend to tell us why."

"Wasn't that performance fun, though?" The jovial Captain was grinning. "But if you're all disappointed Houseman's left us, cheer up. We've got another witness now."

Over the moans of "What!" "Who?" Tony announced he'd just received mail.

"The Boston PD was as good as their word. We've got their video — with transcript. And 'editorial comments,' the mail says. They brought in Gerald Mackey this morning."

"Two acts!" crowed Lopez. "Let's install a popcorn machine!"

"At least, we deserve a cartoon," moped Bruno.

After ten minutes they were back in the Murder Room with fresh drinks, grateful that during this round they would not confront the contemptuous likes of Dr. Houseman in the flesh.

Alvaro turned on the video.

Anyone who had been led by Gerald's newspaper threat to expect a swaggering athlete was startled by the image of the young man sitting in an interrogation room like the one they had just left.

Mackey was small and thin, baby-faced, with horn-rimmed glasses. He looked more like a ninth grade geek than a med school student.

When the video began he was looking off to the side, saying, "Am I supposed to formally identify myself, or —?"

An unseen woman replied, and then Gerald faced forward.

"My name is Gerald Mackey. It's Tuesday, December second and I'm at One Schroeder Plaza, I guess around eleven a.m. — by my own suggestion. The police have a copy of a letter from a woman who was killed in Santa Christina, but they didn't show me it or read it to me."

"Also they have a copy of a newspaper interview I gave, in which I said 'I'll find that girl who killed my sister' — or something like that.

"I'm making this statement to clarify a few points.

"First: The reason I'm in med school now is that I want to spend the rest of my life trying to save people. I hope that someday I can forgive myself for having accidentally killed my sister Sheila. I love you, kiddo. Forever.

"Second point, I'm told the letter mentions there was a witness to the accident in which my sister died. I never knew that. Despite my bragging to the reporter I never even considered going out to try to find this girl — who could be just an innocent —"

The same woman's voice briefly interrupted. Gerald nodded. By the time he resumed speaking, every listener had noted that although he had a weak voice, he did sound intelligent.

"Because in spite of what I said to a reporter — *what she seemed to expect!* — I knew right off, maybe not quite consciously — from that *clunk* when Sheila's head smacked a truck — I was responsible. It took a while to face it. The whole thing, at first it seemed like just all… fragments of air…."

He stopped, grim-faced, remembering. Jaw bones forward, clenching teeth.

"There were four of us in the car. What Sheila did, leaning out like that, was not smart. I never even realized she'd done it. But what I did was inexcusable. Because I was driving.

"My girlfriend was sitting right behind me, next to Sheila. Her name is 'Eve' — can you believe that? I threw that window up fast *because Eve told me to.* Because she was the first girl who slept with me, and anything Eve said, I did not think about. Just did it. She practically screamed in my ear, *'Put the window up!'* Made it sound like — killer bees? *I didn't know.*

"I never saw any girl outside the car. Just, afterwards Eve and Rob explained what happened.

"Uh — what they claim happened.

"It took time… to confess to Mom and Dad. *That sound* — it was Sheila's head hitting! I'd swerved left, nearly sideswiped a parked truck. I can never forgive Eve Gollbart.

"The scraps of nothing came together. I sit too low in my dad's car. Fatally. Eve and me, we broke up soon after. She'll never forgive me, either. I don't care.

"I don't know where she is now. I can't stand to even think of her. Probably she feels the same. I've heard she hates me.

"What's happened now, this lady who's been killed? I've asked myself, Could it be Eve? She'd sure have the hostility, but she doesn't have the brains. My parents? They never gave a thought to that person outside the car. How could they? They'd just lost a child. Were real worried about me, too. Mom would get scared, leaving me alone…."

Gerald paused, miserably shaking his head.

"So — I spent the Thanksgiving weekend volunteering at our clinic, giving flu shots.

"The last thing I want to say is, to the family of this woman who just died — I am so sorry. From my heart, I know what you are suffering. I pray you can learn to live with this. The pain of being without her. Every day, again, without her.

"I wish you peace."

After the blinds were opened, Tony looked over the transcript with promised "editorial remarks." All the Boston detective said was that Mr. Mackey's presence at the flu clinic was verified. Apart from being filled with self-reproach, he had impressed them as even-tempered and credible.

TWENTY-THREE

FASCINATING ACTIVITIES

In late June suddenly Ogy had started spending far more time at home than he used to, acting much more lethargic than he ever had. In Ghazi's view, the man finally understood what was expected of him — faithful companionship, with naps.

Going out to the park or beach all the time wasn't necessary. Ghazi liked having Ogy just lying in pajamas on his sofa, with his own padded basket just the right distance from the fireplace, where he could scent his friend's presence. But recently Ogy had begun leaving home with a briefcase most mornings again, which confused the dog. He'd thought the man comprehended his role here. Ghazi disliked having his home left too long unpeopled.

Which is not to say he didn't have opinions about whom he would tolerate inside his house and whom he would not. He had never needed to think about that at all. He simply knew.

On Tuesday Ogy left home early again, this time in the odd-sounding new car, again without building a fire. It was already December; which, in his dog manner, Ghazi recognized. For a time he snoozed upstairs, where strong eastern sun heated a golden chenille quadrangle on one bed. But later he detected a familiar noise below — at a time when there should not be one.

Barking loudly, he raced down the stairs to arrive in his front hall just as the door began easing open. Growling with more menace than he'd known was in him, he leaped at the person opening the door just as it slammed shut, causing him to bang his nose against carved rosewood.

Then he just stood inside the door, nose smarting, to growl curses and bark, understanding very well that the intruder had not withdrawn. Eventually he heard footsteps receding down the front walk. Unreasonably, though, he could see only sky and partial bunya branches through the kitchen window.

From his water bowl he heard more suspicious noises —

The side door of his garage had been breached! He knew the squeal of its hinges.

Again he started barking. But instead of being scared off, the intruder continued scuffing around inside the garage. Ghazi recalled a recent day when someone in there had quietly installed a thing that connected by a long new cord to the short new car. But these thumping, clattering noises sounded chaotic. Infuriated, he was beginning to feel he couldn't bark any more when abruptly the side door opened and shut again.

With his garage vacated by the enemy, the weary victor took a few laps of water, then went to lie down in his cushioned bed.

Perhaps for a few minutes he did sleep. But after not very long he heard new sounds, this time far behind his house. Since they seemed to originate at some elevation, he decided to reconnoiter upstairs.

Very quickly, from the back bedroom containing a metal item jointed like bodiless limbs, he spotted the trespasser.

At first Ghazi had glanced toward the cedar teahouse in a distant neighbor's yard, where he had detected commotion before; but no, this time there was somebody right up there in his own backyard. The stranger had taken Ogy's tools and was committing violent damage to the flopped wood structure high above the pool, in front of Ghazi's preferred defecation arena.

The ridgeback jumped up with his front feet on the windowsill and roared in outrage. For an exhilarating moment the sledge hammerer looked up at the window and saw him.

Then the trespasser waved —

Which did not seem right at all.

More barking drove the intruder away a second time. But again he returned, carrying a metal box. Despite Ghazi's guttural threats, he set the thing down.

Loud music began to play, so extremely loud that despite the Rhodesian's powerful instinct to chase a stranger from his domain, he felt forced to retreat for the time being. But although he ceased barking he remained vigilant beside the window, noting the interloper's every move.

~ ~ ~

It was nearly three o'clock when Dr. Bradley received a surprising phone call at his medical school office.

"The print in the phone book is just too small," complained Esther Coleman, his next door neighbor to the east. "Took me half an hour to get your number, Ogy. And don't tell me to 'look online.' I won't."

"Esther, my dear! I'm sorry about that, but what's wrong? What can I do for you?"

"Do you know somebody with a blue Toyota Matrix?"

"No?"

"Well, *somebody* up high in your yard has been playing terribly loud music for a long, long time, Ogy. And bear in mind, Manny and I are both deaf."

"But nobody's home."

"Outside, Ogy! Up. Your gardener or somebody, they're driving us crazy! Plus, your dog was barking constantly — at him, I think. Manny needs sleep, he's supposed to sleep."

"What kind of music?"

"What's the diff —"

"No, please, Esther. Ask Manny, what's the music?"

After a short conference Mrs. Coleman returned to the phone.

"It's Vivaldi. *The Four Seasons*. He says, many years of them."

"Esther, I'm teaching in ten minutes and can't come home. Please call the Seagraves. Ghazi knows them all. With Gloria or Lynleigh there, the dog will let him into the house."

It was after five o'clock and quite dark when Ogy turned his spanking new Tesla roadster onto Avenida Placida. Spotting a blue Matrix parked ahead in front of his house, he experienced a soaring fondness for it such as he had never felt for any other vehicle.

Then he saw Anthea's Audi parked in his driveway, and that made him even happier.

For once Ghazi did not come running to the front door when he opened it. But there was talk upstairs, and a short bark, and laughter.

A silk blouse was draped over the upstairs bannister with the pieces of Thea's green tweed suit. Suede pumps lay on the floor. She must have changed into clothing from her bedroom closet.

When he reached the doorway to Caelan's room, his daughter was lying on her stomach on Cael's bed, swinging her legs in jeans, elbows propped and chin in hands, engrossed by the proceedings.

After a few moments Ogy understood. Ghazi was receiving a French lesson.

"Dites-moi 'carotte.' 'Carotte.' 'Donnez-moi une carotte, s'il vous plaît.'

"Alors: Caaa - ROTTE! Ca - ROTTE!" Sounding between a sneeze and a bark.

"Grrr-RUFF!" replied the dog.

Anthea snorted chuckles as Ghazi was rewarded with one of those contracted vegetables cycled through some sort of pencil sharpening device to be marketed as "baby" carrots.

"Très bien, bien fait, Ghazi!"

When Thea's face turned to the doorway and she saw her father standing there, her expression twisted with the same sweet pain he was experiencing —

How cold a place this house had become, missing both its more playful family members!

"Oh, hi, Dad," said Cael, as Ogy went to kneel on the floor beside him and embrace him.

"You really believe he can learn French?"

"You think he's dumber than every dog in France?"

"He's smart!" insisted Thea gleefully. "He's very smart!"

"Watch this, Dad.

"— You want another carrot, Ghazi? *Voulez-vous une autre carotte?*

"Bien. Où est la lune? Où est la lune, Ghazi?"

From the bed Thea softly urged, "Go, dog, go...."

"LA LUNE? Où est la lune?"

Ghazi did not understand what *"lune"* meant any more than he knew the word "moon." But he did recall the command now. He got to his feet and trotted to the telescope beside the window, then positioned his eye beside the eyepiece.

Thea collapsed on the bed, choking with laughter.

"He gets it, Dad! He really gets it," insisted Caelan. "You should move it sometimes, so he has something to look at while you're not home. It's kind of mean to keep it aimed at the sky, when he could watch people at the Casa."

"The Chromstads' teahouse," snickered Thea, recalling their new council member's naughty conduct there last spring.

"I don't know which of you delights me more," marveled Ogy, daring to kiss his son's temple. "You have some purpose in this? — You look so well, Cael. It's a thrill to see you."

"Thanks. If you're wondering, my campaign manager picks the clothes."

"She knows what becomes you."

"He. But one thing I've realized since getting involved in this campaign is, even though my district is a long way from Quebec, New Hampshire still has a fair number of French speakers. So before we all get sworn in next month, I'm trying to cram the language. Listening to tapes all the time."

The notion of Caelan's being sworn into Congress still amazed his father and sister.

"What do we want for dinner?" trilled Thea. "I'm treating."

"You two decide. Take my car," said their father. "It's on the drive, next to hers."

"MON DIEU?" gulped the imperturbable politician as he accepted a Tesla key.

Ogy followed his adult children as they tumbled down the stairs and raced out the front door. Then he went out to water his twenty small potted rosebushes arranged just beyond the patio door. It pleased him to see that a few of his master-gardener neighbor's creations were still setting new buds.

But there could be no greater gift for anyone than having a lost son restored.

During a takeout meal of combined Lebanese and Mexican food, fledgling congressman Caelan Bradley explained that his visit to El Albergue was less a vacation than a working trip.

"Someone pointed out there's another freshman, from Christina County, whose campaign themes were similar to mine. So he and I decided to get acquainted before we move to Washington, to discuss environmental problems. And the other representative who interests me is a woman from Orange County. She's been active in the Sierra Club a long time. She's forty and knowledgable — more than the two of us. I'll drive up to see her tomorrow. Don't wait dinner for me, Dad. Together those two can speak for the concerns of the southwest, and I bring the perspective of the northeast."

"You phoned them?" asked Anthea lightly.

"Sure, we've spoken a few times."

Father and daughter exchanged a glance, but neither had the temerity to raise the subject of a phone number for the New Hampshire congressman. Soon one would be publicly available.

"Have you been to D.C. yet? Do you know where you'll be living?" asked Ogy.

"I have an address, but didn't have to go. I'm moving into a Dupont Circle condo with some other guys. One of the four didn't get re-elected, so I'm the new kid replacement."

"Nice location," said his sister.

"Very. If you want to visit sometime, obviously I can't put you up, but I already have the names of a couple of good hotels close by. You can visit Congress in session. We can eat out."

On that cordial note, the executive in the room realized they should not press their luck. Since Cael had left New England very early on eastern time, she offered to clear up after dinner and allow her brother to go to bed.

Upstairs, the fascinated ridgeback watched the newcomer hang his clothing in the telescope bedroom's closet, remove pajamas from the chest of drawers and cross the hall to the shower. Downstairs Anthea declared she would spend the night, and her father agreed she should. Exchanging smiles, they put away take-out boxes and loaded dishes without speaking.

~ ~ ~

On Wednesday morning both Ogy and Thea left early for their respective hospitals — she to her administrator's office and he to his breakfast cafeteria.

Having arrived home after dark on Tuesday, Ogy had not seen that the termites' twenty-year-old "fort" above the backyard was demolished. Tonight and tomorrow, Thursday evening, also arriving home well after nightfall, he would be equally unaware that the pile of debris had been removed, and that later in the afternoon a delivery of lumber and concrete mix was hoisted up to Ghazi's newly raked and cleared poop lot.

These developments provided welcome entertainment to his dog and the Colemans.

But now that they knew unpredictable Caelan Bradley was in residence again next door, neither Esther nor Manny saw any reason to phone Omar at the university and inform him of fascinating activities in his backyard.

TWENTY-FOUR

SOUTH SLOPE REPOSO

After progressing through endless Adler party reports, on Wednesday Detective Abelove drove alone to the El Albergue home of Laurence and Janet Mackey. After Gerald Mackey's video testimony, he didn't expect to learn anything additional to advance the Houseman murder investigation. This errand was more a matter of filling in blanks to wrap up an earlier report.

Unsmiling but polite, the couple ushered him into a garden area that backed onto the country club's golf course. After Tor and Mr. Mackey were seated beneath a broad fringed green umbrella, Mrs. Mackey returned to the house for a tray with glasses and a pitcher of lemonade. December was performing at peak, the day resembling the best that June can offer in less-blessed climates.

Was it a myth or true, Tor wondered, that doctors took off Wednesdays to play golf? Away in the uphill northern distance, a group of gray-headed men at a tee were silhouetted by clouds with that blank look unknowing of rain.

After thanking Janet Mackey for the iced drink Tor took a sip. He had never tasted lemonade quite like it but had no idea what was different about it. A low buzz over rosemary blossoms skirting the lawn turned out to be a rabble of honeybees. He offered regrets for disrupting the Mackeys' afternoon.

"Don't," interrupted Laurence Mackey. "This is a good thing. We didn't know the Housemans, but Janet and Mrs. Houseman had a friend in common, we've just learned. Imagine. Our mystery woman. One step removed, through a reading club."

"Of course Gerald called last night after his interview in Boston," added his wife. "I wish he could stop apologizing."

"Maybe this will bring some closure," mumbled her husband.

"OH. Larry doesn't mean, because of Mrs. Houseman's death!" hastened Janet. "Or because Gerald got hauled in again by police."

"I was wrong." Laurence Mackey's nod was so insistent it looked palsied. "I didn't think so at the time. He was infatuated with her. I still believe it would have made things worse —"

"*How* can you say that, *still*?

"Detective, I know how this sounds," Mrs. Mackey entreated, "But I *loathed* that girl. *Before I knew…!* Gerald was a shy boy. The inveigler wrapped herself around him, because she was determined to marry money."

"You mean Miss Gollbart, ma'am? She was a student also?"

"NO, she wasn't a student. She was a gold-digger. Showing off how easily she could manipulate our son."

"I thought interfering would be a mistake. He wouldn't have reacted well."

"She gave him orders. 'Get me a drink, Gerry.' 'You don't have to study, let's go out.'"

"Your son was living at home while he attended college?"

"Gerald didn't like dorm life." His father waved a dismissive hand.

"What Larry was just referring to? Last night, Detective — our son told us the truth."

"It wasn't easy for him. I pity him."

"It's not easy for *us*. Tell the man. *Spit out the fly.*"

"You tell him."

Janet's appeared the greater need.

"Not only did Eve coil herself around our son, she'd started exerting power over our daughter. We — are — horrified. Last night Gerald finally admitted — what Eve said to Sheila in the back seat that afternoon? It was something like, 'Look at the Jewish princess! She needs a slap in the face!'"

"Eve… was talking about Lisette Houseman?"

"*Yes!* Have you ever heard anything so revolting? And so our foolish, docile daughter threw her drink at the lady! And died for it.

"*Sheila's last act in this world*" — the hard words pitched from her — "*An antisemitic assault!* Every good thing she'd ever done, nullified!

"We did not raise our children that way. There was an evil influence in that car."

"The boy? Eve's brother? Do you know where he is?"

"We never met Rob, but Gerald didn't like him. After all this he enlisted. I hope the army makes something of him."

"I can still… scarcely believe it." Mr. Mackey's formerly dark hair was edged by white curlicues about his face and ears that suggested a frosted wedding cake. Their cloying sugary look belied his manifest grief.

"Gerald's been suffering three years with this filthy secret, Jan. At least — he knows better. He wrestled alone with it to protect us, honey. But so did Sheila know better. She was a kind girl. Just… *fifteen*. Still meek enough to… be led."

"*Ordered.*"

"I should have bought him that MG he wanted."

"Lisette's funeral service will be at St. Elizabeth's," Tor lightly intervened. He was thinking that this petite blonde mother with a figure starting to thicken had recently been far more attractive than she appeared now. Her face remained contorted in a perpetual frown as she shrugged off his information.

"Eve's disgusting thought, Sheila's offensive deed remain. Regardless of her religion."

Tor just kept hoping to see Janet Mackey smile once. He was reluctant to leave them without verifying that she still could smile.

"You'll have to forgive us, Detective. What my wife says is true. We raised two decent citizens. Respectful of people. All my law partners are Jewish, old family friends. This… comes like something from outer space."

"Grieving my daughter wasn't bad enough," Janet lamented. "Now for the rest of my life I'm also appalled. We have to hold our good memory of her, Larry. But Eve's foul mind dirtied us all."

"Sir," said Tor, succumbing to their despair, "Mrs. Mackey? I have wonderful kids too. And this whole story scares me so bad. I'm sorry it happened to your family."

After being assured by the couple that two years ago Eve Gollbart had moved to Atlanta, Detective Abelove took leave of them and their delicious lemonade. Returning to the SCPD's beige car in this richly peaceful neighborhood, he felt oddly dizzy from the baneful taint surrounding those wretched parents. He had witnessed ghastly crime scenes that did not leave him as perturbed as this scarcely noticed incident of three years ago, the brainless prank of a child who didn't hate anyone, which he must officially reclassify today as a hate crime.

The Mackeys' lifetime civility could not counter the nuclear force of one vicious impulse that in seconds had ignited annihilation of their now cruelly disfigured world.

Realizing that their backyard tableau below the golf course was situated on the opposite side of Mount Reposo from where Dr. Bradley lived left Tor impatient to escape the stain of Eve Gollbart, which seemed to flow down the road in pursuit of him. With scarcely a glance toward the view of Mexico's distant islands, he drove three blocks farther towards sea level before parking again. Then almost without conscious forethought he phoned Ogy and said, "Could you possibly join me for dinner tonight? Linda has lessons at the dojang Wednesdays and Fridays. Mrs. Kimura will have the kids, and it's time you met Piggy."

"As a matter of fact, I'm alone tonight."

This seemed a peculiar statement, from solitary Dr. Bradley.

"So yes, Detective, I can. I have minor thoughts I've wanted to mention, and I've long hoped *to meet Piggy*."

Tor heard a pointed humor in those last three words. But, mentally economical, he accepted that he'd find out what it meant when Ogy was disposed to tell him. He had today's interview to write up, and an afternoon meeting.

Tor surprised himself by leaving Bay Street earlier than usual. After an errand, he could spend a blissful pre-dinner hour with his family before the short walk to Piggy's.

Linda was very happy to have her husband arrive home so early and unexpectedly. With a light heart she left her mother in charge of dinner, and Tor reading *The Swiss Family Robinson* to the children. Because she was not a police detective herself and because she had no idea whether it had ever happened before, she failed to notice as she drove away that she was being followed.

TWENTY-FIVE

WHO'S AFRAID?

"Hey, cop! Want to drive it back to your house?"

Although night had fallen when Ogy arrived at Piggy's parking lot in his new roadster and called to Abelove through the Tesla's window, the spritely vehicle had as much impact on him as it did on Ted Friedland last Saturday. Waiting outside on This Little Piggy's veranda, Tor vaulted the porch railing to lope after the car into the parking area.

While walking back to the entrance, Ogy explained that he had received an unexpected visit from Caelan, who planned to sponsor environmental legislation in Congress.

"I've been hoping you could meet my son," he apologized. "Wanted to surprise you. But it turns out he has work dates filling a short visit here."

"I'll be honored to meet him whenever that happens." Beaming about both the new car and Caelan's visit, the detective fondly escorted Dr. Bradley up the stairs to his favorite restaurant. "I'm so glad he came. He's excited about the new job?"

"Seems to be, but I'm worried. Here we are on the brink of economic armageddon. Bold environmental policy probably sounds frivolous to everyone who feels financially threatened."

"They cared enough to elect him. So the interest is there."

Tor opened the door. Piggy's interior was only slightly brighter than outdoors.

"Ohhh….!" Ogy softly exclaimed. A glance down the length of the dark porkery made it obvious why the Abeloves brought their children to This Little Piggy's. The place was filled with rustic booths, but at the far end were three unique cubicles. The first stall had sides built up from hay bales. The second appeared fashioned of sticks and twigs; and the third, with high sturdy walls, of course was crafted of bricks.

"I reserved us the brick house, Ogy, so you don't have to get scared if there's an earthquake while we're in here."

But Ogy had already observed that a number of the diners were wearing wolves' caps with pointed ears, some with glowing red eyes as well. He started to laugh.

"I'm already scared in here."

Most of the tables were equipped with old-fashioned jukebox selector consoles. The music now playing in the room was "Who's Afraid of the Big Bad Wolf?" from Disney's 1933 cartoon. Some patrons at their tables sang along or stomped the floor with the final five notes of the chorus.

"You're welcome to play the jukebox, but house rules are, 'Who's Afraid?' can only come on once an hour." Tor pointed to a chalkboard listing military times. "Little Piggy keeps track for us.

"Piggy, my love!" he warbled, as a small woman in her fifties or sixties appeared behind the front counter. "Thanks for saving the brick house. My friend Dr. Bradley has been wanting to meet you!"

Tor easily leaned over the narrow counter to hug Piggy and kiss her cheek.

The gaunt, grave-faced woman with severely pulled-back hair might have been Grant Wood's model for his "American Gothic." But a hug and kiss bestowed by Abelove altered the stern old face to a twinkling expression that was downright comely.

"How do you do, Little Piggy," intoned the Persian, with a bow hailing from a place and period in his early life of which Tor lacked knowledge. Nor had such extravagant courtesy been witnessed before in Piggy's porkery. "I am delighted to be here at last."

"I have fantasies of Calamansi Carnitas, Piggy." The policeman confessed his hope with abject doggy eyes. "Is there any left?"

"There's not," pronounced the proprietress. "But I put aside two portions for you."

"She makes it only from her own trees' ripened fruit, Ogy. We are blessed. Thank you, ma'am, we thank you!"

The fireplace was heating one brick wall of their booth. Its confined space with flame view resembled an inglenook.

"Want to sit on this side? Toast yourself?" offered Tor. "Warm bricks. Nice on sore muscles."

"You enjoy it this time."

Sniffing the heated bricks, Ogy experienced a farm memory of damp soil on a hot day.

For starters they ordered the zucchini disks and crab-stuffed portobellos, with calamondin margaritas. It was early yet. When the drinks came Tor emitted a long sigh.

"We have a negative symmetry," he decided. "Your son came. That's great. My dad wants me to come. I will not go. Won't take my kids to those people, no."

"By 'those people,' you mean Russians?"

"No. Russians are a heroic, gifted race. I mean Soviets."

"Care to elaborate?"

Dainty eater Abelove made two bites of one zucchini round.

"Maybe that whole bloc got infected with Soviet disease, I dunno — Ukraine, Belarus? Those nationalities, all salt of the earth people. But the *system*?

"— I ever tell you about Linda's dad?"

"No."

"Hiroshi's family's been here a long time, a few generations. Their old community's in San Jose. They stick together, especially after Manzanar.

"He left San Jose. Met Marjorie, started the nursery — only Asian plant specialist in the county. Like a Japanese maple tree museum."

"You have some at your house."

"All his. The family kept after him — 'Come back to San Jose.' He might have had more business up there, but he wouldn't budge."

"Prefers the climate down here for his plants?"

Tor shook his head. "Feels pressure up there to '*be* Japanese.' My father-in-law sees himself as American. Period. Doesn't speak Japanese but has nothing against them. He just wants to be free of any — imposed identity."

"What about the older generation? Doesn't that seem to them like indifference to what they endured in the wartime internment?"

"And expropriations. 'Course it does. Respect issues crop up."

Ogy said, "I think a big reason my own parents were so happy was, often they were well removed from their worlds-apart families. Teheran and the midwest farm."

"Makes sense. Anyway, I admire the man. No fancy education, but he's a gentleman. Patriot. Who raised his daughter right. Lucky me, I married a beautiful *American* girl."

"You sure did. But — I sense a contrast coming."

When Pink Floyd's song "Pigs" began to play, Tor asked, "You want to wear one of the wolf caps? I can get you one."

"Over my hair? I scarcely need it."

"That's true. You just naturally look feral most of the time."

Tor waved over the waiter and ordered two beers to follow their margaritas.

Then he decided, "I look too tame next to you," and jumped up to collect a wolf cap.

But instead of the ragged cap's transforming Abelove to a wild man, his broad face and long frame diminished the wolf pelt to something resembling an unkempt house pet.

"Two things I want my children to be. Honest people. Good citizens."

"Is that controversial?"

"Oh — you think — *it shouldn't be*?

"To my father's Soviet friends? I am stupid. I am sneered at. *'Why?'* you wonder. Because I became a cop — ?

"OH, no. Because I don't *exploit* my authority, to steal and extort! Because Linda and I pay our taxes.

"Ogy, you would not believe — these people learn every angle to defraud and bilk the government. Disability payments for nonexistent medical conditions? Multiple social security identities? Assistance with heating bills, et cetera, et cetera — even if they're well-to-do? In Soviet-think, that proves you're smart. An operator.

"And don't misunderstand, my disgust isn't because I'm cheated personally. It's the idea — that we collectively, as taxpayers, are ripped off by these ingrates. A rotten system created that culture. But a good system can't function if the culture's crooked. I meet plenty of immigrants. Work with Latinos, assorted Muslims, deal with diverse illegals, and mostly they are decent folks. Without much education, they're all idealistic about the States.

"But my Soviets I'd like to deport."

"It is painful to think, if assistance money isn't going where it's needed."

"It's beyond just money. It's — *they think they're good people.* Respectable, because they won't steal from you *if they know you.* Because they'll help friends set up their own fiddles and scams. The mentality's that nuanced.

"And this is without getting into the drinking problem. I haven't seen any other immigrant group so unAmerican. Cynical. They would treat us friendly, but — I don't want our kids exposed to that casual corruption, it shames me that bad.

"And Mom? She excuses her drunk of a husband. It's expected. Shows you have *soul.*"

Their beers came. Emitting a hummed moan, Tor pressed his back against the warm bricks. He sipped icy beer. Then their pork plates arrived, smelling ambrosial. Ogy sampled the beans before the meat.

"*How does she do this?* These are amazing."

"I think — using the broth from the first cooking of the pork for the beans. Then their flavor gets so rich."

"Wow. Wouldn't even need the meat." He kept eating beans.

"Wait until you try it."

Ogy had picked up the beverage menu and was scrutinizing it.

"Okay," segued the cop. "That was embarrassing. I showed you mine. Now what about your hangup?"

"Which hangup. — The 'Big Bad Wolf' lyrics are on the back of the drinks menu?"

"After ten, the room can sing along for the whole wolf song, if anybody wants. One time."

He leaned forward, planting an elbow to either side of his plate, wolf ears almost tickling Ogy's face.

"*The rug.* Why?"

Tor had wanted to ask for a long time, and was still nervous about how his private older friend would react. But detection skills were of no avail in explaining the perpetually crooked placement of the little carpet beside the Bradleys' front door.

The dignified physician continued reading the list of beers and cocktails, forking up frijoles.

"Look, if it's —"

"Just — I'm thinking what a little bastard I was."

Finally Ogy scooped up a mound of shredded pork, tasted it and flung his hand up, exclaiming *"Mmmmhh!"*

Then he sat a few moments, staring with regret through fifty years.

"My mother, Neda — her education was much broader than you'd expect, given the regime today."

"Is Neda still with you?"

"With my sister Tara. My only grievance with that marvelous woman was that she treated me like an adult. When I was a twerp."

"That's different."

"Sometimes I'd challenge her. Then instead of shooing me out like your mom is supposed to, she'd drop everything to engage me in some ethical discourse."

"I can't imagine, still with broom marks on my behind."

"*Religion.* One of my favorite targets, because her parents were devout. Although she does deeply value her culture, she was candid about not being a religious believer. It was a sore spot for her, so I'd prod. One time she really did seem hurt.

"'Because I am apostate, you imply my dear father would see me stoned to death?' she dares me.

"I fudge when I claim that's what Sharia law says. Knew my Quran, but not really well.

"'No. It doesn't. But if it did? What does this reveal about you, my son? If you choose to see only conflict, not concord? The Quran tells many things, some maybe vague? — Like in the Bible,' she says. 'If you were Grandpa, which attributes of Allah would help you decide whether to stone me?'

"I want to go back outside and play. So I recite, 'Allah is the merciful, compassionate' — expecting such long words will end it.

"She says, 'The Old Testament Christian God is grouchy, but the Son preaches love and forgiveness. From their example, I accept that you and I too may disagree. Remember, when judging me? Your mother is an American citizen now. Here I am allowed freedom of conscience.'

"So, Wolf Man. How I regret that I must have seemed hostile, when I revered her, really. It was just, oh, combative showing off."

"You said once, your Illinois granddad was a minister. Your Quran bother him?"

"Uh-uh. One subject he was liberal about was religion. All God-fearing is good.

"Then another time I walked back into that same mud hole. Caught my mother unstraightening the prayer rug."

"Oh ho."

"I said, 'Mama, that doesn't look nice. Grandma and Grandpa can't see it here anyhow.'"

Abelove just sat taking small sips of beer, gloating too happily to eat. Starting with Caelan, at long last he was hearing bits about Ogy's family.

"I think I said, *'It's hypocrisy,* if you're not a believer, to make the rug face Mecca.'

"'Hypocrite, am I?' Actually, she laughed. Then she asks, 'Do you like the carpet?'

"Well, sure. It's very fine. All natural dyes, in the old way.

"Then — 'You respect the carpet maker?'

"I allowed I did. Our Teheran grandpa told Tara and me the weaver was one of the best of his generation.

"'Because I too respect him. He labored over this small carpet many months. More hours than you spent learning algebra. And to *him?* The carpet was a religious object, filled with meaning. With reverence for Allah.

"'What does it cost me to respect his work and place his sacred little rug as he intended? I do it, and it fills my heart.'

"It fills mine too, still."

Tor nodded and toasted with his beer bottle.

"My thanks — to Neda, then. For you."

Ogy was too surprised and touched by this Russian soulfulness to say anything.

They ate, sitting quietly until "The Big Bad Wolf" began to play again. This time Tor's baritone absently joined the final notes of the chorus.

"You remind me. Since Saturday? Trivial thoughts are niggling at the back of my brain."

"We like those."

"*Singing*. If Houseman were here, and everybody joined in, as you say, you'd hear *him*. Not loud. Just, his voice would stand out."

"I get you."

"It's a gift. Listening to his trio made me recall that diving trip after election day. On the boat I talked a fair while with our Navy oceanographer. You weren't there."

"Work, work."

"So while Doerr was asking about that grad student he liked, he mentioned Houseman is quite political — in the self-seeking sense."

"You should hear Houseman. Very proud of his self-seeking."

"My unimportant insight was — everyone knows we react to a person's appearance. But I suspect far fewer are aware of how affected we can be by voices. In Houseman's case, my guess is he doesn't have to work very hard to influence people to his point of view. When you sound like the Archangel, people just naturally believe you."

"I have to say — I was unhappy about how credible I actually found him."

"Fine, maybe the man was being truthful."

Tor filled in Ogy about Allan Houseman's belated conviction that he, not his wife, had been a murderer's intended victim. Then he told him about this morning's visit to the Mackeys.

"You didn't track down Artie Vaccari?"

"Disappeared. But our interest in him was related to the Mackeys as suspects — in case they'd learned Lisette's identity from him. Gerald was in Boston, and that family do not look likely for it."

"That's good. Although after my conversation with Artie, one thing troubled me — he never explained how he knew Lisette's name

— to be able to check up on her afterwards. Probably it's something simple, like he worked at a banquet where Allan was the featured speaker. I just can't imagine remembering every name of all the customers you've served."

"Another possible," added Tor, "We stopped by to interview Claire Fields. Did you happen to meet her at the party?"

"Attractive girl in the red wig, I remember," said Dr. Bradley.

"What! How did you know it was a wig?"

"I spend so much time in hospitals. It's almost a matter of etiquette, to recognize our oncology patients —"

"She's not an oncology patient."

"No, I'm just saying, you learn to *see* the wigs." Ogy tapped together the toes of his trainers stretched outside the brick house doorway. "I assumed, a fashion statement. I mean, who seriously needs more than one pair of shoes? But lots of women have fifty pairs, as I understand. So — she likes a change of hair, too? What do I know?

"Anyway, what all this is leading to is — there was something fishy in Jon's quite discreet gossip about Allan. He said Houseman was the leader of a research cruise, where — my inference? — maybe something connects regarding this new PhD Jon liked, Cris Harbison. But when I ran into Lisette — was it a week before she died? She didn't know anything. Just said, "Oh, he's sweet." At that point it didn't seem important, except to Jon."

"I should challenge Houseman…?"

"I'd ask Doerr. Only because, that cruise is Jon's last tag to this kid Harbison, where he's worried something is not kosher. It was Houseman in charge, and now he's of interest to you. Whether as potential criminal or intended victim."

Piggy was making rounds of the tables, checking customer satisfaction. When she approached the brick house, Dr. Bradley said with fervor, "Ma'am, it was the best I've ever had, of everything! I greatly admire your talent."

When Tor sadly admitted they were too full for cherry lime pie, Piggy declared with a straight face, "I do have Persian coffee?"

The doctor's eyes bulged and his mouth dropped open. Then one glance at Abelove made him recall that, although he'd arrived early tonight, the detective had been here still earlier.

"I would love some Persian coffee, thank you," he nodded, resolved that it was worth being kept awake until tomorrow morning just to hold up his end of the gag. "Imagine that." He sounded startled. "She must get it —"

"From Iowa, where the pigs come from," agreed Tor.

While a vocalist Ogy didn't recognize sang about joining a wolf pack, he decided that this evening out with Tor in the fireside brick house was enough fun to justify drinking two cups of coffee, sleep be damned. He was remembering the illustration of three piglets in his own childhood book of nursery rhymes, and his distress at the carelessness of the first two. When he lamented their fate to his father, Michael Bradley had replied that *maybe the pigs did not know about the wolf.* Years afterward, he faulted his father for suggesting such metaphysical injustice to a small boy. But at least tonight, he and Abelove both had houses that couldn't be blown down, *tra-la!*

Later they would have no reason not to join the rest of the dining patrons in song, and boast of being unafraid.

TWENTY-SIX

INTERNATIONAL SQUABBLES

There had been few occasions in the life of Tor Abelove when he felt small. One vivid childhood experience was his family's visit to the mothball fleet berthed in Christina Harbor. In proximity to that vast gray palisade of silent steel ghosts even his chronically querulous parents fell mute. Over the years as toxins in the reserve fleet's paint contaminated the bay's seawater and tons of paint flakes lodged heavy metals into the seabed, by ones and twos the ships were gradually disassembled and sold for scrap. Although today their former anchorage boasts transparent cerulean water, anyone who remembers the ghost fleet cannot have forgotten the embedded underwater poisons it left behind.

On Thursday morning when Tor called his fellow diver Jon Doerr, the oceanographer was cordial but explained, "I work in a secured area. If you don't mind driving over here — we're just minutes from Bay Street — I'm more comfortable talking on the base than on the phone."

When he pulled out his driver's license and gold shield while approaching the naval installation's gatekeeper, Abelove noticed his heart rate had quickened. He had to chuckle at himself, wondering what adrenalin reactions other citizens experienced when arriving at Santa Christina Bay Street Police Headquarters.

Jon met him at the parking lot. As they walked back towards the offices Tor noticed arrow signs directing visitors to "Fish Village." He was surprised to see that the casual office complex was similar to the university's oceanography school, except that these buildings were sturdier — and more soundproof, masonry instead of frame.

Taking the chair beside Jon's desk, Tor commented "You have dolphins here."

"That's secret. Although not very. The research facility's off-bounds to tourists."

"I remember — dolphins guarded a political convention on the harbor some years back?"

"Among other events. To date, cetaceans' inborn sonar is still superior to human technology. But as you know, this is getting to be the drone age. In a few years robotics should be able to replace their skill set. Then maybe our finned colleagues can retire.

"Thanks, Steve," Jon nodded as a young man in uniform brought coffees, then withdrew.

"Allan Houseman." Tor's first sip suggested that Naval Warfare coffee was better than the SCPD's. "He's a person of interest. Omar didn't remember exactly what you said about him, the day of the dive.

But at that point Mrs. Houseman had not been murdered. What he does remember is that you hinted at something maybe shady.”

“I certainly didn't suggest anything shady at the level of killing his wife!”

“Understood. But what Houseman is insisting now — and not illogically — is that *he* was the targeted victim, not his nice Lisette.”

“Oh. That must feel strange.”

“Visibly. So the concern becomes, who has enough animus — or some large enough interest — to want him dead? We're almost confident there is something. Awkward enough that, even scared, Allan won't tell us.”

“I'm… gulping. All right. I've spent a little time, and now I'm glad I did. First off, I looked him up. Based on background, committees and so forth, I've got three names and numbers of guys who know or knew him well enough to direct you where else to look. The name on top, especially, he's early in the guy's career — and I got a feeling, about that one.

“Getting to Harbison, if he's a factor? There was an expedition, and I don't know what its mission was. But to prep you for talking to these people, not knowing what subjects they'll bring up — I should tell you about possible projects. Assuming you're not conversant.”

“Am not at all. Thank you.”

“Okay.” Jon shook his head, still looking shocked. “Biggest, but least likely — there's everything associated with offshore oil exploration. You can't turn on your TV without seeing some actress in her perfect kitchen, extolling the blessings of fossil fuels. That ad campaign wouldn't exist if the industry weren't still expanding. On the other end of the spectrum in terms of scale are the medicos like your friend Bradley, who sift sea and soil in hope of capturing any new organism that might provide a miracle cure for something.

"A related subject, of which you might not be aware — but it's a hot topic, would surely appeal to Cris — only recently have we come to understand that possibly as much as twenty per cent of the planet's biomass is hidden deep inside the earth or under the seas. Think of it! Twenty per cent of *all life,* comprised of microbes, tiny worms, surviving wherever heat and water combine! And there's plenty of both underground. Then — after NASA researchers found possible evidence of primitive life in a Martian meteorite, some scientists are suggesting Mars was chemically more hospitable to the creation of life, and that our earliest life forms got transported to Earth on meteorites — no, don't laugh —"

"Somebody… *seriously wants to know… THAT?*"

Tor had spilled coffee on his lap.

"But this is very serious. Look, even if you don't belong to the set of dreamers who worry about having an outpost on Mars in case something bad happens on Earth —"

"I worry about keeping the streets safe because something bad is always happening! *Worms…?*"

"Of course, we megafauna are your own first concern."

"Megafauna with guns and knives."

"But it's exactly from this realm of pure science that a subject which initially sounds silly can yield something world-changing."

"Sorry, Jon, no disrespect intended…."

"Anyway, back to whatever topic young Cris was so excited about, there are other research areas, not at all laughable, that are highly charged politically. One obviously is the health of the oceans themselves. That issue concerns not just effects of pollution, involving wrongdoers and price tags — but also consequences of climate change, which has become 'The Emperor's New Clothes' of American politics.

"And then, saving most up-front for last, there's the boiling controversy about all the world's fish stocks. It's political because practically every country on earth has an interest in it. It's hugely financial, because both industries and individuals in those countries rely on fishing for their survival. It's even cultural, a matter of identity politics. The cod fishermen, the tuna boats, the lobstermen — their lifestyles, even the existence of their towns is as dependent on fish as the miners' are upon coal. And if you think fish stock depletion looks threatening to our antique ports in New England — imagine how scary it must be in, say, the Japanese islands?

"In case that's not complicated enough — we're coming to realize that most of global warming is being concentrated in the oceans. If you can't conceive of a fish feeling too hot, ask yourself, where might she go, in pursuit of her own migrating food stock?"

"North?"

"Or south. So penguins and people in Reykjavik don't starve, but residents of the middling latitudes find it harder to catch protein. International squabbles about fishing rights keep getting messier."

"Okay, Jon. Thanks for the names and all your trouble. You send me off grateful for the relatively small scope of my problem."

"I don't underestimate your problem. We read about it. Sounded very sad."

"'Sad' is one aspect."

After exiting the defense installation, Abelove drove less than a mile before prickling curiosity got the better of him. He pulled over and parked in front of a pizzeria. Ignoring the garlicky aromas wafting into the car even with windows up, he phoned the top name on Jon Doerr's list.

"Hello, Detective," smirked the voice on the other end. "Jon pegged you for an eager beaver. Where do we start?"

"Dr. Graham? Thank you for talking to me. In confidence, the person we're discussing is potentially a suspect in our case, but is also being considered as the intended victim."

"Oh boy."

"Which means — even though we may charge him, there could be greater urgency in protecting him. So I need to know who dislikes him and why."

"Okay. First, I have to say I have no knowledge of what he has been up to for a very long time. I knew him early on, and I can tell you what he is: a thief and a charlatan. And for a guy who's not much to look at, he can be remarkably charming."

"Sir, my pen is poised."

"What do you know about his career?"

"Nothing worth mentioning."

"*Sinks and Sediments of the Pacific Plate.* In some circles, that is a famous title. Revisionist concept. It's the book he published very early in his career. Notice I didn't say, 'the book he *wrote.*'

"If you're in any way close to the university there — even if you just watch TV— you may have heard stories about graduate students who think the professor they're working for has stolen their work, published it under his own name. It's a delicate subject. What you don't hear is any tale about some grad student who steals the professor's work. But so far as some people are concerned — including me — that's exactly what happened to launch this guy's career. In a big way, let me assure you."

"How could that happen? Sounds impossible."

"This was in the 'eighties — when personal computers were coming into use and your old IBM typewriter was getting shunted into the garage sale. At that time, a gentleman who should have been long retired had a few younger PhDs working under him. I was one. Oskar Kisselbaum was considered by all of us a great man — in addition to being a top scholar. Oskar did not own a computer. He wrote with a fancy fountain pen his wife Adela had given him ages earlier. All his writing, all his data — it went into those bound notebooks with the black-and-white covers that look like the snow when your TV's not receiving a signal. I don't think his vision was good. Maybe small notebooks were easier to work with.

"Anyway, he was frail. While the rest of us moved elsewhere, your boy remained with Oskar. The old man interpreted that as personal loyalty. Then Oskar died. Everybody thought he'd been working on a book. Adela insisted there must be a manuscript.

"But nothing. When no traces of it could be found, a few murmurs started about how Oskar must have been getting senile — and pretending he was working.

"His 'devoted' disciple moved on. A year or so later Allan's first book came out. It was a milestone. Some people did see his preparation for it — the data, in different pens at different times. Notes, thoughts, partly typed but some handwritten on lined paper stained with spilt tea. Much what Oskar's notebooks would have looked like... if they still existed. But these were in Oskar's former post doc's handwriting, with later parts on computer.

"To some of us, what happened seemed obvious. He must have copied everything, a weekend at a time, with different pens on different paper. Then at the end, when Kisselbaum was dead? He would have destroyed all the old man's originals. So everything Oskar had been writing remained only in his plagiarist's hand."

"Of course you have no proof."

"Of course there isn't any — just my imagining my former colleague rushing in, grabbing and incinerating Oskar's meticulous notebooks.... But I knew the old man's vision. His student was more interested in success than in science. Allan's talent was for brown-nosing and self-promotion, which he pushed as far as it could take him.

"What I resent most is the money. Oskar didn't have a great deal. The proceeds from that book were meant, I think, to take good care of Adela. Didn't happen. Her son was angry enough to sue. Adela decided she couldn't risk winding up with less than nothing."

"He drives a Mercedes now," allowed Tor. "Big one."

"Small man. If Oskar's son kills him, let him get away with it," grumbled Dr. Graham.

When the detective arrived back at Bay Street headquarters, he did not immediately call the other two numbers on Jon Doerr's list. Officer Lopez was waiting for him, impatiently.

"Sir? It wasn't hard at all to find Mrs. Harbison. Her son lives with her."

"Call and tell her we'll come later this afternoon."

TWENTY-SEVEN

THE NOVICE MARTIAL ARTIST

Ingrid Becker's older husband Matthias had always insisted, "Ingrid is the only kid I want."

Again this year she had accepted Ogy's routine invitation to a restaurant Thanksgiving with him, his daughter Anthea and her occasional fiancé, Dan Griswold. Lacking children, Ingrid counted herself fortunate to share the holiday with even this slippery facsimile of a family.

The truly surprising invitation came the next day.

"Mrs. Becker," sang the young voice on the phone, "This is Linda Abelove. We met at Ogy's lunch party in July?"

More accurately, the two women differing in age by fifty years had been thoroughly delighted by one another, despite or possibly because of mutually exclusive life experiences.

"After that lunch *my husband* remarked to me how pretty you looked in your blue dress. He's never said anything like that before about anyone. — Well, maybe he wouldn't praise somebody twenty-nine to me...."

"I'm flattered, nevertheless."

"Mrs. Becker, I think Tor wants me to buy… something nice to wear. And the truth is, I never learned how to shop. My family didn't have money or need any special clothes. So I was wondering if, as a favor, we might go together to some stores you like? I could pick you up at Casa Bunya, and we can drive anyplace you suggest. I promise not to keep you out too long."

That remark prompted a rumble of low laughter.

"My dear girl — you can't keep me out long enough! And please call me 'Ingrid.' Here's what I propose — yes, I can think of stores you might like."

The emphysema patient had to pause for breath.

"But first — we go just to look. *Just looking* is the primary skill you need — browsing clothes racks is a skill in itself. Another time — you can go back alone or with Tor. Second — in return for the outing, I buy you lunch."

Ignoring Thursday's gusts and gray skies, Linda dropped off Timmy with her mother and collected Ingrid at the Casa. In the morning they visited a high-end fashion outlet. Then, before moving on to boutiques catering to women Linda's age, they lunched elegantly at a window beside a bay tossed with whitecaps — by motorboat only minutes away from where Tor was visiting Jon Doerr.

"Your littlest — he's with your mother?"

"My mom is Marjorie. Dad is Hiroshi."

"He's Japanese. And your mother — ? Forgive my asking, dear. My career was tracing origins and migrations of peoples. But individuals fascinate me too."

"Mom's your generic German blonde."

"Not Lutheran, then?" Ingrid recalled from their first meeting that Linda was Catholic.

"Oh — Catholicism's on my father's side."

Ingrid's expression made Linda giggle.

"Really. His family were from the southwest islands visited by Portuguese explorers. It's a peculiar hybrid that developed down there, but I inherit it from my Grandma Kimura."

"Your husband is Catholic too? Or —"

"I think of Tor more as pantheist. And no, that doesn't trouble me. The way it feels is, we take different paths to the same place." Mrs. Abelove beamed.

"Even if you weren't such good company, Linda — that would make my day! I'd never heard of tropical Japanese Catholics. I wish I could tell my husband. I wonder if Matt knew?"

"What was he like, your famous archaeologist?"

"You realize, he and Ogy's father Michael were best friends? We worked as a team."

"'Becker and Bradley.' Tor says Ogy mentioned — Mr. Becker was like a film star."

Ingrid sighed.

"Ogy probably meant 'spoiled and temperamental.' And, yes, handsome, for what it's worth. When I was young — Matt seemed like the moon. You'd never know where he'd brilliantly turn up…."

"And Ogy? You've known him a long time?"

"Since he was seven."

"Really?"

"He called me 'Aunt Ingrid.'"

"That's incredible! Please, Tor will want to know — what was he like?"

Ingrid covered her mouth with both hands and chortled.

"Exactly the same."

"No! You're teasing."

"Omar — is a constant."

"But — Tor thought — I don't mean to *ask*. But — he thinks Dr. Bradley has… special feeling for you. 'Old feeling,' Tor said."

"Tor's a good detective. When Ogy was sixteen and I was thirty-four…."

Ingrid laughed at Linda's gape.

"…And Matthias was fifty, things did become a little strained. For other reasons, Matt was behaving like an infant. Omar had grown up. But what Tor thinks — didn't happen."

Even as she said it, Ingrid realized Linda must hear an implied possibility.

Young Mrs. Abelove grew solemn. Ingrid waited, sipping tea, and after a minute Linda told her about her husband's insistence that she should take martial arts lessons.

For Tor's sylph of a wife that did sound incongruous.

Cautiously Ingrid said, "I understand how you could be put off by the idea. Any combat — not your temperament. But, even sympathizing, at your age I would have been thrilled to try it. Just being *allowed*."

"You worked surrounded by men."

"Always. And controlled them with my big mouth."

"Let me tell you the amazing part. I've only been going for three weeks, but — I love it. After just these few lessons, I think I understand Tor better — differently, than I ever did."

"That *is* amazing."

"It's not what I expected," Linda nodded. "There's philosophy involved. Our Master Hwan is a quiet, kind man. Tor can seem… bigger than life. Because he's intense about his work. But he has a quiet center. There's a balance inside Tor never loses. And now I wonder if this discipline is where that stillness in him comes from? I always assumed he learned his poise on a surfboard.

"I'm half Asian. But it feels weird, sensing how he can seem more Asian than me."

"*In fact* —" The archaeological anthropologist cast Linda a wicked smile. "Your Russian husband may well *be* part Asian." Over Linda's delighted gasp she continued, "But they must be treating you well at the gym, if you're so comfortable there."

"Wonderfully. Plus, a big surprise was, at my first class I saw Ted Friedland there."

"Teddy!"

"Yes, he's so encouraging. There are two women who are very serious, I haven't dared speak to them yet. Nadine and Jane. I feel… beneath their notice. But then a funny thing happened that put my self-consciousness into perspective. A new girl came, younger than me — Mara. She has little blonde curls — to me curls seem miraculous. And Mara asked me for help. I'd only been there — six or so times? And somebody thinks I know what I'm doing."

"Learn from Mara. If you like Nadine and Jane — speak to them. A friendship is like a seat mate on a bus. Choose yours, or be chosen."

Looking very serious, Linda nodded.

"Tor took me there the first evening, to introduce me to Master Hwan. Then Ted walked in, and… it looks like they're friends."

Ingrid's faint smile acknowledged her understanding of Linda's dubious tone.

"Even though six months ago Tor was questioning him about — well, murder."

"Sometimes men set a good example. *Forward*-looking. What did they talk about?"

"I don't think we exactly told you, at Ogy's — Tor was a competitive surfer, big time. World title. He's been lots of places — Australia, Hawaii of course, Peru, Portugal. Ted knew nothing about waves, but — just as a computer programmer, he did seem really interested."

"The only waves in my experience are in desert sand."

"Some beaches have higher quality waves than others. Every surfer has to gauge what size he can handle. There are waves only somebody as good as Tor should attempt.

"So then Ted had the idea of creating an application surfers could check for information about waves in different locations. If you love a left hand break —"

"But that sounds impossible. What's more ephemeral than a wave?"

"Tor sounded enthusiastic, though. Lots of beaches around the world aren't even evaluated yet. They change, but gradually."

"I've learned so much from you today, Linda!" Ingrid marveled. "Thank you for this privileged conversation. I wish you many rewards from your new friendships."

Totally enchanted by the novelty of what she had been hearing, Ingrid was dismayed to see her companion's lovely face turn somber, as if she had been insulted. Quickly Linda smiled again, but the older woman understood something had disturbed the girl. They continued "just looking" until it was almost time for the elder Abelove children to return from school.

Back at Casa Bunya, Ingrid wondered what might be troubling the novice martial artist.

TWENTY-EIGHT

NICOLA

Santa Christina's Almira district had become a prime example of an old neighborhood's ability to ascend from dereliction and crime to safety and high real estate values. To the surprise of some older residents, this change was occurring largely as a result of the influx of gay homebuyers. The newcomers repainted their vintage houses in sophisticated shades and replanted their yards with creative gardens and scrupulously maintained lawns. Their quickly established Neighborhood Watch remained attentive to neighbors' properties as well as their own. After a home invasion in which two hoodlums were merely wounded by armed homeowners, gang leaders appreciative that their members had deliberately not been killed began to withdraw their criminal activities from Almira.

Santa Christina's police were impressed. Local patrolmen developed professional friendships with local change agents mobilized for crime prevention and civic solidarity. Whether you were Black, White or a member of an immigrant group, if you were sick your doorbell would very likely chime to announce a friendly neighbor arriving with a hot dinner, and flowers.

As they approached Mrs. Harbison's address, Tor noticed that Almira's gentrification was spottier than he had realized. Streets in the south-facing hills had a long view to downtown and beyond, besides overlooking the district's own coffee shops and art galleries. So prosperous did that neighborhood now appear that any house not yet updated would be snapped up even before officially on the market. Although the day was overcast and it would soon be growing dark, he could see that the western area they were entering, closer to the sea, did not look nearly as well maintained. These homes almost surely still belonged to people who had owned them for a long time and could not afford to reroof, repaint or replant.

While driving, even young Alvaro Lopez commented, "Lawns around here look like just dogs are watering them."

Tor recalled that during this prolonged drought the price of water had been going up.

"Linda's father gave us our trees and camellias. Letting them brown out would be as bad as starving the dog."

"Maybe the new people moving in don't like the freeway noise on this side?"

"Could be because there's commercial stuff mixed in. Doctor, realtor. Not as homey."

"Lamp shop. But I'd still choose here, for ocean air. Worse pollution on the other side."

Unlike homes on those more prevalently residential streets, the Harbison house was not an adobe bungalow, but a Victorian frame two-story. A long time ago it had been painted a morose beige, with faded brown trim that reminded Tor of Timmy's dirty diapers. He wondered how many coats would be needed to restore its original white.

The homeowner who answered the Harbisons' door astonished both policemen. Immediately Tor calculated that she had to be at least fifteen years older than he was, but still he could feel that this was a woman it would be possible to get into a lot of trouble over. Not that she would instigate it. Her dignity was evident before she'd even spoken to them. But she possessed a draw, all right.

(*Ignore that at your peril, copper,* he thought.)

"You're different." She looked befuddled. "But — I'm Nicola Harbison."

The pair of officers introduced themselves while the woman busied herself with cups of tea, not much interested in their identities — which was fine, because she did powerfully compel interest in herself. Although her dress did not reveal a lot of leg above those delicately ankle-strapped high heels, it was enough to keep their eyes slowly moving up, up, observing her figure become subtly more full, in the way a widening river need not appear to move to convey its cautionary depth and force.

Despite the neglected exterior of the house, both men noticed that the interior was almost richly furnished. Pictures on the walls were not exactly genuine art, but attractive. Abelove guessed that, if removed, each would reveal a rectangle of unfaded hue. This pleasant interior had not been refurbished in a long time.

"Ma'am, what did your husband do?" Unprepared, all he knew about Mrs. Harbison was that she was widowed.

"He managed a furniture store in the valley here," she said.

"Very nice room, ma'am."

He was thinking that the woman herself, with a slight foreign accent, must have been a dazzler, not long ago.

"Thank you. One thing we never went without was furniture."

After handing each of them a teacup the woman sat with her own, revealing knees sculpted like cathedral carvings and legs that were slim and muscular, as if she still used them.

"You're here about the cars." In a dress and jacket, she was polite but perfunctory, as if they were an extraneous detail to be dealt with before returning to Nicola's greater concerns.

"'Cars'?"

"Yes. I did tell the other officers, if they wanted to see my son they should come later in the evening. He works until nine tonight. Fortunately I was able to get off — to meet you."

Tor noticed her smiling glance at Alvaro. Earlier he had been annoyed that Smithers was home sick today, because he preferred to have her along when interviewing women. But this one was the mother of a son. Her brief bright look made him realize that his officer of about her own boy's age probably warmed her toward them, more than Tina would have.

"What did you tell her?" Now Abelove guessed that Alvaro may have been too cryptic.

"Sir, just that you wished to speak to her." Lopez looked sheepishly apologetic.

"But — Mrs. Harbison — this isn't about any cars —"

"*Of course it is!*" The lady jumped to her feet, opened a table drawer and retrieved a card both men recognized as the SCPD's.

"Your — friends left this, a few days ago!" She handed it to Abelove. "There is some confusement. Last week somebody visiting his doctor on this street reported it — his own car and some others broken into. Glass all over the street. This man saw my son on the sidewalk. Like many thoughtless people he took Cris for some cretin — *which he is not.*"

"Ma'am?" said Abelove softly, almost tenderly, "Mrs. Harbison? This card — those officers were from our Robbery Division. Officer Lopez and I represent Homicide."

"*Homicide* —?" The lady quailed. "I don't know any homicide! What are you talking about? This is some mistake, don't you see? Your people last week came to investigate the break-ins of some cars parked outside my house and —"

"Mrs. Harbison — you must have heard that a woman was murdered in El Albergue, just this past weekend?"

"*No?*" Nicola insisted, shaking her head. "I work? In a department store — even Sundays I do. I scarcely glance at the paper, don't watch TV much. What are you talking about, murder? They accused our Cristoforo of breaking into some cars, because he's handicapped."

"We're not accusing your son here —"

"*Somebody* did! The man whose car was broken into did. My Cris has his doctorate! He was a scientist, until the accident. And now — he works because the supermarket has this policy, like charity. They hire retarded people to stack cans. Cris is not retarded, but — he seems to be. The gentlest soul, but so disabled — so the police believed that man when he accused him of breaking into cars. He never touched any car, unless he stumbled —"

"What was the accident, ma'am?" interrupted Alvaro. "What happened to your son?"

"He drowned. But then — he was revived. So damaged. Why are you talking about murder?" beseeched the aggrieved mother.

Mrs. Harbison," soothed Tor, "Please don't be upset, I'm sure this car thing is nothing. A woman was killed, on Saturday. The wife of Allan Houseman. Do you know him?"

"*Houseman...?*" asked the dark-haired beauty. Those richly balsamic eyes promising complex emotion suddenly darted with fear.

"I can't — I can't talk about that."

"You mean — about Allan? You do know him, then?"

"No. I never met — I'm not allowed to talk about it. Please."

"What do you mean, you're 'not allowed'—?"

"I signed a settlement. *It was a terrible mistake.* I realize now, but I was desperate. My son was dying, I thought —"

"What kind of settlement?" Alvaro interrupted again.

"One hundred thousand. Not nearly enough. I was such a fool. Cris is helpless, so young. What does this murder have to do —?"

They all heard the front door creak open.

Then, *"Nico?"* called a male voice, not young. "I bought baby artichokes and veal. I can make gnocchi, too, if Cris wants —"

Both visitors heard Mrs. Harbison gasp as the distressed woman willed herself to her feet.

"Officers," she announced in a quavering voice, "My longtime *ex*-husband... but still Cristoforo's father. Arturo Vaccari."

TWENTY-NINE

VERY BAD THOUGHTS

On the blond wood table beside Detective Abelove's chair, an edge of a round doily lay folded back on itself. His left hand slowly passed over its crocheted texture, smoothing it with a lingering caress as if it were a lover's sleeve. If Lopez and Mrs. Harbison had not been looking toward the man approaching from the front hall, the detective's expression while his right hand carefully lowered the teacup and saucer would have embarrassed them both.

Tor's normally sober face had creased into a leer of anticipation like lust.

~ ~ ~

Very likely Artie Vaccari had been a flight risk his entire adult life. For the drive from the Harbison home back to Bay Street the officers cuffed him.

Without any discernible communication between them, after parking in the police lot on Christina Bay Street the junior officer politely removed the handcuffs.

"I'm under arrest for something?"

"No, not now, sir."

In the elevator ride to Floor Three the detective said, "Sorry about your artichokes and veal, but you'll have to make do with whatever we have."

"Doesn't matter."

Instead of acting tense, as murder suspects customarily do, the waiter sounded professionally polite, despite looking weary and resigned. If slender Nicola Harbison in her work attire did not cook as competently as her ex-husband apparently did, later tonight Cris might receive a meal from a can or freezer carton. Vaccari's final words had been, "Nico, bake just eight minutes. Or freeze until I come back."

In the interrogation room their captive declined anything but water. Detective Lianopoulos was out, but Officer Bruno Belknap sat in with them.

"It looks like there's a long history here," Tor began, still preoccupied by this ordinary-looking man's extraordinary ex-wife. "Why did you come to this country? When?"

"I was working at a restaurant in Rome. My wife realized she was pregnant. And right then I received an offer — a better job, in New York. So — those two things together? Fate. We decided to try 'the new world.' Our child would be American. Named 'Cristoforo' for the explorer, Colombo. That's it."

"Not yet. When did Harbison enter the picture? And die?"

Vaccari's air of relaxed tolerance was irritating. Now he even laughed.

"I'm not *Sicilian,*" he protested, and grinned at all three younger men. Then, looking tired, he sat back in the chair, resigned again.

"After — two years? Another offer, back in Italy. So I went. My wife was working too, nights, for a while. That way a neighbor could keep Cris. So we lived separate. I sent money back, but — . It's not a way to stay married."

"What are you leaving out?"

"New York's expensive. Nicola was — real good looking. Started selling dresses. And then there was a chance for her to move to a new store being built out here. Brand new shopping center. California was cheaper to live. Nicer than New York for our boy.

"So — I was in Italy, and Nico and Cris here. Two plane fares away. Santa Christina wasn't a real big town then. Not so many restaurants. — Not *quality* restaurants. But after, it grew fast. Lots of houses built. New people buying furniture."

"That's when she met Harbison?"

He became quiet.

"When?"

"I don't know. But I don't blame her."

"She didn't do anything you weren't doing."

"Hardly."

"You make yourself sound remarkably open-minded. We've seen Mrs. Harbison."

That earned Tor a look that was almost a glare, but of ill-humor tempered by decades.

"What you're asking? Yeah. I could have killed Don Harbison. But I didn't. My wife — my son too — they were better off with him. I could see. Don bought him a skateboard. Bicycle. *A house.* He was a good father to Cris. Better than me.

"The letters talked about gymnastics lessons. Soccer. Until the letters stopped.

"Cris had no use for me. I was no use to them. I — got used to that, long time ago."

None of his three listeners looked convinced.

"Sir," persisted Tor, "Everything we've heard about Cris is that he is a fine young man. But now in a much worse way he's been taken from you — again."

"Why — are you doing this? I thought you wanted to ask me about the party Saturday. I was there, all over the place. Why handcuffs? Why all this about *me*?"

"Sir? Please answer directly. Do you blame Allan Houseman for your son's accident? For the brain damage it appears he suffered on that expedition led by Dr. Houseman?"

"I — *yeah! Yeah, sure I do!* But how does that — you don't — you don't think I would *hurt Mrs. Houseman?* Because of HIM?

"Is that it…? You're thinking — to hurt him back? But — that's crazy. You don't know him. It would pain him more to scuff his English shoes. To scratch his German car. He thinks only of himself, that one. Mrs. Houseman disappeared at the party and *he never even noticed.*

"I thought she went home. Maybe because of me? It's not a long walk."

"Mr. Vaccari — it appears now that Mrs. Houseman may have been killed by accident. That her murderer intended to kill Mr. Houseman. When his group went to sing he handed her his mulled wine. It was poisoned."

"The red? I never served it, the other two did. I served the white in stems, they couldn't balance the trays. I never went within ten feet of Houseman. Once, he came to me. For a glass of white."

"You've just been explaining to us — you have nothing to lose."

Lethargic no longer, Vaccari was thinking hard now. He looked genuinely surprised.

"Mrs. Harbison —" he stared at the exigent detective. "— She wants nothing to do with me. I understand that. Caring for Cris is on her now. But she has to work, and I can cook. There's no chance of moving in, but it's a big house and sometimes I stay over. For the first time in my life, I do things for Cristoforo. That's what I live for. I feed him *well*. He's still Italian."

"What does 'TRAITOR!' mean? On the Housemans' wall?"

"Don't ask me." The witness shrugged.

"Speaking as a father, sir, I just can't believe you don't want revenge on the man responsible for his accident. In your situation, I would harbor very bad thoughts."

"With God as my witness — *I do*." murmured Vaccari.

"I'd think, death was too good for him!"

"That's right. Too good. There is no suffering in death." Sadly Vaccari shook his head.

"This — it's something different. From when somebody with more money steals your wife."

"How do you mean?"

"There'd be no satisfaction. No satisfaction possible. Nothing to make better. Not for my son."

"Why spend so much time on the Strand? You've hung out there, off and on, for a few years, we've heard."

Vaccari almost smiled.

"...All three of them. At first, just because of Cris. He was a student at that ocean school. Happy. Sometimes I'd see my boy — without him seeing me. From a distance. After living two continents away? That was a feast for me.

"But after he went on that trip with Houseman as boss? I'd go there... just to hate. To be near Allan Houseman, where he lives, works — thinking what I'd like to do to him."

"Which is?"

"I'd like to hold him under water a long time. Until most of his brain dies. Until he has just enough intelligence left to know he's lost his intelligence. I would like that."

"But you didn't...?" Young Belknap sounded out of his depth.

"I'm a weak man, not an evil one. Then one day — there was that accident with Mrs. Houseman. I left, didn't want to be involved. But after, I worried. I should have gone to the police. Told them — 'What the paper says happened isn't true.'

"So now, after poor Lisette? I dream Houseman spends his life in prison for murdering her — especially if he didn't do it. That would hurt him, in his pride. To be despised."

Then he added, "Some people are nice to Cristoforo. But most people think he's a creep. That's what I want to happen to Allan."

"You admit you have these elaborate fantasies. But claim you've never acted on them. I have to say, that invites skepticism."

Vaccari shrugged again, as if to deny he was any kind of thinker.

"'Never acted....' No. Maybe because — in my work, all I ever did was serve. — I don't mean like, in the army. Just, putting pasta in front of people. It doesn't make you feel important. In a way, maybe that turned out for the good. Saved me. I'm a failure at life. But I'm a good waiter. One step up from being a nun."

"How's that?"

"You can leave."

"We're taking a break."

After Bruno removed Arturo Vaccari from the room Tor grabbed Alvaro's arm and growled, "Something else is going on here! *I'm not sure anymore what we're talking about?*"

THIRTY

THREAT LOOMING

Allan had not enjoyed his stay in Elinor's mountainside apartment. The alpine hamlet had one main street, oriented entirely to tourist business. As good as the pines smelled, he did not want to see another candle shop or Christmas trim store, ever. After two dinners out they had used up the town's best dining options. In the evenings Elinor watched TV. Even going early to bed — and it was a terrible bed — he was still annoyed by the sound of her television and tried to pass time reading. But after an old issue of *Time* there wasn't worthwhile print left anywhere.

He did feel guilty about his ill-humor, especially since his sister had rushed down to El Albergue to stay with him as soon as he told her about Lisette's "accident." Surliness about her habits in her own home when he was the intruder was worse than unreasonable. But what wasn't unreasonable was his shock at discovering a grand strategy brewing in that little blonde head.

On Wednesday over a cold sugary cereal breakfast Elinor apologized, "Sorry I can't take the time to fry up something nice, but getting ice off the windshield is a lot of bother. Each time I waste gas running the engine to warm it, I think about how it's probably sixty degrees in El Albergue."

"You've got a really short drive to work, though. In El Al, the mile into town can take twenty minutes in morning rush hour."

"Allan, you're so busy and work so hard, I'd be happy to come take care of you now —"

Allan was aghast.

How had he not seen this threat looming?

For a few seconds he felt more panicked than he had when fleeing Santa Christina, constantly checking the rearview mirror, to reach Elinor's anonymous mountain refuge.

"And I'd pay you a fair rent too, gladly. That's no problem —"

The idea of her moving in with him was an enormous problem!

"I can see how that might actually be fun, a brother and sister sharing a house. — If it were some big old New England colonial," he improvised.

"You're looking awfully thin."

"— Where we each had our area like a private reserve — we'd meet at dinner — sometimes. Not be forced to share a bathroom —"

I'm wondering if you'll eat properly, without Lise to cook for you? I'd be happy to do all the cooking —"

"But I prefer eating out — alone, mostly. Lets me think my deep thoughts. Besides, hon, in our tiny house in the Strand every belch and fart is a public event, ha ha! Neither of us would have any privacy. If Lisette walked about half dressed, that was nice. But I don't want to see anybody else headed to the shower. A twenty-foot bedroom you can comfortably hide out in, but ours are tiny. I won't be taking in roommates for fun and don't need extra income."

He could see she wasn't deterred. Elinor apparently had no concept of "a fair rent" in El Albergue Strand, if she thought it wouldn't be a problem for her. The attraction of saving money by sponging off him must be powerful, since she had never finished college and worked at low-paying jobs since she quit.

Besides, the idea that Elinor could match Lisette's cooking was crazy. Of course he was willing to help her out if needed. But he would not subsidize her lack of ambition.

Thinking further about that unpleasantness left him in a foul mood. For one thing, it brought to mind the stark reality that after their mother passed his half-sister would be his only heir. Allan was quietly infuriated by how distasteful that idea was. Without Lisette or a child, it forced him to face the bleakness of his own unmourned mortality. But more than that, he simply disliked the idea that Elinor, who had never done anything, should receive everything.

Already she was gaining too much weight.

Lisette he had never begrudged. She worked. Her work was respected. Most of all, she had been putting up with him for many years now. Certainly Lisette had deserved the house, the car and whatever else they accumulated together by the time he died.

The more graphic his visions of Elinor moving into Lise's house, stuffing Lise's cupboards with awful sugar-coated cereal and denting his Mercedes, the more noxious an irritant she became.

The antidote, marrying again, was equally scary.

He decided to leave Norwald earlier than he had intended. His excuse was that he must visit the office and make arrangements for Lisette's memorial service, if the police were ready to allow it. With bad weather forecast, on mountain roads? Leaving earlier Thursday would also avoid crossing east county during rush hour.

The jubilation of escaping Elinor made Allan temporarily forget why he had fled to the mountains in the first place: no one knew she lived in Norwald. Once on the road, though, his anxiety that he might be hunted by an unknown assailant returned. *If I were the murderer, I could find out where Elinor lives and soon recognize my Mercedes in Norwald, then wait to ambush me.*

After the first half of the drive, near panic caused him to stop at an isolated country restaurant where no one might look for him — except Elinor, who had mentioned it to him. But at even this short distance he could feel affection for her again.

The Fairwaye Inn's dining room boasted a large stone fireplace, despite the fact that wood fires were now disapproved in Santa Christina County. Seated beside it and confident no one here would try to poison him, Allan entertained himself by staring at a nineteenth century American flag, trying to guess how many stars were on its complex field without actually counting them.

He ordered a much heavier meal than he was accustomed to. The Coquilles St. Jacques were a bit glutinous but he enjoyed them, eating slowly and reading the newspaper. But when pot roast in gravy with potatoes was served he became suspicious. It seemed to him that this meal was not freshly prepared — that it was an entrée the restaurant must have purchased frozen, then reheated in their kitchen. The gravy was too thick and everything was too salty.

So much for trusting Elinor's recommendation, so much for her delusion she can cook.

No sooner had he forgotten his annoyance that his sister would inherit all his worldly goods than Allan Houseman was struck hard by the reality of losing his wife. Lisette would have prepared these dishes beautifully, creating the sauces from stock she made herself. He missed her greatly. Especially in this dim room's firelight, he remembered how the sheen of her dark hair always reminded him of fresh blueberries. He missed her pertly poetic face, so pretty in each graceful detail of brow, cheek and lashes, her ardent smiles always with such fond humor and anecdote across the table.

This sudden misery at comprehending she was gone caused him to linger at the Fairwaye Inn. He consumed the entire dinner because it was all he had, and aromatic wood fires were becoming rare. Even though there had been nothing much to do in Norwald besides eat local apple pie, despite misgivings he ordered pie too.

It wasn't Lise's tarte tatin, but he crunched each tough chunk.

Resuming the trip home, the sky was overcast. Today's paper had warned that rain might really be on the way tonight. Without any precipitation yet, the air felt wet. He drove with the defroster on. Dallying beside the fireplace for almost two hours had brought him to the city's outskirts as rush hour was beginning. Around four, when he reached El Albergue, a patter of rain had begun and the wipers were running.

Allan pulled his Mercedes into the garage beside Lisette's Honda. Rather than fight through book boxes to the garage's side door, he came around the front through the gate in the defaced stucco wall that still proclaimed "TRAITOR!"

To close the garage door, it was simpler to reach its switch just inside the garage's side door from the brick-paved walkway leading to the kitchen entry.

The sudden sharp stab of pain in his heart made him regret forking up so much dense gravy and over-sweet pie.

THIRTY-ONE

BELL JAR

For patrons of Strand area restaurants it was possible to arrive at Thursday's Happy Hour, order drinks with appetizers and converse beside windows that thrummed and streamed from the brief staccato downpour, then return to their dripping cars without ever feeling a raindrop. The misty evening air seemed to create a bell jar of still warmth over the beach area, insulating strollers who were not discouraged from visiting the sand or boardwalk. Later, whitecaps and stormy surf revealed by the beachfront Posada's high spotlights would provide a dramatic spectacle, since the waterline was high, the noisy tide incoming throughout the hotel's dinner hours.

Having taken public transport to work, Dr. Bradley was lucky to exit the bus with his umbrella just as the first drops began falling on Bunya Road. Before heavy rain began he hustled around the corner into Strand Road's Mariscos Valorosos, which served martinis. After dallying over fish tacos and flan with berries, he noticed that the rain had stopped. Feeling victorious, ten minutes later he unlocked his own door and greeted Ghazi. Neither Cael nor Thea would be home for dinner. The new congressman had finagled a short appointment with one of California's senators today. With a view to finding common ground between the environmental priorities of their two states he had taken a plane to meet her and would not return until late. Ogy in his slippers was grateful to Mrs. Park that his infant roses were newly drenched on the patio instead of still staining the hall floorboards.

Dr. Bradley's upstairs bedroom was in the front of the house, with a view over Strand neighborhoods to the sea; and his den and family room at the back of the house were equipped with wood shutters to prohibit sunlight from creating glare on their TVs. During the past few days he had had no reason to look outside beyond his patio or to inspect his small segment of Reposo from Cael's and Anthea's southern rooms. So, despite having recently gained very small fame as an amateur detective, he remained oblivious to the construction project that had been ongoing in his own backyard during the shorter light hours while he was away from home.

On Friday morning he made an early breakfast for Cael and promised him a special dinner with Anthea that evening, before his early Saturday flight back east. As the two Bradley men drove off, it would be impossible to say which felt more content.

For Ogy the only downside of driving to the university was that, since he began taking the bus, he had received much satisfaction from being able to circumvent the sculpture garden which he must pass while walking from his parking lot to the medical buildings. Where the fine arts were concerned, he scarcely considered himself a conservative person. His own artist wife had expressed enthusiasm for much contemporary art, which more often than not he shared.

Dr. Bradley did not require art to be uplifting. Whimsical creations could be worthwhile as well. But the pervasive tenor of pieces assembled in this sculpture garden was sniggering — all of them purchased by an individual who was not so much the garden's guiding spirit as its plenipotentiary. O.G. Bradley remained baffled that the administration should allow such absolute decision-making authority for a substantial component of its art collection to one man of no conspicuous qualification besides a facility for smiling while expelling bombast.

Recently Ogy had conceded ground regarding the garden's centerpiece, a crayfish in awkwardly executed Grecian drapery. He now allowed that the crustacean Demosthenes might seem witty to the undergraduates who left flowers behind its flopped antenna. But that thin charm withered quickly after one learned that every campus installation represented a similar rude joke.

A student who was unlocking the brochure case smiled at his approach. He smiled back. Her head was partially shaved in complicated paths. The shaved strips were tattooed in an intricate formal pattern. Between the strips, fine braids coiled in a repeated Grecian wave motif.

"There's a new flyer." The art major extended one from her sheaf.

"Thank you very much," he nodded, accepting it.

Strolling past a sourly cross-eyed takedown of Rodin's *Thinker* scratching his head, Ogy glanced over this latest directory to the sculpture garden.

"THE NEW IRONY" was the headline over the introductory essay. It was accompanied by a marginal inset photo of the grinning curator who had selected all these pieces.

Inauspiciously the essay began, *"What are the functions of a liberal rats university?*

"To perpetuate understanding of proud traditions, but create a capacity for constructive iconoclasm? To delineate eternal principles of beauty, but reevaluate them? To analyze historic institutions, potentially to challenge and overturn them?"

Ogy folded the paper and slid it into his briefcase.

A short time afterwards he was slipping on a white lab coverall when his phone rang.

"Good morning. There isn't background noise to your sukiyaki omelet," detected Tor.

"Cael was home this morning. Flies back tomorrow."

"So glad you've had the time with him. What I'm calling about is to tell you, before you see it on TV tonight — we brought in Artie Vaccari yesterday. Talked to him 'til late. Vaccari is Cris Harbison's natural father. The kid drowned on Houseman's trip, suffered brain damage."

"That's what it was…."

"Vaccari looks good for this. Very. The Captain and the Chief both like him for it — for the attempt on Allan, not intending her."

"But I told you —"

"You told me he was upset about her. Remorseful — well sure he is, he would be."

"You're saying — he totally conned me. All right. I concede — he may be smarter than I am. But *not that much.* I just happened upon him, sitting there —"

"Doc, he had days to perfect his story. For any audience. That part I have no problem with. Not smarter than you — cunning. And rehearsed."

"I've just been reading this flyer about our sculpture garden. What the man writes sounds okay. Trouble is, there's a disconnect between his logical paragraph and the reality of his silly art."

"Now you're doing it. What you say sounds plausible except it doesn't at all accord with *what I observed.*"

"There's just one thing I can't make gel. I exaggerate, to provoke him. To get a genuine reaction. But instead of denying it — the man escalates. Raises me, I feel like some poker novice against a pro. He makes himself sound worse than I was doing. Something is odd. I don't know what game he's playing."

"I wish we could talk —"

"Can't."

"I'm sorry. I shouldn't interfere."

"No."

Tor ended the call.

THIRTY-TWO

THE POM-POM CULTIVAR

"CAELAAAN!"

It happened as fast as when the ridgeback leaped for him on Tuesday. But this time as soon as he opened the door the vacuum cleaner sighed off and he was nabbed. A tactical error, to forget after decades that the cleaning dominatrix swept through on Fridays.

"Why you no call Daddy! He so not happy, have heart attack and still his boy not call, why that?"

"Hi, Mrs. Park. For a long time I didn't have a phone. I've got one now."

"Miss Thea work and work seven day, but she come see him. Make him Grandma fish, bring other Persia treat with pommygrant.

All good heart, Miss Thea. You call him. Big empty place for him now, without Mama. *You know* — Mrs. Bradley, *she not happy* how her boy not call Daddy."

"No, I'm sure you're right. Good to see you, Mrs. Park."

He started up the stairs — shadowed by Ghazi dragging a mortified tail.

"Cael, you leave towel wet in hamper always. I don't come, mold grow everything. Hang or good enough like Daddy spread across washer."

"Okay. I rubbed down Ghazi, thought I shouldn't rehang it after that."

"Now make Ghazi miss you too? Think better, Cael."

The vacuum cleaner roared back to life.

"Nobody misses me — now."

"*Oh?* I dust airplanes. I miss you."

Cael lay on the bed beside the dust-free Warthog, Tiger Shark and Corsair models — mostly constructed by Daddy, although he had at least stuck on their decorations. He was not thinking about whether Ghazi would miss him. He was thinking that he would miss Ghazi.

If he asked, would Ogy give him the dog? Probably he didn't much care. He was far too busy to keep a pet.

Only of course Cael was going to be even busier himself soon — and living with three other congressmen, to boot.

But the congressional term was just two years. Afterwards he might have to go home.

Home.

His cabin was twelve feet by eleven. He couldn't expect Ghazi to live in a space that small. It wouldn't be fair even to a Shih Tzu. The cabin was adequate for just his solitary self, able to shower at the

"Y." Whenever he stayed away for a few hours, his wood stove grew cold.

He would return to find his dog frozen solid.

Although — how would it be possible ever to go "home"?

He had all these necessary clothes now. Suits and shoes and ties and —

— And pounds of folders full of homework.

After a week of getting up very early and staying out late Cael napped, lightly enough to hear Mrs. Park leave. Soon clicking toenails alerted him that Ghazi was racing downstairs.

Earlier than he would have expected, Anthea had arrived. In his socks he followed the dog down to find her already in the kitchen, putting on a pot of coffee.

"Oh, my dear, were you sleeping?" she crooned as he came forward to claim a hug with kisses on both cheeks. "Go on back up, if you need to. I'm going to have some coffee, and then some wine, and then maybe I'll go lie down too. I know this murder at Adlers' party — just months after losing dear Babby, incredible! — has Daddy worked up, he sounded very disturbed just now. He called to say he's asked Ingrid. When they get started, evenings can run late."

"Oh, great. I thought this was for me. My last night."

"But it is. Only she's his oldest friend, just a hopscotch down the street. How would it look, not to invite her for a peek at you? You think a seventy-eight-year-old's feelings have all dried up with everything else?"

"You're the one running a hospital," he deferred.

Fiercely loyal to his mother, Caelan had always resented Ingrid Becker, perceiving her as a threat even when she visited with Mr. Becker. No matter that Sylvia herself attempted to placate her young son, "But she's known him since he was a wee sprout with training wheels!"

Since Dr. Bradley's locked heart never admitted any rival to Sylvia Brownell Bradley, he was too oblivious to recognize Cael's jealousy. But both his wife and daughter understood Cael's rancor well enough to mollify him without strong challenges.

"Besides, being fair — those two pals from their camel-riding days are quite a comfort to each other. Matt's been gone a long time. Who else cares about Dad? Talks to him?"

Like rich mahogany observed through bourbon and crystal, Anthea's Mideastern eyes offered glowing depth worth lingering over. Since childhood he'd understood how ardently his sister loved him, and that she was destined inevitably to preside over something big, besides him.

"Mrs. Park just gave me that speech, thanks."

"Did she? Well… good for her. She's not afraid to. I am."

"She says *you're* doing fine at looking after him. By the way, I've meant to say again — there's no reason for you to keep sending me money. It's very generous and well-meaning, I know. But my new job pays plenty, and even if it didn't —"

"It was never intended as a bribe. Just if you want someday to buy a house —"

"You haven't bought a house."

"I don't have time even to want one! Always hoped you'll do better than me, on the personal side. But in little dollops, it's been tax-free. Whereas in a big lump someday you would have to pay —"

"Anthea, no. And please spare me the guilt trip about Dad. I don't think he gives me a thought, frankly."

"Untrue!"

"It's always been like that."

"You've always been like this! If they respected your privacy, nobody gives you a thought. If they expressed any interest — 'how was school?' — they were meddling —"

"I don't say he didn't love Mom."

"She flowered with him! And he let her. Never tried to turn her into 'Mrs. Dr. Bradley.' We were treated the same, never pressured to do anything."

"But apart from Mom, his head was full of — the Nobel Prize."

"WHAT! — On earth? *When* did you ever — *ever?* Hear anybody mention *the Nobel Prize?* Where does this come from?"

"I heard it. From — friends."

"'What friends? When?"

"Friends in school."

"*— High school?"*

He barely nodded.

With a cascade of laughter, Anthea threw her arms around him, squeezing to expel idiocy.

"My *dearest* incorrigible…. Daddy's seen princes with soil compacted in their skulls. You know how little he was, learning to think in time writ large. He knows too much history —"

"No, he doesn't!" Cael backed away, almost angry with his sister. "I know what he studied in college, Thea. Don't make him out some universal genius!"

"I meant — what Neda instilled in him."

She banished her mug of coffee to the back of the counter and began arm-wrestling a bottle of wine. He took it from her and opened it, then brought two glasses.

"You don't realize how easy we had it. You and me, we know zero Persian Empire."

"Full?" he asked, pouring red wine.

She nodded, touched glasses. Kissed up at his forehead.

Very few people — not even Caelan — had heard about the Arab potentate who came to America in search of a brain surgeon and learned of an Iranian-American in California. Months after his operation when they met again, the Arab was cancer-free.

"Ghazi," he asked, "What in this world do you desire?"

The academic had not anticipated such a question. But an answer was easy to frame.

"The free enterprise system in this country is a good engine of economic growth," he professed, "— Handicapped by one big inefficiency. I'd like to pursue medical research, to hunt for cures. But to do that, I should be working for Allah. Not for big business."

They discussed it with the university, and a deal was struck.

"Maybe you don't know this —" Thea was opening a pretzel box. "But your father's research chair in the med school is endowed by a private philanthropist. What that means — there isn't any pharma group with automatic ownership of anything he discovers."

"Nobody told me."

"So if it's ever seemed he's felt rushed about his work? That's why the haste. On the remote chance he actually does discover something? Dad thinks cures for Parkinson's and Alzheimer's should be as cheap as aspirin."

They sat quietly, both thinking that in a few hours he would return to New England.

"Not to be rude, changing the subject. A while ago — you wrote he seemed interested in picking up Babby's hobby. The roses?"

After Babby Blenheim's death her nephew Ted had made Ogy a gift of her last crop of seedlings, probably because one group was labelled "Sylvie's Persian." As a tribute to his wife, even just the new plants' name moved Dr. Bradley. But when they bloomed, he understood how much admiration of Sylvia had gone into Babby's witty cultivation of this flower.

Dr. O.G. Bradley possessed densely voluminous hair mostly disposed to stand up. Years ago Sylvia made an ink portrait of him interpreting that rampant jungle as a crowded "conspiracy of ravens" perched upon — or nearly sliding off his head. Always when Babby visited, she wanted to go upstairs to view the drawing again.

In August the yearling plants had revealed what was in her mind when she bred "Sylvie's Persian." Not only were its petals a near-black red in color, but there were so many, so crowded, that they formed a ragged pom-pom. This new cultivar's name did not refer to Sylvia's husband himself. Instead, its flower was Babby's botanical homage and riposte to Sylvie's whimsical cartoon of him with bewildered ravens trying to stay upright over his ears.

"I saw Babby's plants outside. But I didn't notice any — signs of breeding?"

"Oh. Well — when Teddy detected that interest, he immediately offered Dad free run of her rose garden. So next spring, if he wants, he can start experimenting with Babby's stock. I've ordered him a few catalogs, so he can choose new varieties to be additional, ah, genetic building blocks. I think it's a neat development for him."

"Me too. So, that's 'Teddy.'" Cael smiled for this new neighbor he didn't recall from distant childhood. "And the other person you haven't mentioned?"

"Tor Abelove?"

"What's that about?"

"Aaaaaaaahhh…? I have a feeling…? *He* may be a prime topic tonight."

She took her glass, yawning, "I'm so drowsy. Heading up to beddy, half an hour…."

"Are you drinking too much?"

"Not when it's unsafe."

THIRTY-THREE

HEARTFELT

Opposition mailings had styled political novice Caelan Bradley's upstart "toadstool" campaign for a congressional seat "up from nowhere, soft and bad for you." Its pivot point was the decision by his opponent's advisers to expose him as a poseur. Since he was a graduate of a prestigious university, they suspected his background might not be so humble as his current hand-built "toadstool" house pretended. After a campaign worker returned from El Albergue del Valoroso with an arsenal of incriminating photos of that luxurious locale, Mr. Bradley was aghast to discover a five-inch photo of his nearly naked twelve-year-old self, portrayed in bronze with wings uplifted, on his local paper's front page. Of course the strategy of infantilizing Cael properly credited the candidate's mother for that statue of him fronting his family's home — which made clear his well-off upbringing. His head drooping with girlish hair, the skinny bird-boy in the photo must surely define him as unmanly and ridiculous.

Instead, over time, the image's impact was to convey a sense of the youthful activist as a sorrowful angel. That emotional bronze portrait *by his mother* seemed to authenticate the gravity of the candidate's conservationist commitment. Concerns he'd expressed for New Hampshire's citizens came to be viewed as credibly sincere. Best of all, the statue of a thoughtful child world-weary beyond his years galvanized donors who previously had liked the tall muscular fellow, but had not yet taken him seriously.

Young and inexperienced Mr. Bradley certainly was — but he was not a fraud.

Thus the woman who throughout his life had given so profusely interceded even after her own death, when her son had floundered for too many years — gifting him one more time, by delivering the only job he truly longed for.

Cael had not wanted to come home. Knowing he might be able to invite his rump family to visit him in Washington D.C., for a long time he scarcely thought that they too must still be grieving. Dutifully he read his sister's gently entreating letters. The astonishing newspaper story regarding his father's heroic involvement in solving Miss Blenheim's murder last spring he read long after the fact — with a sigh at the man's gift for grandiosity.

Away campaigning when Thea's letter came, he also learned belatedly of his father's heart attack. Still, dread persisted at the thought of returning to the house his family had moved into in celebration of his own birth. Only after being elected to Congress, when he realized he could visit El Albergue for appointments with other freshman representatives, did the thought of entering his parents' home become tolerable.

Then — at the moment when he turned the key, prepared to confront the remarkable space created by the most delightfully surprising personality he had ever known — he was attacked. With bared fangs someone scarcely one year old and all unknowing had leaped at him, ready to defend that devalued home with his young life.

Bitterness vanished. Amusement soared, as Cael began to befriend his family's innocent new member.

On Tuesday it had been fun to drive the pristine roadster up Bunya Road with Anthea and select takeout foods for dinner. He'd expected to repeat that expedition tonight. Instead, when he heard the Tesla arrive and looked out the kitchen window, there were his father and Mrs. Becker, laughing like high school sweethearts, carrying satchels of dinner.

Caelan felt the old deep anger burning. He strode towards the front door, as if to bar their entry, until he realized, "I'm worse than Ghazi."

"Cael!" exclaimed Mrs. Becker, first to appear. "How splendid you look! And congratulations! Are you pleased by the new car?"

"More than a little extravagant?"

"He didn't care. Bought in honor of you, after all. Right after your election."

"You're awake." Ogy came in with a shopping bag in each hand. "Good, your sister said you were napping, so we hit the favorite take-outs. The *meze* items you like and Italian from Volpe."

"He's not mentioning the onion rings from Burger Basement, he's besotted — flavored ones. But be quick. They disappear."

"Hi, Ingrid, I heard that about the onions." In jeans Thea came heavy-footed down the stairs, still sleepy. "Let me deal with the food, you sit and visit with Cael. We're sad, he leaves us tomorrow."

Telling himself that she could be any elderly constituent, Caelan was prepared to chat politely with Ingrid Becker. But as if she'd anticipated that her appearance might be awkward for him, she reached inside her handbag and produced a gift-wrapped package.

"I thought this might be useful."

"Thank you." Any conversation topic made him genuinely grateful.

"How I wish she could see you," sighed the white-haired woman. "So like her. I believe, at your age — Sylvia was just expecting you."

"Good memory. I was about halfway here."

"I wish you could see her, too. She was so radiant. So thrilled about you."

"She was often radiant."

"Caelan — what I just said — about how you resemble her? It was Babby who said once, 'Cael is Sylvie's child. Thea is his.' No harm meant. But — that was unjust —"

"You have trouble breathing?"

"Agh. With a bad knee — you lay it aside a while. Breathing — can't escape it.

"— So many times, when we would visit, I'd think, 'No, Babby.' I would be struck again. Your parents each loved both of you, boundlessly."

"What do you have there!" called Thea, passing with a stack of plates. She set them down and reached. "Let me see, please."

"Mrs. Becker, thank you — I'm a little shocked."

"It's D.C.!" Thea cried, "Dad? Ingrid gave him an appointment book — D.C. art prints."

"Did I hear 'shocked'?"

"Besides all the interesting art," Cael explained, "It's full of blank spaces. To program in every blessed day of the year. What have I done?"

"Oh, you'll need way more calendar space than that," wheezed Ingrid. "Keep this one for just — social interludes."

Cael became anxious again, about dinner seating. But Mrs. Becker showed no inclination to claim his mother's chair. Instead Anthea sat in it, with Ingrid to her right. Given her position at the hospital, his sister was accustomed to heading tables.

As dishes were passed, their guest inquired politely which congressional committees interested the new representative.

"New Hampshire's not called the 'Granite State' for nothing. Not much topsoil out there, so a lot of our agriculture has been greenhouse farming." Cael passed Ingrid her preferred riesling. "It's remarkable, the difference in a vegetable grown in a glasshouse compared to one from the ground. At least, out of *my* ground. But now a new system is coming into favor, using plastic tunnels that hold heat. So one Agriculture subcommittee that interests me is Horticulture and Biotechnology —"

"Cael, darling? Forgive me. That *is* interesting, but — Dad? What's up? You're all flustered. Cael doesn't know anything about this and I don't know much, so spill. Please."

"I yield," practiced the House freshman.

Feeling sorry for himself, Ogy selected the largest remaining onion ring and took a bite.

"Today — stupid thing — I stepped on Tor's toes. The situation is way too important for mistakes like that —"

"A breach?" gasped Thea.

"Can't happen," declared Ingrid tersely. "They're blood brothers."

"I disagree with what the police are doing, but — no call of mine. Can you imagine me, letting some uninvited amateur into the O.R. to dispense surgical advice?"

"He's angry with you?"

"No, I don't think that. You know, six months ago he invited me to spend a Saturday with them, after a dive. A beautiful family, he has. Ghazi was in heaven, with their dog and three fabulous kids —"

The dour expressions on his own unmarried children's faces prompted Dr. Bradley to abandon this undiplomatic subject.

"After that, he said if I felt I needed to abandon our friendship, he would understand."

"*Why?*" From Ingrid and Cael together.

"Because — this is in confidence — they might arrest someone… close to us. Didn't happen. But Tor was gracious about it. Said he didn't want me to feel compromised. And today I pushed him."

"Story time," demanded Cael.

"Yes, Dad."

He told them how Allan insisted he was the intended victim at the Adlers' party, and for Cael explained the death of the fifteen-year-old whose trapped head crashed into a truck's mirror.

"Then her attorney identified Lise as the 'girl' the victim's brother held responsible."

"Telling coincidence, that Lisette was killed?" asked Cael.

"More likely, misleading coincidence," was Ingrid's hunch.

"Then," added Thea, 'TRAITOR!' painted gigantic appeared on the Housemans' wall."

"I met up with one of the waiters from the Adlers' party who says he witnessed the accident that killed the girl." After elaborating his chat at with Artie, Ogy added, "But the latest revelation? This same waiter's son — with a PhD — was seriously brain-damaged on an ocean expedition led by Allan."

"There's a connection!" Anthea looked grim. "Closed circle?"

"Maybe not, dear. Not to me. Even if Tor thinks so."

"Parse this, please." Ingrid was ever clinical.

"Ingy, I don't have words to describe how *sad* that man is — a potential suicide for sure, but not homicidal. I tried to explain to Tor how guilty Artie feels about not coming forward when the accident happened. He assumes Lise got murdered because he didn't clear her when he should have. What Tor took from my inept retelling was that Artie feels guilty because he accidentally killed Lise with poison intended for her husband. So I boorishly implicated Mr. Vaccari — for a murder I'd swear he didn't commit."

"Dad — the way you relate this waiter's conversation? If anything the story is too pat. As if it were *composed*. And rehearsed. This is a problem I've experienced, delivering the same speech over and over to voters. First it gains structure, great. But later it just sounds stale."

"That's what Tor said. 'Rehearsed.' I understand, I can't convince you. But even if Artie were the greatest actor alive, the way this all came out? It just happened spontaneously. I can't reproduce that."

"I have to say, Dad. Based on these facts, I'd believe Houseman and suspect Artie too."

"But, dear girl, these are not *all* the facts. And the others argue against it."

"Tell."

"This tragic accident to Cris Harbison — his stepfather's surname — happened around three years ago. *Three years.* In which Artie travelled back and forth from the States to Europe. During which he could have murdered Allan Houseman anytime! In a dark alley. Totally anonymously. Staged an accident. *Anywhere.* And slipped back to Trieste, or.

"Why would he finally elect to do it at a party where a named crowd of people were congregated, when he's the *only one* whom the dullest cop — and that's sure not Abelove — would identify quickly as somebody with a major grievance against Houseman?

"WELL? Even if Artie is not some master criminal, even if he's just average IQ, would he be that uncalculating? Wait so long? Not sneak, while still at high temperature fresh fury?"

"Point. I like the dark alley," Cael nodded. "En route to Venice."

"And then, how was the poison administered? Artie never served mugs of glögg. Only the other two waiters did, those two are sure of that. Allan was in a little huddle of people until he handed off his mug to Lise — who almost immediately drank it.

"So either Allan poisoned it himself, or someone else did it while they all gabbed there. "There's also the matter of this interesting poison itself. Somebody created it, presumably from a concentration of potato eyes."

"What?"

"Anecdote for your hospital. Toxic but not likely lethal —"

"I never — ! Okay, onto Woodward's 'household hazards' list."

"— Unless somebody works at it. Now, consider — this man is homeless. Probably not educated much, but he does know food. Has access to his ex-wife's kitchen, where he cooks for them sometimes.

"Okay — accept that he knows old green potatoes can make you sick. Accept that there is a kitchen he might borrow when not sleeping on the street.

"Then explain to me: How did he know to prepare poison for a job at famous *economist* Hiram Adler's house? How could he guess *oceanographer* Allan Houseman would be there?

"And I have to say — to me, maybe Allan could be a poisoner. But Vaccari? Not super-macho, no. But, sorry — his revenge for cerebral injury to his only child would not be spud juice."

"Already, Dad, you're putting me in a mood to call Abelove and tell him to think again."

"Tor isn't just smart, he's honest," sighed Ogy. "In fact, Wednesday when we went to Piggy's I learned something about how important personal honor really is to him."

"Interesting you say that. Linda and I just had a girls' day out. She talks about him more — like a priest than a policeman. Wouldn't think it, to look at him."

"No. But Chief Margolies? — That one is a politician. From his perspective, prosecuting an indigent Italian waiter is far less risky than bringing down an illustrious academic. I'm so worried about Artie, with no advocates.

"And one other thing. Did you ever hear the saw, 'It's easier to say "I love you" in a foreign language'?"

"A century ago, I think I did," allowed Thea.

"Artie's Italian. Very much so. I'm sorry, but whenever I visualize that 'TRAITOR!' sign? I think, 'No way.'"

"But he couldn't write it *in Italian*, could he," grinned Cael.

"Abelove is shrewd. Thought there was a chance Houseman wrote it, to confuse the cops. But — call it the Persian in me — I think that ugly message on poor Lisette's wall is heartfelt. We just don't get it."

They all considered this possibility of their missing the point.

"Omar… what bothers me? Vaccari is *presumed* — the independent variable here. That 'given' leads to the deduction… Allan has to be the intended victim."

Mrs. Becker could finger a fallacy.

"But how can they be certain — Lisette wasn't the real target?"

"And why *a priori* reject the chance Vaccari wasn't involved at all?" appended Thea.

"Thank you both. Focus only on Cris and his dad, and it so easily falls into place. But that is arbitrary. Selective tunnel vision."

"Bias," deplored the congressman-elect.

"On the evidence so far? We can't know whether Allan or Lisette was meant to die."

THIRTY-FOUR

SURPASSING RESPLENDENCE

On Saturday morning there was scarcely time for the Persian coffee Cael had requested before he had to leave for the car rental return.

"Wait!" Thea rushed to bring Ghazi's leash before her brother opened the front door. "He knows what the suitcase means. But we have to let him watch you drive away, so he can believe you'll come again."

On the driveway Cael stooped to kiss the dog and whisper "*Au revoir.*" To hug his sister he lifted her off her toes. Then he embraced his father as well.

Ogy said, "Thank you so much for giving us all this time together. It's been the best Christmas gift I could have dreamed of."

Suddenly Caelan broke into a grin so humorously dazzling that both his father and sister were incredulous. It wasn't just the presence of Sylvia in his face — those changeable pond water eyes his mother described as "mud and algae." But Cael had always been disinclined to smile for photographers. If any of that determined profession had penetrated his obstinacy and transferred this laughing young presence to campaign posters, his opponent hadn't had a chance.

"I never got around to telling you how well all my meetings went. Being with you both was fun, with some relaxed hours I needed. It was great to see Mrs. Becker again. And please, Dad — give Mrs. Park a message for me? Tell her I miss her."

Leaving his family looking forlorn on the walk, Cael got into the rental car shaking his head and chuckling, surprised by how nourished in spirit he felt after four days in this house.

As the Matrix backed onto Avenida Placida all three watched him waving at them, laughing to himself as he drove away.

Since Anthea had a pancake date with Dan she declined breakfast. At nine when Ogy's coffee and newspaper both were exhausted, the phone rang.

"My friend! I need advice. Can you help me?"

"What's wrong, Ted?"

"I've been seeing Ginger Guardian. Last week, I told you —"

"Not a night I've forgotten."

"'But I've just invited her out — planned a special evening. Dinner, then the symphony — I thought she'd like. But she said she can't go."

"Why —"

"She was vague, is the trouble. Evasive. Isn't like her. And I don't know what to think. Honestly, I'm scared now. Don't know what to think."

"How often have you been seeing each other?"

"Often. All she said was, 'I'm afraid I can't, right now.' Well, *that* is not encouraging. Is she seeing somebody else, too, and I don't know?"

"How many times a week?"

"Oh — twice. More, when we've had time. Should I think she's getting tired of me? I want her to want to see me *more often,* I want her to want to spend *all her time* with me, not —"

"Teddy — Ted! By chance — have you ever offered to help her pay the babysitter?"

"…Babysitter."

Ted sounded as if he wasn't sure what that was.

"Ginger must be hiring someone to stay with Peter, while she goes out with you. No? You weren't planning to take her son along to this dinner and symphony, were you?"

"I… never…. Don't kids charge like a dollar an hour for that?"

"Did. When you were a child. Mrs. Guardian could buy food for a week for what the sitter would cost her for the evening you have in mind."

"But… Ginger can't afford that."

"No. She can't."

"Ogy, what… how should I…"

"Broach it? Well for starters, it would make sense to learn first what the real world costs today. Why not try Gloria Seagrave? Lynleigh might know what the older kids are charging now. Also — since Peter has Down's, it's possible Ginger might employ someone a bit more expensive. Like, say, a university student."

"Okay. Okay."

After wishing Ted good luck Ogy could not help thinking, not for the first time, that an elementary school teacher was exactly what he needed in his life. He recalled the university's dowagers surrounding Ted at Adlers' party. Despite being smart, he was easy to recognize as a softie. And those *Old Ladies Who Plan,* who had kept reining back the polite and handsome fellow had no idea how well-off he was. Dr. Bradley was displeased at the thought that they might try to confiscate Mr. Friedland away from the toffee-haired teacher, for one of their own.

If the hopes Ted had expressed last week came true and he wound up not just marrying Ginger but having children, Babby's house could quickly become too small for his family.

On the other hand, Ginger's father was a resident of Casa Bunya's Alzheimer's wing. She would value living just two doors from Peter's grandfather. For as many years as that situation continued, neither would want to see the retirement home torn down — which might happen, if Babby's substantial property came on the market and attracted developers.

Solemn thoughts that Babby's century-old fairy castle and cathedral-like gardens might eventually be demolished prompted Ogy to go out to the patio and check on her infant rose creations. Despite the lateness of the year, they continued to make new growth.

This morning had begun with crystalline air, instead of the overcast skies customary at early hours in El Albergue. Sunshine on the damp patio was piercing today. Although in December the sun dipped behind Mount Reposo early, at this hour it was high.

As Dr. Bradley glanced up at the flank of the mountain, he experienced a sensation that he associated only with movies about space aliens — a perception that just ahead, above him, loomed a structure of brilliant light — meant for him, waiting for him and transporting him upward to interplanetary weightlessness.

At first he actually felt befuddled about *where* he was looking. The termite-ridden wreckage of Caelan's childhood fort fronting

Ghazi's poop lot was supposed to be up there — and to be grimly replicated by its mirrored doppelgänger in the swimming pool.

Instead that space was all shimmering facets, with resplendence that surpassed even the tessellated field of stars that now opaqued the brilliant pool.

Within seconds his disoriented mind re-sorted its confusion to a perception of how his world had just altered. But even after he recognized that he was staring at a glass-encased greenhouse, he could not comprehend how it had landed here.

He had not brought his cane outdoors. But removing his gaze from this wonder now would be impossible.

He crossed the yard. The old "stairs" that were just shovel notches in adobe soil looked newly sharpened. Carefully he climbed the bottom dozen feet of Mount Reposo to the small plateau where Cael's haphazard fort had formerly swayed.

This greenhouse had a door. Peering through it, he saw a second door in the west wall.

Across this one was a wooden plaque painted in floral pastels.

Examining closely, he discovered that its hand-painted ribbon traced script that appeared to be Persian. Despite the botanically undulant Farsi style of writing, though, its vine of words gradually sorted itself into English.

It spelled, *"Sylvie's Persian."*

His first thought was that only Sylvia could do this.

But that was not true.

THIRTY-FIVE

A HYPOTHETICAL

The interrogation of Artie Vaccari had provided such a wealth of self-incrimination that news of it rose straight to Chief Margolies. Informed that he was being held, Mr. Vaccari said he had never been in jail before, and asked if there were showers. On Friday morning when he was cautioned and told he was under arrest for the murder of Lisette Houseman and the attempted murder of Allan he replied with lingering surprise, "I had no idea they would even be there."

Abelove was getting nervous. When the minute hand reached eight o'clock in the morning he telephoned Hank Smithers. It was one of those short coded conversations.

"How's Tina doing?" ("I really need her back here.")

"She's asleep, but she still had a fever yesterday." ("You've got a lot of nerve.")

"Sorry to hear that." ("The others aren't as good at research.")

"She has cabin fever. Wishes she was on the job." ("My wife does not malinger.")

"Tell her she's missed. Something big is popping here." ("I dare you to tell her *that!*")

"Will do." ("Fat chance.")

One of Officer Smithers' efficiencies was that she didn't need to be told to delve into minutiae. When a person of interest was found, immediately she made inquiries about him. But the sheer volume of the crowd at the Adlers' party last week had resulted in all manner of loose ends remaining unsorted. Now trivia about this or that probably irrelevant party guest or caterer's worker felt like unsettled lint tumbling in Tor's head. His next phone call, informing Ogy that they were holding Vaccari, did not leave him feeling any less muddled. Tor did not want to hear Bradley's objections to the congenial waiter's arrest.

He was smacking the end of his pen on the desk pad when the Captain walked by.

"Tony — did you ever go inside the Adlers' house?"'

"Me? No. That kitchen has two dishwashers. All the mugs were through the cycle when our guys showed up. They just taped off the yard, catalogued guests and staff, and waited to search in the morning. Why?"

"I scoped it from outside. It's a bigger place than it looks when you drive by. And the photos, of inside? Like a subway station."

Captain Marcos pulled a chair to Tor's desk.

"You're getting cold feet. Again."

"Last night, I admit it. I was hot for Artie too. But… even if I hate the idea — Houseman could be in danger. Tony — in my dreams now I see that video…. That clump of people in front of — visually, under the stage? At some point while they're listening to the piano, Allan's poison mug gets passed to Lisette."

"So what about the house."

"People milling all though it, even outdoors. That family room with the stage — all rooms open to the guests. Everything way off-scale from my house. And when you add up the people? Just the guest list was fifty invitees. But lots more could've come than that — one, for sure did. You remember Ted Friedland?"

"The computer guy, yeah. Blenheim case."

"He came. Not invited by Adlers. Dr. Bradley took him, to introduce him around. Because he can. Probably nobody walked up to challenge Ted — 'Who are *you?*' Bradley could bring Jack the Ripper, and so long as Jack wore black —"

"You're not accusing Friedland, so what?"

"So when you think about the makeup of that party? There were some of Adler's economics mates, and ocean people from the institute next door —"

"Claire Fields, I recall, a staffer."

"Who also knows Priscilla from some women's committee — so there's another population. And maybe a few more yet. But the point is, all those people knew some of the others. But even the Adlers couldn't know all of them, when you figure in spouses. And very few could have known most."

"So the Adlers were mixing it up. Not just intimates."

"Then — to that partial anonymity — you add that everybody's in black."

"I think I see where this is going."

"There's something we never considered, Tony. Way more people at the uni would have known about this party than got invited to it. Just suppose — somebody uninvited walks in. Maybe some legitimate guest knows that person. Or — maybe not."

"Who."

"Just — hold off on that. But you see the picture — this big affair could run over a hundred, and probably every individual knows somebody somewhere — except at any given moment, few are recognizable. Another thing, from the video and the photos we've collected — during the Gershwin medley and the trio after? Mostly people are looking *up* — at the stage. Even while they talk, their eyes are mostly checking the show. Any amateur could have dumped that poison in front of half a dozen witnesses who just weren't... looking *down*."

"WHO. The walk-in fake guest?"

"Only as a hypothetical? This sister of his. Suppose she slips in. Wearing black. Finds Lisette, tells her she wanted to see this bash, as a lark. They share a laugh about that. When Lise sets down her mug, that's it. In minutes she's sipping bad potato juice. Her sister-in-law says, 'I'll go say hi to Allan' — and leaves. If her hair hides her face, nobody notices her in photos. Neither does brother Allan, off in that Monopoly corner politicking the whole time.

"I'm not accusing her. The surreptitious guest could be an enemy of his. Show's on, lights are low, and a rival or a ditched girlfriend tips a vial in someone's mug."

"You did this about Babby Blenheim. You wanted it to be some unknown, a stranger."

"As we later discovered — it was. My problem again — we don't know anything about the Housemans, really. I'm not insisting it's not Vaccari. But he does seem awfully passive."

"Has anybody spoken to this sister?"

"When Chuck went to the house just the minister was there."

"Houseman gave us her name when he informed us he was planning to hunker out of sight. In Norwald, that was. No other suspects?"

"Have we started to look? Honestly?"

"Don't say that again. Check this one quietly, if you want. But it's worse than far-fetched. We have an arrest. Righteous."

"No dispute, Captain."

Lacking any better idea, Tor phoned Reverend Jim Mannering.

"What can I do for you?' asked the Reverend, guardedly.

"Sir, we're routinely speaking with everyone associated with the Housemans, just looking for insights. The only family member around this area is his sister. You met her last Sunday. What can you tell me about her?"

"Nothing."

Tor gave the representative of the Lord time to reconsider that regrettable response to an officer of the law. They both listened as the ponderous silence burgeoned.

Finally the clergyman relented, "What do you want to know?"

"Anything. How old is she?"

"Oh, younger. Quite a bit. Told me they had different fathers."

"Did you get the sense that she was close to Mrs. Houseman?"

"Didn't get any sense of anything. Except that she was anxious about leaving Allan alone, but had to work that afternoon."

"She mention what she does?"

"No."

"Allan and Lisette were married a long time. Had she been crying?"

"I don't know."

That was information of sorts.

Now the woman who ten minutes ago had been a purely hypothetical suspect sounded a shade more plausible. He guessed that if she were a teacher, attorney or nurse she would have mentioned that to her brother's minister. But without a career of her own she would be more likely to chafe at the difference in their incomes.

Tor had noted dynamics causing a sister to feel she should be more entitled than a wife.

To fish or not to fish?

Although the case against Vaccari was a priority, Chief Margolies was still annoyed by the "TRAITOR!" graffiti. Nobody offered a convincing explanation for it. Residents on Calle Canciones del Mar had made more than one call protesting that desecration of their neighborhood. Early this evening when those stewing citizens should be in front of their dinners or TVs, a team would canvas with photos of Vaccari, asking if anyone had seen him lingering in the vicinity of the Houseman home (hopefully, late at night with a can of spray enamel).

After this week of grace, the Chief wanted Allan told tomorrow that it was time to clean up the mess. He said he should be able to paint the wall himself in a day.

"Tell him, put a sealer coat over the lettering first. Or it could come back. Boo."

Although Margolies was planning to speak to the press, that meeting was not yet scheduled. A public defender for Vaccari was being arranged.

With luck, tomorrow Officer Smithers might return.

Plagued by misgivings, Abelove decided that he needed to rebalance in the presence of his wife and children. As he braved Friday's rush hour, vague but ongoing dread made him overlook the fact that Linda might be passing him on the road, headed downtown to the martial arts class he had arranged for her.

THIRTY-SIX

WALLOWING

"We have new people in the dojang today," began Master Hwan. "Let me mention —my name is 'Hwan.' Is different from Spanish 'Juan.' I wish I was named after a saint, only I'm not. But if anybody is more comfortable calling me 'Juan' instead of 'Hwan,' that's okay."

Through their titters he continued, "People who brought your handouts, in case you forgot already — last week we talked about achieving *zazen* —"

On one foot Hwan pivoted, better to see a nine-year-old among the boys at his left.

"Hey, you boy — is that some kind of little camera? You're not putting me on that internet thing?"

"Never to post, Master Hwan," bowed the boy. "Just to review class at home. My dad says, everything you tell us is your property."

Nodding, their master resumed, "So if sometimes you maybe struggle towards this meditation, and can't find it? Yeah? And other times, like here, in the dojang, you notice *zazen* meditation just settles over you. Like a butterfly lands on your head, and you didn't notice. You ever feel that happen?"

Over his hair he waved two fingers, flexing butterfly wings.

"And you think — 'How did that come?'

"Tonight's topic later will be 'indomitable spirit.' After practice. In your groups now."

After the students bowed to Master Hwan and divided into their separate small classes, Linda could not help counting the yellow belts again. She wondered how long she would have to wear the beginner's white belt — even though it looked nicer with her white dobok than the lemon-colored belts of the next class up.

That such a concern even occurred to her was puzzling. She was not aware of having formed any commitment to continue with these classes.

One foolish incentive for doing so, she realized, was that she wanted to deserve the regard of the two eldest and most proficient female members, who so far had mostly ignored her. On the other hand, Mara, the lively young newcomer, seemed oblivious to the two older women's circle of privacy and was forwardly friendly to all three of them. Because Ted Friedland had mentioned them on that first evening, Linda knew that auburn-haired Jane was an attorney and pale blonde Nadine a businesswoman. She admired the elegant French braids that circled Nadine's head to culminate in a twist that never came loose during practice.

When the evening's instruction began, such little thoughts soon dissolved into *zazen* meditation.

Tonight during the break between the instruction portion of the class and practice in the second half, as Linda was heading for the water fountain Jane smiled at her.

"You seem to be doing well, and you certainly have the right look for martial arts. Are you enjoying the class?"

"Thank you, I am." Linda tried to pin her bun of not purely Asian hair back together. "He's wonderful. And I was just thinking, it felt like that *zazen* butterfly visited me today."

"Good. *Zazen,* one down," laughed Nadine. "How about you?" she asked Mara, who had just walked up.

"Maybe next time." The blonde's shrug looked embarrassed.

"Tuesday when Ted Friedland was here, he mentioned your husband is working on that murder case," said Jane. "We were talking about breathing and tao, all Master Hwan's principles —"

"'Indomitable spirit,' later," Mara reminded them. "That sounds motivating."

"— And asking ourselves, how on earth?" continued Nadine. "Is it possible to sustain 'self-control' dealing with something so awful?"

"Mara said it, actually," Linda nodded sadly. "I do believe his 'indomitable spirit' keeps my husband going. But your question does concern me, yes. It was a terrible death. Tor — I can tell, he's grown quite attached to Mrs. Houseman."

"I was close to someone who was killed," said Mara quietly. "A beautiful friend."

"I'm sorry," said Linda. "Was she blonde like you?"

"She was black."

Suddenly Linda felt confused and mortified. Had Mara's friend lived in one of the gang-infested neighborhoods where innocent passersby got shot?

— And had she just slighted even herself, with dark hair in a blonde-ascendant world?

To move past this race-tinged blunder she continued, "The two of you work so gracefully together. Mara and I watch you drill. Have you been doing this a very long time?"

"My husband is Korean," said Jane. "We converted the master bedroom into our dojang, with mats and a heavy bag."

"I started because of a friend of mine," said Nadine, who although very slim was clearly much stronger than she appeared. "She was a corporate vice president. After some years of sexual harassment, she finally complained. First board members put her on administrative leave. Then she was terminated."

"You wouldn't think that was possible today," grumbled attorney Jane.

"I decided it wouldn't happen to me," continued Nadine. "After I started coming here, I noticed people treated me differently."

"They realize you can do them serious damage," gloated Jane.

"I don't think the men are afraid of me, exactly. The sense I get…? Even though I don't behave or dress differently, it's as if I've acquired some invisible veneer of maleness. Not fun to oppress."

~ ~ ~

When Tor arrived home Linda had already left for her lesson. Mrs. Kimura was just serving the children chicken fricassee with dumplings.

"Stay, Marjorie," he said. "You cooked it, you should at least enjoy some."

"I will," promised his mother-in-law. "My deal with Linda is, I cook and then take home enough for Hiroshi and me."

"Okay, didn't know. I realize I haven't been around."

"No criticism. Everybody's rooting for you. Good night and good luck."

Andrew, Clematis and Timothy were entertained by the novelty of dinner alone with Daddy; but Tor was unhappy, because he wanted Linda to be there and had only himself to blame for her absence — and because this situation hardly commended his foresight. Afterwards he and Clemma cleared the table and loaded the dishwasher. She had homework. Tor read to Andy. Already the boy could read simple children's books from the school library, but Linda insisted he enjoyed hearing better ones that were still too challenging for him to navigate alone.

Abelove was floundering in doubts about their suspect pool, while with every hour the department's commitment to convicting Vaccari grew stronger. Since the "TRAITOR!" sign had appeared on the Housemans' wall he could not stop spinning explanations.

Could some confidante of Lise's at the university be hinting that Allan was unfaithful to his wife, if only they would bother to investigate? Was some member of Lise's family convinced of his guilt but reluctant to accuse him openly?

Or had Allan done anything his sister viewed as treacherous? Might she have asked for a loan and been refused?

Nor was he crossing off Claire Fields, at least not until he could ask Smithers to investigate her fiancé-on-hold, Pat Connell. The "traitor" angle certainly suggested a lover scorned.

And so far as he knew, nobody had questioned the senior member of the ocean sciences department, Dr. Rebecca Savage — although since she was near retirement it was hard to imagine any involvement with Houseman.

Right now, a team should be canvassing the Strand area with photos of Vaccari. Tor didn't expect useful information from that inquiry. Artie had frequented the Strand for years.

At this point, the most foreseeable conclusion of the case was that quiet, civilized Arturo Vaccari would be convicted of a sadistically cruel murder.

He could not help feeling anxious and glum.

"Good evening," smiled Linda as she walked in wearing street clothes, her new dobok and belt properly stowed inside her gym bag. "How are your *harmony and balance* today?"

"Not. None."

"Now, now. Where's the 'indomitable spirit' that inspires us?"

Without even removing her jacket she went to check Clemmie's homework. Soon he heard the hair dryer as Linda pre-warmed Timmy's sleepers before dressing him for the night. Clemmie and Andy still shared the second bedroom. Timmy's crib was in the dining room, so after Tor heated a plate of dinner for his wife he carried it into their bedroom.

Relaxed by her shower, Linda sat on the small boudoir chair to eat her chicken and dumplings. Happy just to sit back on the bed and watch his wife eat, Tor sipped tea.

In pjs, with bare feet, very likely Lisette had looked this pretty.

He pictured Lisette's face now, destroyed by her fall onto boulders.

Then he recalled her parents' faces, when he had to insist it would not be possible to view the body of their only child.

Linda took her empty plate to the kitchen. When she returned she climbed into bed even though it wasn't even nine yet.

"What if I bleach my hair blonde? With fat Brunhilda braids?"

"What?"

A long spasm ran the full length of the mattress.

"Don't — do not — make me worry about *that!"*

"Tonight I realized, my German half doesn't show at all. Nobody sees any German," she giggled.

"They hear it. In the choir. Your German half is musical."

Linda giggled again, musically. The concave softness of her high-arched foot was sliding slowly down his leg.

"What a magnificent detective…! Of course. Music's the best part of me."

The children weren't asleep yet. Since the hour still wasn't late, Tor kept wondering whether Bettina Smithers might be over her fever and awake, or if he would have to talk to Hank again — if he called to ask if she could look up Patrick Connell, supposedly in the U.S. Army and stationed in Afghanistan.

Tina would understand how he would rather not do it himself, and then maybe later be awkwardly tempted to lie about that to Captain Marcos.

But any further calls now would leave her resentful husband exasperated, if not outraged.

He whispered, "Music is just one of your best parts."

THIRTY-SEVEN

A POSSIBLE

Early Friday evening, a weak drizzle caused Detective Lianopoulos to suspend his officers' canvas of the Housemans' Strand neighborhood. Already several Bay Street personnel were out sick. Without slickers the canvassers were likely to catch cold. A few soaked copies of Vaccari's photo were disintegrating. California was engaged in its autumnal dance of fire and rain. So far, the kind of storm system that might dampen the chance of a forest conflagration during the holidays was not visibly forming. But even without a downpour, homeowners would not hold their doors open on a blustery Friday night as willingly as on a sunshiny weekend morning.

Before the returning canvassers even reached El Albergue on that cloudless Saturday, Chief Margolies called the M. Room.

"Did you tell Houseman yet that he should paint his wall? Neighbors are complaining. They're scared gangs will move in, start breaking their windows."

"Sorry, Chief," explained Alvaro, "I keep trying but getting voicemail. He's supposed to be in the mountains, so depending on where his sister lives he may not have reception."

"Sounds nice," said Margolies. "But it's time to get the Sheriff after him. I hope you fellas have street pants in your lockers. Because if you don't have Houseman working on that wall by noon today, you're going out to do the job yourselves."

Alvaro wondered if Bettina ever got such calls. And when she was coming back to work.

Last night it had not been lost on Tor that Linda arrived home from the dojang preening with renewed spirit after her experience of *zazen* meditation — while he was inwardly curled, almost fetal with frustration, rehashing his interview with Artie Vaccari and trying to grasp what it was he had heard but not understood.

"Linda *is* Asian, even if I never thought of her that way," he noted defensively. *"Meditation's in her DNA."*

That excuse didn't make him feel any less stale.

Abandoning Vaccari, his thoughts slid back to Allan's sister. After asking Officer Lopez to dig up whatever might be found about her, he was still trying to decide how much time to invest in her as a possible — starting with the question of where she had been early last Saturday evening — when a call came, specifically for him.

"Detective Abelove, you don't know me. I'm Judy Herndon, office manager at the Oceanographic Institute. I was out of town when you met with Claire Fields. This might be nothing, but Claire says she promised to let you know if — anything."

"Please thank Ms. Fields for me, Ms. Herndon. I appreciate your taking the time. What did she think of?"

"That's not it. She received a phone call from Allan's sister in Norwald. Yesterday, actually. Last week when Claire was the only one in the office, Allan gave Elinor Claire's number, in case Elinor wanted to leave a message for him. He told her he was going to buy a new cell phone and change the number. After that he went up to her apartment and stayed part of this week. He didn't tell us here about that. And so far Elinor doesn't know about any new phone. She's tried calling the old one, but there's just the voicemail message."

"He left her place?"

"Thursday at around one, she said. He said he'd call Thursday evening. He needed to check with you — police — about going ahead with Lise's memorial service. And he needed to come into his office, but nobody's seen him. His mailbox hasn't been emptied for a while.

"Detective — I admit, Claire told me all this yesterday. She wasn't sure it amounted to anything. Even Elinor thought Thursday night he probably just forgot to call, or fell asleep, or still hadn't learned about the funeral. But yesterday she was getting nervous. Then I thought, 'Maybe he's at an electronics store, buying that phone?' — What?

"Excuse me, I have Claire on speaker phone. — Oh. Claire says, 'Allan is very fussy about his phone and computer.'

"So, you see how we weren't sure what to think? I can believe Allan would forget all about his sister, out shopping for new toys. My brother would. But it doesn't explain his silence this long."

Tor called Elinor Burns, Allan's half-sister.

"He left your place Thursday at one?"

"I was at work. My neighbor thinks, maybe before one. He did want to beat rush hour."

"Is there anyplace else he might have gone? That you can think of? Did he say?"

"No. Because he had these important things to do. And I needed to know when was the memorial service scheduled, because I'll have to take time off work again. — Well, unless he stopped at the restaurant."

"You have one in mind."

"I'd been telling him about it. On the road maybe halfway back to Santa Christina. It's the old Fairwaye Inn. With a huge antique fireplace. The golf course there just gradually burned out.

"I know Allan was scared. Please, somebody let me know where he is."

Minutes before the Fairwaye Inn opened for lunch, Abelove's call representing the SCPD's Homicide Division got the full attention of the front desk hostess. From Houseman's waitress he quickly learned that Thursday during the time interval he suggested, Allan had been dragging out a large lunch in their dining room.

"He sat two hours at our best fireside table and left a chintzy tip," groused the girl. "Is he dead?"

Surprised that he was still capable of being shocked by the law-abiding citizens he served, Tor jumped to his feet and mumbled about seeking a witness.

Captain Marcos was not in today. But the Chief in his office was planning his press conference about the Vaccari arrest. Tor raced upstairs.

Mrs. Voorheis, Margolies' receptionist, glanced at Abelove. She left her desk, rapped on the Chief's office door and opened it herself.

Tor hovering in your doorway was impossible not to notice.

"What do you bring?" asked Margolies, looking away from his communications director.

"Your press talk — is it fixed yet?"

"Just about to let the sweethearts know."

"Thursday, probably *after* we picked up Vaccari — sounds like Allan Houseman disappeared. Almost definitely — *after* Vaccari was in custody."

The Chief considered that.

"You think — he made a run for it?"

"Got to check the house."

The communications director had been leaning over Margolies' desk. As he straightened again his mouth fell open and his chest seemed to collapse.

Tor barely nodded.

Bypassing the elevator, he ran back downstairs.

TENSION

From Floor Three Tor called Bruno, the canvassing team member he knew best.

"HI, sir!" Officer Belknap sounded more enthusiastic than seemed warranted by just recognizing the name on his cell display.

Immediately Tor told him that Houseman was missing. They were instructed to enter the house and search it for any indication of a crime — or that Allan had absconded.

"But *wait!*" rushed Bruno. "We have news! None of us expected anything to come of this, but there were some sightings of our homeless guy — very near the house. Calle Canciones is one of those ones with an alley. Somebody taking out their trash saw him pushing his grocery buggy. And then another person saw him pushing it toward the Strand.

"We found a neat eatery down there. We're going to the Burger Basement after this."

"When! Did somebody see him pushing the cart?"

"Night before last."

"Not possible. We had him in custody."

"These people recognized him immediately, though. Knew exactly who we meant. One lady said she'd swear she recognized him."

"Recognized who?"

"This homeless person. Gray hair. Not tall, not short, not fat."

"Recognized your photo as their Homeless Guy? Or recognized *the man in the alley* as the person in the photo? Night before last Vaccari was at Bay Street. They must've seen somebody else."

"So they got the date wrong. Sir — this blah time of year, dark before five? Who can tell them apart — Friday, Wednesday?"

"Search that house. Luggage, medicine cabinet, clothes. We have his passport. Did he go someplace without it?"

~ ~ ~

The lightness of discovering his new glasshouse had not abandoned Dr. Bradley. He decided this sense of weightlessness had something to do with Caelan's being still miles overhead and by now almost a thousand miles northeast. In celebration of his talented son, he returned to the upstairs storage room for the first time since last June, when he had retrieved his wife's sand paintings from their twenty years' sleep. It was a difficult place to visit, Sylvia's small catacomb. There were boxes of old letters. The children's report cards. Despite how well she had organized the shelves, they presented many distractions.

But he knew what he was looking for. It was a cardboard box — of a size to contain a pair of boots. Within it were stacked smaller boxes, formerly containing Christmas cards. They had become repositories for his wife's seed collection. With considerable excitement — because finding the correct box made him feel close to her — he extracted the one devoted to tomatoes. Inside was a hodgepodge of open seed packets, along with labelled envelopes and plastic baggies. Momotaro and Jaune Flammée were favorites, he recalled. Other packs were annotated "green striped from road stand N of Flagstaff," "gift from Roberta" or as similar finds.

The notion that with a greenhouse it would be possible to grow flavorful fruit during the winter months was inspiring thoughts of all sorts of dishes. He peeked inside the box of herb seeds. But although pizza with clams and lovage suddenly swam through olfactory memory, he resolved to leave the herbs until later.

Finally he chose eight packs of tomato seed with which to start a small winter garden. No sooner had he replaced the box in the storage room than the phone rang. The displayed name surprised him. Yesterday Tor had been abrupt — or maybe just rushed.

"Ogy. I apologize for interrupting your Saturday. But we have a situation, and I thought you might be able to help with information."

"Anything."

"First — Allan is missing. Don't know what that means. Next thing — Vaccari was spotted very near their house, pushing his cart down the alley behind Calle Canciones."

"I don't think so. Artie doesn't have a cart."

"So far as you know. But we have two sightings of him already, down in the Strand area, pushing the thing or just sitting by it."

"But — was he smoking?"

"Both of these were at night, by the way. Maybe he just keeps it hidden someplace other times, then moves house in the evening."

"He spends nights at the shelter. If you ask at St. Rita's —"

"You remember Mel at the diving club? Works with the homeless. They've got pretty complicated living arrangements, social structures — more than you'd guess.

"Anyway, we're worried now about tracing his movements around the Strand. So I was hoping you could tell me places you know he hangs out, to get us started. Because now he's been seen behind that house at night — he could be the angry person with spray paint after all.

"And I've got a nightmare here — a just conceivable slat of time where after buying groceries he could murder Allan before arriving to cook dinner at Harbisons.' Unlikely, but —"

"All right. Chiefly, he likes those two benches, the one outside Mariscos Valorosos and the other outside Burger Basement. Good smells there. He smokes and reads whatever is lying around. Then, as you said, the boardwalk benches.

"I should add — a place I've never seen him, but — maybe of interest — you know the big pedestrian bridge over Bunya Road? At the base of that, under the struts, there's a protected area where you typically see a few homeless congregated. It's shielded from rain, of course. And being right by the gas station, the sea wind must be blocked too. So in winter it's a dry place on a wet night, even if it isn't scenic like those hills north of Adlers.' But still just two blocks from Strand coffee shops."

"Thanks, that's a help. Is Cael still there?"

"Left this morning."

"Glad he came. I'll let you know."

"One other thing. If you're looking for witnesses. *You* might not see *them,* but — it's worth asking at the lifeguard station. Or if this was strictly at night, they might not be there then. But a janitorial service comes to work on the restrooms right beside the boardwalk, and those cleaners do stay a while."

"That's a thought. Thanks, Doc."

Not long after Tor had phoned Officer Belknap, Bruno called him back. Tor could hear Saturday afternoon restaurant noise.

"Sir? We're at the burger place now. The menu looks good."

"The *house?*"

"He likes very modern furniture. White leather —"

"Bruno!"

"But, sir, everything seemed fine. Except — I fed a cat in there, has one of those pet flaps in the kitchen door. Bed's not made, as if Allan left in a hurry. But perfectly ordinary interior. Garage with two cars. The big blue Mercedes we figure must be his. And in the back seat? The twenty-two-inch wheelie airplane carryon.

"The way it looks? Houseman came home, sir. Or else somebody drove his car here.

"Car in the garage, garage door down, but luggage still in the car. Then either he took off, or somebody grabbed him. There's just a cereal bowl in the kitchen sink, with dried milk. We don't think he went back inside at all."

Officer Belknap sounded pleased at being ordered back to the beach. He happily promised to talk to the lifeguards and find out when the restroom cleaners came. When Tor mentioned the pedestrian bridge Bruno said he knew exactly where it was, and that they had lots of photos of Vaccari left to show anybody under it.

Two hours later the four canvassers returned to Bay Street in a frolicsome mood, having scored again under the pedestrian bridge when a homeless veteran Marine assured them that the gray-haired guy had idled much of a damp evening there, napping beside his cart. Inconveniently, like Houseman's neighbors this veteran assigned the visit to Thursday evening.

They also brought back a double bag of flavored onion rings to share. While everybody in the room was sampling them, Chief Margolies walked in unannounced. Immediately he spotted the pile of onions on paper towels and went to help himself.

"Looks like I had three good reasons to come down here," said the Chief, selecting a ring. "The first was, I came to ask for volunteers. There's still some hours of daylight and no rain expected tonight. You go back to Canciones, take a stucco chip off that wall to the hardware and get some matching masonry paint. Also a quart of sealer to cover the black lettering. While the sealer dries, you're all painting the rest, around the letters. You can get a coat over the entire front of Housemans' wall *by tonight.*"

He took another ring and looked poised to grab a pile of them, staring around the room until some hands went up.

"Good. Thank you.

"'Why?' The volunteers have a right to ask.

"Primarily because the Housemans' neighbors are having their weekend spoiled by that unfriendly message in their faces, and I don't blame them.

"Also, Dr. Houseman will not be painting his own privacy wall. Yes, he has been found.

"You all detect, I didn't say, 'We found him.' Not us. Could scarcely be expected. The will of the currents was that he arrived to bide a day with our *amigos* in Rosarito Beach. His lightish hair and

L.L. Bean jacket suggested to them he might belong to us. And, lucky for us, he still has one hand. So they were able to fax his prints. Got those an hour ago.

"I've never met this gentleman who called from Rosarito. Maybe he was having fun with me? Sounded very businesslike though. I'll call my Tijuana buddies and ask about him. But according to my new *amigo* down there, who knows way more about sharks than I do, great white adults like to hang around in San Francisco Bay. Says he read that. But their great white shark minnows just six or eight feet long prefer the surfing down here with us, Tor. Which, according to him, is why we're getting back most of Allan Houseman. Instead of none of him.

"On your own time, you all should say a prayer for him.

"If you're thinking it would have been a drag on our investigation not to find any body at all — that's true. But something you would never figure is, we're lucky he still has his clothes. We're getting back his zip-up jacket minus the left sleeve, and the tops of his trousers."

Margolies was almost smiling.

"This is wonderful to me. In all my policing career, I have never heard of a floater who beached so distinctively outfitted as this one fished out by Rosarito's *policía*. This excites me.

"What do you think our *compadres Mexicanos* discovered in every single one of Houseman's pockets?"

Despite the silence, there was an air of tension in the room. The volunteers were impatient to leave on their painting job.

Finally Alvaro guessed, "Spanish doubloons from the wreck of *El Valoroso?"*

"Aspirational thinker! But no. I'd say, Houseman's pockets eliminate any possibility of suicide.

"They're all stuffed with raw hamburger."

THIRTY-NINE

A CRY OF LIGHT

Allan Houseman had not requested police protection. Nor had any been offered, in view of Floor Three's openness to the likelihood that he himself had poisoned his wife. Until the medical examiner announced his conclusions they could not be positive he had been murdered. But they might presume as much, given his pockets full of bloody meat and the 'TRAITOR!" message screaming that someone did not like him. If Allan really had been the intended victim, as he'd insisted, Chief Margolies felt much relief. Now their investigation of Lisette's incomprehensible death could focus on motives relating to her husband.

Nevertheless a second life had been taken, in ghastly fashion. Everyone in the room felt the shock of it, and the four who had just left the *casita* on Calle Canciones in a blithe Saturday frame of mind were stunned to realize that the lovingly kept home was orphaned. Alvaro begged permission to return later for a tabby whose water bowl identified her as "Peaches." He promised he and his mother would keep her at least until some family member claimed her.

All their witnesses who observed the gray-haired homeless man with a cart had insisted they saw him Thursday, after Arturo Vaccari was in police custody, instead of on Wednesday — much as the police wanted to believe Vaccari had been lurking in wait for Houseman. Informing the Chief was not a pleasant prospect. But with the Captain absent the job fell to Abelove.

"Two things, sir." Tor shoved the diminished pile of onion rings toward Margolies. Then he explained that the derelict whose sightings had so encouraged them earlier today could not possibly have been Mr. Vaccari. Seen around the Strand on Thursday evening, he was apparently one of Santa Christina's numerous other gray-haired homeless men.

"First business now," Margolies grimaced, "Is we drop the charges and release him fast, before Herman calls and demands we do. Better keep as much upper hand as I've got left."

Tor could see in the eyes of some of the younger officers that this sounded petty to them. But he and Lianopoulos understood the importance of political capital — both in negotiations with even someone as lowly as a young public defender like Frank Herman, and in maintaining the public's cooperation and good will. The Chief did not want anyone languishing in his custody after the case against him collapsed.

"Your second thing."

"Sir, this may be premature, but — nobody's spoken yet with Houseman's half-sister. Elinor Burns. I suspect she'll be the only heir. — Well, there's a mother, beneficiary of his life insurance now — but that leaves Elinor with enviable prospects. She placed a call to one of the secretaries, expressing great worry that she hadn't heard from Allan. We all accepted it at face value. Now I wonder if that call wasn't tactical and sly. And then — our guys who visited the house today found Houseman's car — with suitcase — in the garage. They think he must have been ambushed. We know for a fact, a receipt printed with the time — that Houseman dawdled nearly two hours at a restaurant his sister basically sent him to. Which means, she could have easily beaten him back to his house."

"Have a look, why not."

"We don't know yet where she was during the Adlers' party. If she has no alibi —"

"Wonder if she has a kayak. Where's Tony?"

"Out sick."

~ ~ ~

After Tor's call informing him of the gray-haired person seen with a grocery cart, Ogy lost interest in tomato seeds. Although he often walked his leashed dog along the boardwalk, he did not recall ever noticing such a character. In fact Gert, the mildly demented lady who never roamed far, was the only person he had observed with a pushcart in the beach area.

The whole situation seemed curious. Especially the mystery man's presence in the alley of Calle Canciones. That neighborhood was totally, quietly residential, with no businesses within four blocks. Couldn't the stranger guess that his presence in the alley behind their homes might seem threatening to locals who did not recognize him?

Although — evidently people had claimed to the police that they *did* recognize him.

So although he was not, *could not have been* Vaccari, he could be mistaken for him....

No doubt many homeless men resembled him.

Vaccari's release was already being arranged downtown, but Dr. Bradley was not apprised of that. Near four o'clock, when it was growing dark, he put Ghazi into the back seat of the Lexus and drove to the Strand. In early December there was ample parking adjacent the boardwalk. The beach was nearly deserted. But on any evening of the year, there were always some spectators milling on the sand to watch the sinking sun, hoping that the disappearance of Earth's near star would be accompanied by the phenomenon known as the "green flash."

Tonight, maybe because after rainfall the air was clear and cloudless, the flash did occur. It didn't very often. Each time, it caused amazement — displaying either lime-bolt rays, or else a soft green echo like a cry of light, as the sun was consumed by the sea.

After that welcome blessing, Dr. Bradley walked his dog to Volpe's outdoor patio at the south end of the beach, then turned back. The boardwalk's mid-section along the swimming beach wasn't as popular in December as the surfers' province farther north.

In this area abutted by the parking lot, he found the person he had hoped to encounter.

A thin woman with wrenched-back silver hair, she often came at nightfall with a bag of bread scraps for the gulls. As she tossed handfuls down to them, the birds rushed screeching about her. Ogy wondered if by now they recognized her when she arrived to sit on the sea wall. The eager gulls appeared oblivious to the Rhodesian ridgeback looming just a few feet away.

"Good evening," intruded the ridgeback's walker.

The stern-faced woman looked up as if annoyed. But after a moment her mouth relented in a faint smile.

"I know you," she realized.

"You work in the library," he recalled. "Reference desk."

"And you...."

"Don't feel nearly that useful."

Now she really smiled.

"Maybe you expect too much," she teased.

"I'm at the wrong end of life for expectations," he chuckled. "But I still do have curiosity. Do you mind my asking, were you by chance here either Wednesday or Thursday?"

"As a matter of fact, I came both evenings. And being a reference librarian, I'm captured by your curiosity."

"I'm wondering if you happened to notice a homeless person, gray-haired, with a loaded grocery cart on either of those dates?'"

"Why — yes. I did see him. At dusk he came slowly strolling by, then settled on a bench farther up. The one beyond the restrooms, where it's darkish and private. On Thursday, it was."

"You're quite sure it wasn't Wednesday?"

"Oh, no question. Wednesday was a perfect day, although with too many clouds at sunset for the flash. But Thursday in the late afternoon it rained for just a little while. I remember he had protective trash bags carefully spread over his bundles in the cart. Even though it was quite dark, like now, those metal rungs glistened from water drops still clinging to them."

"You're an excellent witness. Literary."

Now the librarian laughed.

"Did you happen to notice whether he was the same homeless man who seems to spend a lot of time here in the Strand?"

"Well… I can't say for certain," she decided. "He did have the untrimmed gray hair. Could have been. But — of course it was dark, and rather foggy. Besides, one does try not to look, doesn't one… Dr. Bradley."

Ogy nodded,"Was he smoking?"

"No. Definitely not then."

FORTY

BEING EDUCATED

Although every violent death represented someone's loss the police might marginally grieve, many of the homicides Floor Three dealt with seemed sadly predictable, almost inevitable. Even those left investigators discouraged by humankind's vulnerability and most primitive impulses. The Houseman case was different. Two civilized lives had been snuffed with contemptuous cruelty. Lise apparently had been entirely likable, Allan less so. But to have both coldly slaughtered, five days apart? That made you doubt the viability of lawful society. It cut close.

From the date of his marriage, Tor had made a principle of leaving Bay Street's uglier business behind each time he crossed the threshold of his bride's new home. But the Chief's revelation of what had become of Allan Houseman left a horror not quickly purged from anyone's blood.

He left Bay Street early. A Saturday dinner with both parents was a party to the children.

Later while they played and watched TV, Tor and Linda relaxed in their bedroom, leaving the door open so the youngsters would feel free to join them. He brought tea in Russian glasses and she presented homemade cookies left by her mother.

When both were comfortably sprawled across the bed he said, "You didn't show me what you bought. When you went shopping with Mrs. Becker."

"Oh."

Linda set her tea on the bedside table and slid closer to him.

"That was a lesson in 'just looking.' So I think before I buy."

"So have you thought?"

"A lot. You know — I love my parents very much. I really do."

"You've got great parents."

"But, honestly, darling? I'm crazy about Mrs. Becker."

"I guess that's no surprise."

"Isn't it? We saw all kinds of nice clothes and I even tried some on. But when I got home? All I could think was, 'Tor's giving me *five hundred dollars!*' Because I realized then, I don't want new clothes. I don't even have use for them. I just want to go to school."

"You're going. I promise. As soon as I work out the logistics."

"But *how?* Timothy's not even sixteen months old."

"Doesn't matter. Lots of people do it."

"You really wouldn't mind?"

"All I mind — is knowing you are going to outgrow me. But that's on me."

"What! What are you talking about?"

"You're not on the phone or watching TV. You don't have girlfriends, not really. And when you finally choose yourself one — somebody you actually invite to go out shopping — who is it? Someone with emphysema, pushing eighty years old. What does that say about you?"

"Just… I find her so interesting, that's all."

"No. That's not all. Linda, one time Ogy showed me a book her husband wrote. On the back there's a photo of the two Beckers. That book matters to him — or, the photo does. He almost didn't let me touch it. I said, 'So he was pretty famous,' or something like that. He said, 'Not as much as she was, among people who know.' And of course I had to smart off, so then I said, 'But not as famous as you,' and Omar said, 'Oh, more than I could ever be.' So that's your girlfriend, Linda."

"Okay. I'm embarrassed. I made a fool of myself, wanting to be friends with her."

"No, you didn't! Ingrid likes you too. My only point is, you deserve an education. Long past due. And you're going to get one."

Linda had sat up in distress. He pulled her back onto her pillow.

"The community college is a long drive. It's not realistic, it wouldn't work."

"We'll move."

"What! Where? How?"

"We can rent out this house and lease an apartment two minutes from the campus. We'd be closer to your parents, closer to Bay Street. There might even be child care offered at the school, so you could just bring Timmy for a couple hours. I'm sure he'd like that."

"Why are you thinking about this stuff now, all of a sudden?"

"Mrs. Becker won't live forever. You need more people in your life than just an uneducated klutz like me. Who should not be trying to buy you off."

"What's come over you? You have an awfully challenging job, the toughest job I've ever heard of. You're thinking hard all the time. You think as much as Ogy Bradley does!"

"Not as well."

~ ~ ~

On Saturday night Allan Houseman's remains were received by the SCPD. On Sunday morning Tor called Dr. Bradley to explain that his department was awaiting autopsy results. He wondered if Ogy and Ghazi could join him and Contrail at the dog park somewhat later than usual, say at eleven thirty?

Since it was December, both doctor and dog were content to snooze a little longer and breakfast later than usual on a Sunday. The ridgeback was clearly excited when Ogy told him, *"Contrail!* Romp at the *dog park,* with Contrail!"

Ghazi's human friend could not help being infected, as well as grateful to Cael for reminding him that Ghazi did to a degree recognize a few words.

By the time the two dogs were set loose on the park's beach it was nearly noon. Harnessed and tethered, Timmy ran about happily behind them, pulling his father after him. Although they toured the bay for almost an hour, the dog guru was nowhere in sight.

They must have arrived too late today. Both men wondered if their pets gave any thought to launching their week without their guru's Sunday benediction.

Tor rattled along semi-quoting Medical Examiner Ariel Davies' report, "Shark damage to the extremities is all post-mortem. Lividity was conspicuous in Allan's head, neck, upper chest and single remaining forearm, likely from being transported in a car trunk. Houseman was killed by a single knife thrust to the heart — from behind. To me, that greatly increases the likelihood the killer was a woman — certainly suggesting a very personal interpretation of the 'traitor' aspect. If she was stealthy Allan didn't have any chance to fight back. I'm not abandoning interest in the other females in his periphery, but now I'm really eager to meet half-sister Elinor Burns. She vaults to becoming a priority because she benefits — grandly."

"Of course."

"— Has the biggest motive, in fact. I'd assumed Elinor's not as bright," he said, "But maybe she's as calculating as he was. Maybe Mom was the one with brains. Or deviousness. We don't know yet if she has an alibi for Saturday, but at the moment she's not picking up.

"— And just as well. The truth is, now I've got something else in mind. Do you remember, during the Blenheim case, at one point you said something like, 'Your instinct may be just as valid as some logical explanation you think up?' I forget your exact words."

"Sort of, maybe. Instinct acting up, is it?"

"Something's bugging me ever since Thursday and I've been pretending it's not there. Today I admit it, but I can't talk about it yet, before I clear this with people."

"You've given up on Vaccari's being the man with a cart who went everywhere?"

"Now you put it that way, he did seem to go everywhere. But yeah. All our witnesses saw some other gray-haired man with a cart, just scavenging trash cans in that alley. Not because the Housemans lived there, but because in that well-to-do area where people don't bother taking in recyclables, he maybe can find lots of deposit bottles for his cart or — hate to think — something decent to eat."

"I have to disagree. I'd say the fact he wasn't Vaccari makes him far more interesting."

"Say more?"

"Just by pure chance, he happened to be noticed right behind the Housemans' property, the same date Allan disappeared?

"On that night only, he dawdled in so many places. *For hours.* But he's not been seen there since, and was never noticed before?

"You have to think of Poe, of the boldness of hiding in plain sight. But to justify any risk, surely he was grappling with an overwhelming necessity.

"Then the question becomes — what necessity?"

Tor strode silently, then realized he'd left the sixty-year-old with a cane behind, and turned back, apologetic.

"What you're saying. You have a suspect in my case."

"Only a notion."

"You're not going to tell me."

"You should follow your own instincts, not mine."

"*'Hypothesize and keep an open mind'?*"

"Not if you know a better way to proceed."

"He's some other homeless guy. I accept that. Artie's made me respect that even homeless lives are more complex than we might…."

Tor trailed off, fretting over several topics jostling in his head.

"One thing I've got to do — or get my colleague to do when she's back, is make some calls. When I visited Jon Doerr he gave me three names of scientists familiar with Allan. The first had plenty to say. But with the other two, I got the idea they didn't want to talk. Now that Houseman can't retaliate, maybe they'll be willing. But this time I'll have Smithers get me a handle on those two."

"Sensible."

They had reached a bend in the bay where the path ascended to skirt a broad open area with three picnic tables shaded by huge eucalypts. Tor parked the stroller beside one of the tables, then removed Timmy's harness so that he could run free, safely away from the sea. Ogy sat on the far end of the bench.

"Tor, have I upset you? Is that your *name?* I don't even know."

"It was 'Viktor.' After my father."

"But you don't like it."

"I don't like him. And in my job, a 'vic' is a corpse."

"Since a 'tor' is a sort of peak, hilltop? At first I supposed it was your… surfer brand."

"Never knew. — I'll tell you what does upset me. I wish you could listen to Houseman's interview last week. The way he brags about what a get-ahead ruthless climber he is. Wants Adler's job, or comparable. Makes friends with people on the basis of how useful to him they can be. Even Lisette. His best argument for why he didn't kill his wife is, nobody else would be as convenient to his career."

"Maybe his circumstances were somewhat extenuating? Being suspected of murder? I can imagine fear might make some men act brash, in that show-off way."

"I get that, but most people would say these things a bit apologetically. This guy is so proud of his own coldness he's kind of intriguing. And then he does mention he loves her. So, probably he did."

"I'm not sure what you're telling me."

"I haven't yet. Did you hear about the shopping trip? Ingrid and Linda?"

"Heard of it, not about."

"We didn't hate Houseman or anything. But with cops, that kind of pipsqueak cheekiness is annoying. Later, though — after Linda's great lunch out with Mrs. Becker — I realized. "How am I so different from Houseman? Yeah, he was being outrageous to make a point. But in what way am I better?

"When we got married the Kimuras weren't pleased about it. Not because they disliked me for some horrible fault, just because they wanted their daughter to go to college. When we just wanted to be together."

"Best reason."

"After ten years? I can say she's made me very happy. But Houseman's example made me ask myself, what have I done for her? And I don't like the answer. While I need so much escape."

"I recall your flight lessons."

"Maybe you don't understand how shy she really is. The way she just called Ingrid —?"

On his feet again, he checked where Timothy was headed, and remained standing.

"— That floored me. Linda is such a dedicated mommy, she doesn't think she has a right to go to college yet, but she does. I have to make it happen for her. She wants it, but she's too good to demand it."

"Sounds great to me. …Oh. You have a problem."

"Hundreds. Every man she's going to meet. They'll all be more educated than I am. All. *Everywhere around her.* And eventually… she'll find the one … she'd rather have. Even if I get promotions, I'll still — even if the department sends me to take classes in forensics, criminology — I'm not asking permission to keep her a house slave! But over time, more and more, I'm still just the thug with the gun. That's all."

Dr. Bradley was bewildered. This new frantic tone, almost distraught, betrayed a despair he could never have conceived in the most accomplished and courageous athlete he had ever met. But Tor was no longer a daredevil celebrity. He gave that up for Linda.

Abelove could not help noticing that Ogy didn't scoff. He appreciated that respect, at least.

"She was out of my class to begin with —"

"You want a reaction?"

"I just always thought — yeah. I need to —"

Timmy shot across the open field in a straight line, but Contrail went after him and herded him back like an errant lamb, while Ghazi loped ahead glancing back at them. As if being able to run was still too novel, the giggly child dropped and reverted to crawling.

"In your place?" While Ogy thought earnestly Tor sank onto the bench, his son in close view. "I can imagine — how the thought of having an educated wife might make me feel insecure, in the sense that — here I am with all these years accumulated in the force, without a degree myself and not qualified for other work. Suddenly my career looks maybe not good enough for her higher standards. But, in my mid-thirties, I lack better options.

"So. First of all — I'm back to being me now — *I want to shoot that idea down, dead.*

"Police work is public service. Perpetual, committed, stressful, dangerous service to the people of this city. You probably do more good in one week than our new councilman will manage during a year in office, where he'll be in business mainly for himself.

"On top of that, not only is Linda proud of you — Ingrid picked up on that — but you happen to be very good at what you do. Purely in self-interest, as a citizen, I'd hate to see you give it up.

"And I don't say this just because you're smart, relentless and fearless. I believe it most of all because you have integrity. In any work that confers power, the people can't afford to lose the rare public servant with integrity."

"Thank you."

"No, thank *you*.

"So then my question becomes, Why equate being 'educated' with having a degree? Apart from all the time lost driving, do you need calculus, geology, Portuguese or whatever —"

"Geology? That sounds cool —"

"Fine. In a formal program for a degree nobody gets to elect many courses just because they're cool. But you aren't constrained that way. Lincoln, arguably our greatest president, had scant formal education. But he read — selectively. He knew law. The Bible. Shakespeare. Something I learned from my wife — art makes us more than we were.

"In your case, with your profession and good mind, I'd guess law — or history — is a useful place to start. American, if that's most comfortable. If the department is concerned about terrorism, I'd urge you to read Mideastern history as well. Should you have interest in any branch of science or philosophy, if I can't recommend readable books I'll know someone who can suggest some — including about geology."

Tor rose again, monitoring Timothy's vector and Contrail's attentiveness.

"When I was a kid, a history of the Second World War came out that was a huge success. In my impressionable teens I read it and was astonished to find the author was a blatant homophobe. I thought, 'He knows a lot of history, but this is not some wise man.' 'His head was of fine gold,' but his feet were clay.

"You're an adult with both an unusually broad perspective and experience. You'll see when even idols — like Jefferson — fall short. So please give Linda credit and don't assume she'll find every man who's piled up college degrees superior to you. You thought Allan was a stinker, right? Would she see him differently?"

"Oh, she'd see through him."

"Library books are cheaper than flight lessons. If you read important books while Linda studies, *she'll* have trouble keeping up with *you*."

Still frowning, Tor shook his head.

"She keeps me possible."

FORTY-ONE

PERFORMERS

After their visit to the dog park, Tor's follow-up call interrupted Ghazi's sand rinsing shower.

"Doc, I've got permission to hire you for a consultation, if you're willing. Ever since the night we brought in Vaccari, I've been bothered by that wildly self-incriminating interview. I got the sense that we were talking on parallel tracks, somehow. I have no idea yet what he was really telling me. So even though I have these other logical suspects left to check out, I've decided to home in on my anxiety and try to fathom Artie.

"My big gap — it concerns Allan and Cris Harbison. It just feels like, there's something there. The problem is, according to his parents

Cris is brain-damaged. He drowned, his mother said, and was resuscitated. Has a PhD but works now in a grocery, stacking vegetables. He's clumsy. Artie says people see him as a freak. I want to interview Cris, but I'm worried we may need a specialist to communicate with him. If you're willing to come down here."

"You have his medical records from this accident?"

"Nothing. Don't know if any exist. It didn't happen in this country."

"Okay. First — this is *pro bono,* I'd like to assist you and the lad both. Second, not at Bay Street. Please bring him here, to my house. You and one of his parents, if they can. My guess is Artie is a better choice than his mother, who'd probably want too much to help. I'll try to do a quick evaluation, just to aid you in talking to him. From the sound of it, both his verbal and motor functions were impacted. The question is, how much cognitive impairment did he suffer as well? If he can keep even the grocery job, that's encouraging. His parents aren't the best judges of how far his mental acuity is degraded. They're likely reacting more to his physical than to his mental state. We'll try to get him talking to you. After that, as an experiment, I'd like to invite two or three people over. Social interaction is another potential indicator of how comprehensively his intellect retains function after a major insult. Indifference to other people would not be a good sign."

If this sounded off point to Abelove, he was happy to agree. He'd begun to feel almost like a lover, in the intensity of his desire to plumb the significance of Vaccari's voluntary initial statement, which had displayed the bitter abandon he would expect of someone being escorted to execution.

Meanwhile, Elinor Burns remained through Monday evening in Santa Clara with her grief-stricken mother. Tor did not begrudge the mother that. Losing her son right after her daughter-in-law was very rough. Rebecca Savage, the outlier of his concerns, could wait a while. But he was not yet satisfied writing off Claire Fields. Regarding her as dishonest just because she fooled him by wearing a wig would be egotistical. But even with a supposed fiancé in Afghanistan, she was an attractive young woman in the same office block as Allan Houseman. He could not believe Houseman had not noticed her, whatever her hair issues might be.

This morning Hank Smithers said Bettina had gone to church, and planned to return to work maybe on Monday. With a backlogged wish list of topics for Tina to investigate, Tor was cheered by that news. At the same time, Claire had taken a cheap shot at her when they interviewed her at the Institute — and Tina was offended by his overt admiration of Claire. Right now was late enough on Sunday afternoon that the traffic jam exiting for the water park had cleared. In summer there might still be crowds arriving in anticipation of the evening show; but not in December, not with a possibility of rain.

He decided to take a chance and visit the park without an appointment. He could call Linda and offer to pick up pulled pork sandwiches at Piggy's, which was not far, thus salvaging the trip if there was no one in the park's offices to interview. By now he realized he did not want Officer Smithers present during any discussion of Claire Fields, even if that wasn't fair to Tina's professionalism.

He was lucky. Despite the unlikely hour, he was escorted to one of the park's administrators, a woman probably in her fifties named Candace Willoughby. When the plainclothes detective introduced himself, Ms. Willoughby said, "Police? Well, I'm surprised. From the look of you I thought you'd be asking for a job in the show."

Immediately Tor was relieved he had not brought Bettina.

"Thank you, ma'am, but I'm afraid I'm way past the age limit."

Ms. Willoughby's eyes looked even brighter.

"Can you swim?"

"Oh, yes, ma'am!" laughed the surfing champion.

"Well, if you'd ever like to audition —"

"In fact, right now, ma'am, I've come to inquire about one of your former performers."

"Our 'former performers'?" Candace snickered at the awkward phrase.

Tor prided himself on having become a master of bland. But this woman was not allowing him to employ it. Still smiling, though, he explained, "This is regarding a married couple who were murdered this week in El Albergue."

"The man in today's paper?" exclaimed the woman. "From the Institute? But what does that have to do with our people?"

"Probably nothing at all. It's entirely routine that we have to do a background check on anyone closely associated with the victim in these cases. Of course including their best friends and associates at work. The next name on my list is Claire Fields."

"Oh...."

"Our understanding is that before joining the administrative staff at the ocean school Ms. Fields worked here. Is that correct?"

"Yes. Claire was with us... I'd guess, a bit more than two years."

"How was she? In the job?"

"Fine, in a word. Claire is bright. Beautiful. She'd been a rough water swimmer in school. Has dramatic flair. And she truly loves animals. Not everyone does, we've learned."

"How did she happen to come to the job, do you know? I have no experience of show business," he lied.

"As I recall — she'd been in college. But when her boyfriend enlisted in the service, she was...frightened. Lost patience with schoolwork. Went back to what's most comfortable to her, I guess you'd say. To not just sit and worry about him."

"I can understand that. But he's still over there?"

"I'm not sure. I do know people in the service get pressured into doing more tours."

"Why did she leave, then?"

"Ohhhhh…" It was a deliberating sigh. Ms. Willoughby was staring down, her long fingernails playing with the SCPD card he'd given her. "More reasons than one."

"Okay…."

"First problem, her father. He thought this job was mindless. Wanted her back in school, or at least working at something with… a more useful resumé.

"And then — we had an incident. One of our animal stars injured another girl. Mr. Fields went ballistic, at that point. Insisted Claire should quit before she got killed."

"Fathers. But, I am one."

"The way it ended, the animal was euthanized. When Claire came back and found out what had happened to her co-performer, she was angry."

"I can sympathize."

"We all can. But she wouldn't let it go, sulked about Lupe. I'm not saying that was unreasonable, from someone very young. But the animals she worked with picked up on her mood. If you have a pet —"

"Do I ever."

"Then you know, they're sensitive. Claire was upset. And pretty soon we noticed, the seals were on edge, high strung."

"You fired her?"

"No. That young woman is a talent, so we gave it time. But her father won out. I was sorry to see her leave, but probably he was right that this was not where she belonged."

"I do get the sense she's appreciated, at the Institute."

"That's no surprise. She works hard and she's principled. Claire was the kind who saw all animals as innocents."

"More than we are, anyway."

"I don't know about that. I'm honestly not sure Claire — and you — give them enough credit. I'll always wonder if Lupe didn't attack Alison just because she preferred doing shows with Claire."

"May I ask — what's wrong with her hair?"

"Her *hair?* Nothing…?"

"She wears a wig."

"She worked *in a water show. Wigs are easy!"*

Laughing, Candace swept a hand through her own shoulder-length hair as she told the surfing celebrity, "Convenient laziness, that's all that's about."

When Tor rose to leave, saying he was pleased to meet her, she smirked, "Oh, I'll see your face again. My son still wears one of your T-shirts."

As nearly as Abelove could recall, this woman's information was exactly what Claire had told them herself. The only thing he hadn't found out was whether Pat Connell was still her fiancé. It had not occurred to him before that he and Claire had something in common — both had performed before audiences.

Claire Fields was an impressive young lady, but remembering her snipe at Tina made him impatient to pick up some sandwiches and hurry home.

FORTY-TWO

COGNITIVE CONTROL

It was mid-afternoon when they approached the winged statue of twelve-year-old Caelan atop the western pillar of the Bradleys' gate. Cris stopped to stare at it, while his father mostly stared at him. The statue's bronze head hung slightly, making the viewer uncertain whether his arms were raised in triumph or surrender.

Tor wondered if Ogy knew what Sylvia had been thinking.

With a shambling gait the former gymnast climbed the wide stone stairs. Surely his fashionable mother had outfitted him. He wore a good tweed sport coat with a dress shirt and a beige silk tie. Although gravely disabled, he did seem strong, as might be expected of someone who three years ago had been an athlete. At the top of the stairs he turned to note the expanse of ocean visible from this elevation, even glimpsing the Oceanographic Institute of which he was a graduate. But what the masterful sea might signify to Cris Harbison now was beyond imagining. For years Abelove had lived with a significant risk of drowning, and for that reason never let himself contemplate it.

The rosewood door swung inward, opened by a heavy man in a starched white lab coat. Although Tor had infrequently visited O.G. Bradley in his med school lab, he realized he had never seen him working as either a lecturer or a physician. He hadn't anticipated this frisson of excitement from witnessing a friend in his professional role.

The only stipulation Ogy had insisted upon when they made the appointment was, "Please, do NOT become impatient. Young Harbison will be enduring far more stress than you. Don't make it harder on him by letting him see your reactions."

"Thank you so much for coming," beamed Dr. Bradley, shaking Arturo Vaccari's hand and greeting him like an old friend.

"And Dr. Harbison. I'm very pleased to meet you, sir," with another hearty handshake.

The young man made some comment of demurral which Tor couldn't understand.

"But of course you are, sir," insisted the physician serenely. "No one can ever take that from you."

Leaning on his metal cane, Dr. Bradley led his guests slowly over a stone and rosewood floor to the back of the house. In his family room a fire was burning. The dog in his basket raised his head, inquisitive. But apparently Ghazi decided nothing here merited getting up, not while soft jazz music from a CD player encouraged lethargy. The four men took seats around the coffee table, where a tub of ice held plastic water bottles and a pitcher of lemonade. A hand-thrown ceramic bowl decorated with painted shellfish contained pretzels.

"Dr. Harbison, I'm told you like Neapolitan pizza," said Dr. Bradley. "Later some friends will stop by and bring us the local product. If there's a pizzeria you prefer to today's, Detective Abelove and I would be interested in your recommendation."

For a short time they sipped beverages, speculating about how many years of drought Christina County had endured already and whether coastal desalination facilities might be built.

Then the doctor announced, "Lacking any report on Dr. Harbison's condition, I'm going to perform just a perfunctory examination. A thorough one to protocol would take much longer, but there's no need now. This is just to assist Detective Abelove in questioning his witness."

They filed through a doorway in the back corner of the room. Tor had never even realized this additional small room existed. During Mrs. Bradley's illness it had been refitted as an exam room where her nurse could sleep. Cris understood he should sit up on the examination table. Abelove and Vaccari took plastic chairs against the wall. Oh his feet, Dr. Bradley then proceeded with the sort of routine physical exam familiar to them all. Occasionally he sat on the small bed and explained what he was doing.

Tor watched Ogy more than Cris. Gradually he realized that what he was observing was not discipline and not a performance. The physician possessed skilled perception, purged of aversion or fear. This young man's painfully awkward movements and the contortions of his face while he labored to speak comprehensibly never jarred the examining doctor. All he saw and heard was young Dr. Harbison, injured in a nearly fatal accident. Ogy talked to Cris so slowly and quietly that they might have been sharing a beer in front of a baseball game. While he spoke, his right hand might press the younger man's arm. Or his left hand would settle briefly with light reassurance over his patient's.

Tor told himself, "Any other top specialist this leisurely about a consultation would be charging a fierce hourly rate."

But as those casual minutes meandered by, he noticed that young Harbison was visibly relaxing. So was Artie. So was he.

When the blood pressure, heartbeat and breathing portions of the exam were finished, Dr. Bradley remarked, "You're a healthy young man, as you no doubt already know. Clearly you're very well nourished. I don't detect any lung damage, one of the big dangers from submersion."

"Nicola — they told his mother somebody on the ship knew first aid," volunteered Artie. "They cleared the water when they got him up. Did CPR."

"Good, that's very good. Now let's go back into the other room and try to evaluate somewhat the losses you've sustained. If anyone would like the bathroom, it's across the hall."

No one did. Ogy opened one of the lower cabinets and removed a small chalkboard and some papers.

"Next thing, sir — you're having memory problems. So here's our first experiment. Take your time, and don't be nervous. You are not being judged.

"I'm going to tell you a short story about what I did today. Then I'll ask you to repeat as much as you remember. Okay? Here's my morning:

"First I drove to the drugstore and bought the newspaper. Then I went to the coffee shop, ordered a latte and read the paper. Next, at the grocery store I bought eggs, bacon and English muffins. On my way home I stopped to buy gas.

"Now, sir — can you remember any of that?"

"Uuuuuuuuuuuhh…" Cris grunted. "Gas?"

"Don't recall any more of it? That's all right."

With a look of dejection and disgust Cris shook his head, moaning under his breath.

"It's all right. Don't be discouraged. We're not finished. You mustn't let yourself become discouraged — *ever.*"

The visibly resigned young man sat up straighter and nodded, clearly more from courtesy than optimism.

"The next experiment is similar to the first one. But instead of my telling you the story, you will read it. Then after I remove the page, you'll try to recall what you read. Okay?"

Cris looked defeated but attentive as Dr. Bradley produced a sheet of paper on which one or two sentences were printed.

"Please tell me when you're done, sir."

After staring at the sentences for at least a minute, Cris muttered, "'Kay."

The paper was turned face down.

"Able to remember anything?"

The young man's eyes glazed. "Ro' bi'."

"Yes, good. 'Rode the bike.' Anything else come back to you?"

Harbison shook his head, looking so mortified that Tor felt angry. He was becoming exasperated with his friend, who appeared to have forgotten the point of the interview. Ogy was making Cris miserable and tired. Already his witness was bitterly demoralized, and they had not yet begun trying to elicit information from him. Despite Artie Vaccari's normal finesse of movement, even he appeared to coil with anxiety.

"It's fine, Dr. Harbison," assured the doctor. "These tests are a small portion of the profile, you understand.

"Now we'll try an exercise less verbal. I'll write a problem on the blackboard, and you tell me the answer. All right?"

Tor was looking for an opening to interject somehow that all this was not just futile but counterproductive, when suddenly he realized he was doing exactly what the doctor had warned *not* to do — getting impatient. Glancing again at Vaccari, he was softened by the father's harrowed face. He recalled Ogy's attempt to describe this man's sadness.

If Harbison and Vaccari can stand it, I guess so should I, he decided.

On the left side of the chalkboard Ogy was writing:

$$\begin{array}{r} 10 \\ +10 \\ \underline{+10} \end{array}$$

Cris looked at the sum and grumbled, looking displeased.

"Thugh," he tried. *"Thught —"*

"That's fine," the physician assured him. "You're doing fine, take your time —"

But Dr. Harbison uttered a croak of something like suppressed outrage. He jumped onto his unsteady feet and shuffled to the small chalkboard. Grabbing up the chalk, with difficulty he managed to scratch out a pair of numerals on the upper right of the board.

They read, "17."

When he saw that figure, Vaccari's face dropped so far that Tor was afraid he would weep. But his brain-damaged son was in something of a frenzy, emitting guttural noises while he continued making squeaky scratches on the board. The tension of that pitiful scene was excruciating, but no one had the will to interrupt him.

Finally, the effort of his uncooperative fingers completed, Cris straightened up, somewhat. Summarily his palm wiped away the left column's addition of three times ten. The older men all stared at the new column filling the vertical space on the right side of the board:

$$17$$
$$34$$
$$51$$
$$68$$
$$85$$

"Thank you, Dr. Harbison," purred Dr. Bradley. "That is lovely.

"Mr. Vaccari? What your son demonstrates with his multiples of seventeen is that despite the neurological damage causing his motor and speech problems, his brain substantially retains what's called 'cognitive control.' That is, the ability to plan, to reason — to function in the complexly coordinating way a brain is supposed to. It also remembers some arcane facts it knew before his accident.

"Dr. Harbison, I wonder if your having *written* '17' did not assist your concentration in continuing the sequence? And it could be that seeing the summation of the '10's served as a reminder of the operation you were performing, helping you stay focused. Your success in this exercise suggests that annotating such organizing cues might help to override your loss of memory function.

"Exemplary performance, sir. Next let's try a game."

From a different cupboard the doctor produced a lumpy canvas sack. The bowl of pretzels had been nested inside a larger bowl, from which he now removed it. Shifting the pretzels and tub of drinks to a side cabinet, Ogy emptied his sack's contents into the large bowl.

"Organize those, please, Dr. Harbison. Any way you like."

Cris reached both hands into the bowl. He pulled out two colored wooden shapes. One was a standard wood block painted purple. The other was a green pyramid. Working clumsily but with both hands he pulled out what appeared to be all the purple and green pieces. Next he arranged two columns on the coffee table, one of each color. Then he began reordering the green pieces so that the cylinder, the heart and other shapes were all next to the same shape in the purple column. But at this point his scheme was frustrated.

Rummaging in the bowl, he could not find a purple pyramid or a green ellipse.

The young man muttered unintelligibly as he pulled out pieces of the other colors. Soon he had emptied the bowl and placed each of six hues into a new column. For scarcely longer than a minute, he tried aligning shapes across the rows, stymied when some shape was absent from each color.

Then he abruptly stopped and stared at his erratic array. Instead of correcting the horizontal rows, now coordinating both hands he quickly moved entire columns into a different order. Suddenly the six same-colored columns and six matched-shape horizontal rows formed a complete square — bisected by a diagonal of empty spaces running neatly from the top left position to bottom right.

"Haaah!" exclaimed Cris Harbison, as Detective Abelove applauded.

"Rapidly done!" intoned the deep voice of Ogy Bradley, and he left Cris's elegant grid on the table to be admired.

Then again he covered the young man's hands with his own.

"Dr. Harbison, I know you already understand that my friend here from the police department would like to question you about what happened on your expedition. Your mother told Detective Abelove the ship was the *Cirene,* is that correct?

"Detective Abelove is most interested in events before your submersion accident — before cerebral hypoxia left you disabled. Now you do have difficulty forming new memories, but you didn't prior to that day. What happened to you on the *Cirene* is important. One thing I hope you're convinced of, sir. If you try, if you can construct your times table of seventeen, *you can recall what happened on that ship.*"

Even though this young man was near Linda's age — and Congressman Caelan's — Tor could not help thinking of him as a boy, so desolate did he seem. Since Dr. Bradley did not look inclined to give up his sofa seat beside Cris Harbison, he pulled his own chair closer, shins pressed against the coffee table. Ghazi lifted his head to note the source of the minor vibration on the floor, then ignored a friend who'd neglected to bring the wolfhound.

"Sir, Dr. Bradley and the Santa Christina Police Department thank you for your prolonged patience here. I have two areas of questioning, if you will allow me. One subject — later — is Allan Houseman and what he was up to during that expedition on the *Cirene.* But the first one is your accident. We'd like to know who was present when it happened. And how it happened. But let's begin with the question, What were you doing before this accident occurred? Do you recall the scene?"

"'Curse. Un deh. W'Al'n.'"

"'On deck,'" interpreted Artie. "That much I get."

"With Allan?" verified Tor.

"Talk." Cris's hands began disassembling his puzzle grid.

"What were you talking about?"

"Fish. All fish. Buh… Al'n keep loo'… loo'… loo'… kin' my… foo', foo' —"

Cris's legs appeared to throe with nervous distress. Angry with himself, Tor no longer remembered why this interview had seemed so important to him. Returning to his shaped wooden blocks, Cris had placed a green pyramid in the purple column that lacked one, continuing that green row with an orange ellipse where the green was absent.

"He's getting upset," Tor complained, in a more accusing voice than he had intended.

"He's always upset, wouldn't you be?" shot back the father.

"Please help us understand," soothed Dr. Bradley. "Show us, if you can, please? What did he keep looking at?"

"Foo' —" Exasperated, Cris raised his leg above the table and grabbed his foot. "FOO'!"

"Thank you. But why was he looking at your foot?"

"Foo'n *jin.* Stan' *jin. In jin!* Stan' 'ole time —" He positioned more orange pieces.

"I'm sorry," despaired Tor.

"In jin!"

With an exhausted sigh, Cris touched the tip of his left forefinger to the tip of his left thumb. He did the same with his right hand, linking the two circles. He tugged, to show he could not pull them apart. Then he returned to his new freeform design, conveying urgency as one hand linked the orange sequence with a red line that suddenly also completed the blue.

"Chain?" asked Tor. "You were standing on a chain?"

The witness was removing his tie, as if he felt overheated. But instead of folding it to place aside, he bent to wind the tie around his ankle, leaving its ends on the floor.

"Al'n! Keep loo' my foo' *in jin.* I's stan' in jin, talk'n' bou' fish."

"The chain was around your foot. He saw."

Tor's usual pleasure in this kind of quest deserted him. He was starting to feel disgust.

"I's lea' on rail, talk fish w'm. Jus' — 'ow ma'y tu'a? 'Ow ma'y?"

"And then, Dr. Harbison?" Again the physician's slow voice dropping to a bass register restored a note of calm. "What happened while you discussed how many tuna?"

"Th' mo'or — it wa' —"

For Tor, Cris's struggle to communicate had become almost too much to bear. As his words began to seem a little more coherent, his father became increasingly nervous. Tor could not pull his gaze away from Vaccari's anguish now. Grieving for his child, the man sat with teeth clenched, jaws taut. That pressure seemed to be making his eyes bulge out.

"I her th' mo'or star' — !" An alternate blue row took shape under his twitchy fingers.

"You mean, the motor for the anchor?" asked Dr. Bradley.

"Th' mo'or star' — wi' *foo' in jin*!"

With all his heart, Tor willed the physician to shut up, abandon this interview that he himself had begged Bill Margolies to allow.

But Dr. Bradley was relentless.

"The anchor chain pulled you overboard?"

Even though Cris enunciated so poorly, all three understood his next words perfectly.

"Al'n killed me."

FORTY-THREE

LOST SON RESTORED

Trembling, Cris clung to the doctor's hands in horror at describing the day he woke up dead.

It wasn't that he ever forgot what happened on the *Cirene*. Only that, after the long adjustment to his metamorphosis, now he was experiencing it fresh a second time.

"No," insisted Dr. Bradley. "Allan did you great harm! But he's dead now. Sharks got him. *And here you are…!* Still mathematical."

Unable to endure watching the son's distress, Tor had been focused on the suffering in Vaccari's face. But Artie's taut expression suddenly went slack. Tor turned to see what caused the father's surprised reaction.

For perhaps the first time in three years, Cris Harbison was smiling.

Ogy's arm was wrapped around the shuddering young man's shoulders. As Cris clutched his own biceps, even through tweed sleeves Tor recognized the musculature of a gymnast.

"There's more Detective Abelove still needs to hear," Ogy apologized, "But I think a glass of wine now might be a good idea. In honor of our two Italian guests — and one more coming later — we have Chianti."

The bottle was already open, and glasses without pesky stems stood close at hand. When Cris's health had been roundly toasted the young man nodded, "'S okeh. Go 'hea'."

"This was a sneak attack," Tor resumed. "Planned, or opportunistic? I take it you weren't involved with Mrs. Houseman. So why he did he want you at the bottom of the sea? Do you even know? You're certain it wasn't an accident?"

Harbison grinned briefly at the notion of an illicit liaison with Lisette, but his head shake quickly turned to nodding on the subject of Houseman's murderous intent.

"Al'n was 'n *charge*. Whole trip. 'N' we ma' un-*sched*-you stop. Wake up — *where?* In por'. No' *s'posed* stop —"

"You were in port? Where? What country?"

"Do' know."

"Wait, Detective," interrupted Vaccari. "When Cristoforo says he 'doesn't know'? He just can't remember any names. Of anything or anybody. But if you *say it* — then he recognizes it."

"This *Cirene* trip was a Pacific expedition. Um. Was it Peru?"

"Nuh."

"A prompter." Ogy rose to retrieve a globe from a shelf. He handed it to Tor.

"Was it Chile?"

"Nuh, nuh."

"Ecuador?"

Cris was concentrating hard.

"Manta? Esmeraldas? Guayaquil?"

"Sí!"

"So you stopped in Guayaquil. What for?"

"Women."

Abelove was taken aback. — This was a shipload of mostly married scientists?

"You mean — everybody…?"

"No' me. I's s'prise' too."

"Was that… *all*… this port stop involved?"

"III — do' — knoooow…."

The statement was so burdened by uncertainty, Tor felt sure it must carry something.

"But you think something else was going on?"

"Where?"

"Detective," interjected the doctor softly, "I'm afraid that Dr. Harbison has just lost you. Try rephrasing the question to jog his memory, like this — 'When the *Cirene* docked in Guayaquil to visit women, did you have the sense that *something else* happened too? Someplace Dr. Houseman went, or something he did?'"

"Yuh. Nes' day o' — ? I do' know when."

Tor asked, "What made you think Allan did something in Guayaquil?"

"I rea' Spa'sh."

"You read Spanish. What did you see written in Spanish?"

"He lef' i' ou'. O' ta-ble. Boo' fruh bah'."

"I'm sorry, sir?"

"Baaah — *k* booo — *k*."

"*Bank book?* He has an offshore account?'"

"*Sí. 'Bah-co....'*"

"Did you see — what was in it?"

"*Bi'* buzz! Bug-z. *Buh* — kiss."

"Remember how much?"

"Nuh."

The doorbell rang.

"Any idea why? What he was doing?"

"Nuh. Sorr — ee, nuh."

"Thank you very much, sir. We can proceed from here. Is there anything else you'd like to tell us?"

Cris was clutching his wine glass, thinking intently.

"*Bah-co de Uaaa-yaaa-quiii'.*"

"Fabulous job, sir!" Tor scrawled *Banco de Guayaquil* on his pad, then reached across the table to shake his witness's hand.

Dr. Bradley had ambled off to answer the door. Although it was not quite dark, pizza was arriving. When they heard more voices, the other men politely rose.

Seeing who had just walked in, Abelove's first reaction was astonishment. Excluding himself and Ogy, two of the five people with whom he was about to share a meal were men he had considered as murder suspects. Arturo Vaccari was released two days ago. Only a few months back, kindly Ted Friedland had come closer to arrest than he ever guessed.

But immediately Tor reconsidered, and mentally congratulated Dr. Bradley for his choice of guests to meet Cris Harbison. The woman, Ginger Guardian, was ideal. An elementary school teacher and the mother of a boy with Down syndrome, Ginger had worked very hard to bring her son to an impressively high level of function, instructing him herself and also providing team sports to assist Peter's social and motor skills. Peter was here too, hugging Dr. Bradley, clearly delighted to be included. According to Ogy, at the aquarium's fete last June nine-year-old Peter Guardian and boyish but high-I.Q. Ted Friedland had met and glommed onto one another.

"You're the Italian?" asked the waiter, possibly recalling this face from the Adlers' party.

"Adopted and raised Jewish," nodded Ted.

Encountering Ted Friedland at Seoul Dojang last month during Linda's first lesson, Tor had been happy to chat with him about waves and Ted's wild idea for some sort of surfing app. But Avenida Placida was territory where he and Ted had history. It seemed best to confront that awkwardness head-on.

"So you've decided to live in your aunt's fairy-tale castle?"

"That's been strange. My own notion of home decor is beanbag chair plus futon, and Uncle Nel's taste was awfully French. But it seemed unfair to Babby's cat to change everything in a hurry. The surprising part is, I've gotten really comfortable there. It's like, I live inside this video game. Always expecting some secret panel to slide open."

While the others introduced themselves and Ogy put the pizzas into the oven Peter said, "Dr. Bradley, can we go upstairs? To see my caterpillar?"

"Of course we can." Then he suggested, "Maybe everyone would like to come up and meet the caterpillar? He's quite special."

"I'm Peter," the boy announced to Cris. "My caterpillar is a monarch."

"Pe'er."

"That's right."

"He's certainly monarch of that wall," laughed Ogy. "Tor, would you please turn on the patio heater? It's pleasant enough that we can still eat outside, with the heat."

All the guests trooped upstairs to admire the gloriously striped caterpillar Peter had drawn with colored pencils. Viewing the bedroom wall covered with the Bradley children's artworks, Ted became wistful.

"I've never seen anything like this. I want a talented family someday, like yours."

"Then I'm sure you'll have one, sooner than 'someday.'"

Still chuckling over Sylvia's rakish cartoon of Ogy with birds crowded on his head, everyone returned downstairs. Ginger and Ted brought paper plates and Caesar salad to the picnic table.

To say the least, this was an odd social gathering. But Ginger and Ted had been briefed about Cris's near-fatal accident. That event was so prominent in all adult minds that no one gave a thought to Abelove's current or past murder cases. From the backyard of Casa Bunya Retirement Home at the end of the street, a faint operatic love song wafted from the Italian bocce bowlers' CD player. Mr. Vaccari earned a small laugh commenting, "I feel at home."

No one observed when or how, but sometime between pizza and cannoli Peter and Cris wound up seated on the glider beneath swags of twinkle lights. When Ginger noticed them, Mr. Harbison's arm was around her son's shoulders. It had to be, because Peter's arms encircled Cris's back and chest as if to prevent the young man from dropping out a window.

Their eyes met. Cris smiled at Ginger and shrugged his right shoulder, not disturbing the child's head pressed against his heart.

Then Ginger and Ted were staring at each other, wide-eyed. Not because they were in love, but because they were astonished. Each knew the other was thinking the same thing. They had long observed the delicacy with which Peter treated earthworms and insects. He was instinctively a tenderhearted child. But neither could have imagined this degree of protectiveness exhibited toward an adult human being.

The sky had grown quite dark when Peter exclaimed, "Dr. Bradley! Can Cris and me go up and look in your window house? I need to show him something."

"I'm not sure your mom will want you to? Mount Reposo's darker than down here."

"It's fine," laughed Ginger. "Ted bought him a pocket flashlight."

Immediately Peter's flashlight was on.

While the others watched, the two youngest crossed the yard, Peter leading Cris by the hand, waiting for his half-staggering gait to keep up. They mounted to the glasshouse. Inside, the small flashlight filled the transparent space with a faint glow. Then they exited the structure's west door and continued, still holding hands, along the children's path toward Casa Bunya.

"I never thought of them as a children's space, but those secret paths like overgrown tunnels, and the stairs — Babby's gardens are quite a fantasy kind of environment," observed Ogy. "Have you found anyone to take charge of it all for you?"

"Not yet, he hasn't," said Ginger. "There are gardeners, but not to Babby's standard."

"I know where they're headed!" realized Ted. "Down to my backyard. He wants to show — to *introduce* Cris to Mrs. Bradley's twisty metal Green Man on the tree. I'm glad he's not still afraid of it. But the surprising thing is, he's become fond of the thing."

"Ohhh, Ted!" gasped Ginger. "Don't you see? — Ogy, Peter loves Sylvia's sculpture. Green Man is strange and mysterious, yes. But Peter sees him now as a beautiful being — even though *he looks far from most people's idea of 'normal'...!"*

OVER THE ABYSS

When Tor got home after dropping off Vaccari and his son at Nicola's house, immediately Linda announced, "Alvaro left a message. He got his answer from the Army. That fiancé Patrick Connell is in Afghanistan. Here's his parents' phone number."

Tor nodded. He cuddled each child and wished all three good-night. Then he took Linda's hand and led her into the bedroom.

"You need to sleep on the sofa tonight." He spoke very softly, cautious not to sound upset. "You can say 'Daddy's sick,' because I will be. I love you with all my heart. I've never done this before — and I hope I never will again. But before tomorrow I've got some serious drinking to do. I don't know how much it's going to take. It

won't be pretty. I'm sorry. It's not at all about us. *I've never loved you more."*

"What on earth?" In disbelief Linda stared at a husband who preferred milk with any meal. "What's happened to you?"

"It hasn't — yet. Maybe it won't. I hope, I hope it won't. But right now I just can't take the waiting."

"Can't you at least tell me —"

"I can't tell you. It's only the job. I can't stand thinking about it myself, not now."

He took her head in his hands and kissed her slowly, gently. He kissed handfuls of her perfumed hair, then pulled her to the bedroom door.

"I'm sorry. It doesn't involve you. Just me. Tomorrow — I hope then I can face this."

He raised her favorite bed pillow to her chest and kissed her nose. Then lightly, firmly, he pressed her out the door, feeling miserable because this was her bedroom. But he didn't want the children to see him and wasn't willing to leave his family alone all night. When he heard her removing the extra blanket from the hall closet he went to open the whiskey bottle.

He needed to get started.

At first he kept remembering all that waterlogged gray hamburger in Allan Houseman's pockets. It debased the man even if it hadn't done its job effectively, hadn't attracted a truly *great* white shark to gulp him down entire. By luck of the currents Houseman would receive a funeral for most of him — better than what he'd had in mind for Cris Harbison. Right now Detective Abelove felt about as iron-rich as those dingy glops of soggy meat collected in the ME's tray, all smelling past their sell-by.

He drank the first glass slowly, disliking it, especially after Ogy's voluptuous Chianti.

The damnedest part was, his best instincts had brought him to this hellish place. He'd started out doing the job better than his fellow meatballs rolling around the M. Room. Yes, he'd pursue those female suspects tomorrow, do methodical procedure efficiently with Mrs. Smithers.

But today he'd taken the great leap. Enlisting Ogy's help, he performed the Knievel over the abyss — with no motive other than conviction there was something deep down there they needed to uncover, something in a place where eagles fly but ordinary human eyes don't plumb the depths.

Regardless of whether it had been learned upon a longboard, Abelove's reputation for discipline was well deserved. Whatever personal reactions he might have to witnesses, he was careful not to allow them to intrude. Never in his conduct toward them and not much in his thinking.

But today everything, all of it became personal, almost from the start.

He could not help being moved by Cristoforo Vaccari Harbison — or noticing the similarity between Cris and himself. Except that the youngster had earned a doctorate in oceanography.

Except that his muscular coordination seemed so poor the chances were he was incapable of swimming or ever again visiting the underwater world — and that he could not speak intelligibly, and that the total impression he created was of a cerebrum reduced to decomposing meat.

Sharing Vaccari's grief for Cris, he'd mounted the Bradleys' stairs with little hope they would learn anything. But then — came the phenomenon of Dr. Bradley. Never for a moment forgetting who and what Cris was. Determined to reach and raise intelligence so long degraded by failed neurons but still at least in part alive inside him.

As he watched Cris struggle to be smart again, guided by Ogy's prompts, unexpectedly Tor's own self-regard flared with bitter envy, raging, *What could I have been, with such a father?*

Almost praying for Cris's success entirely for his sake, his own purpose here forgotten, he'd marveled at the resolute patience of the white-clad doctor like a priest of hope and health.

WHAT DID YOU SCORE BY THAT? his cop part cried as he poured the second glass.

The answer was, Truth.

Useless truth.

His brain surgeon friend had met Vaccari. Talked and drunk with him, described him as a charming man in deep depression. But Tor had preferred to attribute Artie's"sadness" to simple guilt about the unintended death of Lise. Then when he himself interrogated Vaccari he had quickly been confounded. Those repeated avowals of hatred for Allan Houseman displayed indifference that seemed mad. Something festering in this man's mind rendered him so abject he scarcely seemed to comprehend the jeopardy of flagrant self-incriminating statements.

Clearly his arrest surprised him. But it did not appear to frighten him. Eventually Tor wondered if what Ogy saw as charm was not the guilelessness of low intelligence.

All this made coherent sense, so long as you believed Vaccari guilty. But when Allan was murdered after Artie was in custody, the evidence suggested he was also innocent of Lisette's death.

From today's dramatic exploit the SCPD learned....?

That Houseman tried to kill Cris Harbison, inflicting grievous injury? That he was engaged in illegal activity, its nature still to be determined?

So what?

That criminal was dead, his crimes repaid.

The Houseman murder cases had advanced...?

No. Not at all.

Tor poured another glass and almost dropped it. From fear of losing any of that necessary poison he gulped half fast, choked by its toxic taste.

Since the first interview he'd admitted to himself, if not to Tina: He favored Claire Fields for the perpetrator of their crime. But he also admitted he couldn't find a reason. Only that she was the one attractive woman near Allan's office. And that she seemed quite spirited — which he admired, without remotely trusting her. At the water park Candace Willoughby corroborated all that about her, but added not a word the least suspicious.

Impugned by him for absolutely nothing, Ms. Fields appeared a dead end. Tomorrow they would interview Ms. Burns, returning tonight from Santa Clara.

So far, he could make a circumstantial case against Elinor based on partial knowledge. The financial motive. The fact that she could have driven to El Al and killed her brother there after he lingered too long over lunch.

Viewed realistically, this speculation about a sister killing her brother seemed implausible at best. It could be shot down as quickly as they learned she'd been in Norwald on the evening of Black Saturday.

Among Allan's associates, that left only Dr. Savage — a staid, stout gray scientist in her sixties. The thought of her spraying "TRAITOR!" on a wall was laughable.

But it was still so tempting to interpret that blade in the back as a woman's crime.

Today he'd tried to follow Ogy's example, maintaining an impassive face, revealing neither pain nor pity. Although while Cris struggled to speak his distorted grimace made it difficult to see, he did have very handsome features — much more so than his dough-faced father. Watching that fundamentally attractive young man suffer through responses during Dr. Bradley's interview, a slow realization gripped Detective Abelove almost with panic.

True, he had not talked with Savage. Must interview Ms. Burns. Remained open to new evidence more indicting of Ms. Fields than just her attractive animal energy. But gradually he'd admitted that in their scrutiny of female suspects *one woman was completely overlooked*. They'd been so focused on the father who was present at the party that they never once considered her.

Yet she loved Cristoforo devotedly. Maybe enough to kill.

It seemed unimaginable she could have known about the Adlers' party. She inhabited a different world, lived miles away. Had no connection with the university, surely had never heard of Hiram or Priscilla Adler.

Impossible.

But Tor had met this woman. Felt her power. Seen fierce feeling animate her when she spoke about a damaged son.

Now that he knew what had transpired on the *Cirene?* He could imagine something else — far, far less shocking than Professor Houseman's treachery. He pictured this woman spraying the Housemans' wall with "TRAITOR!" in huge letters.

It would be righteous.

It would be in English.

Couldn't happen, no way, his mind insisted. *Too unlikely to consider.*

But his heart with logic of its own felt otherwise.

"Please," he begged the Roman beauty, *"Please do not have done these things."*

Tonight on Ogy's patio while assembled guests watched a ten-year-old with Down Syndrome hug Cristoforo as if he'd never let this new friend go, Tor had thought about his own family, the hugs and kisses every day. In that astonishing moment, he'd wondered how much affection the seemingly deformed young man had received these past two years — and how much love he might receive during the long remainder of his life.

Everything of value that endured in the future of likable Cris Harbison revolved around one cherishing woman who provided care and comfort, friendship and familial love.

One thing the detective felt certain of —

— If she did slip briefly through the Adlers' party…?

— If the waiter recognized her there…?

Even at the price of being sentenced for two murders he did not commit, Artie Vaccari never would betray her.

The man who must betray her was Tor Abelove.

FORTY-FIVE

FLYING WILD

Officer Smithers returned on Tuesday, not entirely recovered from flu but pleased at having lost weight. Last night Tor had intentionally bought cheap whiskey so he wouldn't like it. This morning he disliked it even more. But he'd done that to himself. As a courtesy to Smithers he didn't make her drive the winding roads to Norwald. Tina was short. Traveling toward morning sun, she kept her eyes lowered.

Such brilliance through the windshield reminded him of the pleasant house in Almira shared by Mrs. Harbison and her son. Those tall living and dining room windows would capture warm early light. The rooms' cherry and golden oak furnishings must glow on winter mornings.

His reverie was interrupted when Tina began softly singing with the radio, Frankie Laine's rendition of "The Cry of the Wild Goose."

Despite her flu-roughened voice, this young policewoman demonstrated she knew all the lyrics to the 1950 hit. Afterwards Tor exclaimed, "That song's decades before your time!"

"When my brother Carl sang it," she laughed, "Suggestion was our Grandpa's! Carl's group was popular in high school. Their guitarist made a long gooseneck and head. Glued-on pillow feathers. His mom basted costume-shop angel wings to his sleeves. Elaborate, but it looked fantastic with stage lighting."

"Wild goose guitarist."

"Pink feet goose legs too. Cut toes in swim fins."

Certainly, the country they had entered was suggestive of migrating geese. To the detective driving, the surrounding terrain implied a likelihood of all manner of wildness. But at this hour, with light filtering through the evergreens along the alpine town's Front Street, it offered such painterly serenity that Tor and Tina both felt blissfully composed when they reached Norwald a half hour before their appointment with Elinor Burns.

When they made a cop stop for coffee Tor chuckled, "As geese go, you're looking underfed. Have a chocolate frosted, on me."

He finally felt awake enough to brief her about their case, but from reluctance to admit his recent suspicion of Nicola did not mention Houseman's murder attempt on Cris.

Elinor Burns had a sales job in a gift shop. When he spoke to her at her mother's house in Santa Clara she had said that if she must take an hour off work, first thing in the morning was least inconvenient. When they rang her buzzer a couple of minutes early, she came to the door immediately, in work attire. Judging by the coarse red bark and pine boughs visible outside her small apartment's windows, it might have been nestled on a Yosemite mountainside.

"I know what you want," she said hurriedly. "Here's the safe. Allan didn't give me the key. I was just supposed to be his — you know, secure storage facility."

Tor felt embarrassed and stupid. Certainly he should have anticipated such a possibility. But if keys to this strongbox had been found, no one reported the fact to him.

"Thanks, that's useful." He lifted the steel box. It contained paper, not gold bars.

Elinor did not resemble Allan, he decided. Luckily. But hers was a vague, generic prettiness, like on a greeting card or in an animated film.

"Ms. Burns, we are very sorry for both your losses. Please give the department's condolences to your mother, too. But the box isn't all we came for. You understand, in a murder inquiry we have to question everyone. Family members as well as associates. So we have to ask you — where were you on the evening of Saturday, November twenty-ninth?"

"You mean —?"

"Yes, ma'am. The night your sister-in-law Lisette was killed."

Bettina cast him a reproachful look. Reminding Elinor of the sister-in-law's name was maybe a mite heavy.

"I — Saturday. I think… I went to a movie. With Patsy."

"Can you please give us Patsy's phone number?"

"Sure." She wrote it down. "Here. Patricia Dowling. Is that — can I go now?"

"Not just yet. I'll go outside and call Patsy. Officer Smithers stays here with you until I've spoken to your friend."

He started toward the door, counting seconds.

"NO. *Wait*. Please. I'm sorry. It wasn't Patsy. Or the movies."

"Who were you with, Ms. Burns?" sympathized Smithers.

"It was — oh, God. You're not going to tell my mother?"

"Not without need."

"Jim Beddoes. At the Old Oak Post Motel. That's where I was when Allan called to tell me what happened. I drove right out, got to El Albergue before midnight. To stay with Allan."

"We'll need his number."

"He's married! Okay. Okay, but it's over. No need for her to know."

They phoned Jim Beddoes at work, visited the Old Oak Post Motel to verify his booking and were out of Norwald before eleven.

"Short and — dumb-lucky?" yawned Tina, her boot tapping the strongbox as they climbed the freeway ramp. "We should think what might be hidden. In places *we* don't see."

Forty minutes later when a billboard ad announced they were approaching the Fairwaye Inn, Tor saw no purpose in stopping. Smithers noticed his long gaze.

"Sir," she asked, as he checked his watch. "What's wrong."

"Not yet."

Mentally following Allan, Tor pictured strong box keys on the ocean floor.

No matter how formidable the personality and motive, he kept telling himself, w*ithout evidence there is no case.*

Still he could not help fearing that this morning's journey had brought them much closer to removing Cris's mother in handcuffs.

The contents of the strongbox recovered from Norwald revealed that Allan Houseman possessed not one but five offshore bank accounts — two in Latin America and three in Asia.

Not long afterwards, when it was late afternoon on New York's Long Island, Officer Smithers reached the office of Avery Law, who had not been willing to say much during their previous conversation.

"Professor Law, good afternoon," Tor began. "I wonder if you've heard that Allan Houseman is dead? He was stabbed and thrown to the sharks. No idea yet if he was on some boat or bridge. We've just learned he had five offshore bank accounts comprising a balance well over one hundred thousand dollars."

"Good heavens!" choked the New York academic. "What's going on out there?"

"Sir, we invite your speculation. Houseman's work is outside our expertise. Any idea what all this money is about? We know you've served with him on some committees —"

"Now, hold on! Membership on any board aside, I only met the guy in person a few times, mainly at conferences. But about that money — *sharks?* You mean, *literally?"*

"Hard to mistake."

"But… cash accounts…. Phew….

"Okay…." Mr. Law's sigh was audible. "For you, a southern Cal example.

"Say somebody's a botanist. And you hear he's spending most of his time in the orchards, counting avocados. You wonder, 'Why isn't he in the lab researching that blight damaging the trees? What's he doing? Hijacking avocados? A truckload's big money, with disease lowering the fruit yields.'

"That's been the type of curiosity, the rumors about Houseman. Instead of sticking to research he seems to be out on expeditions counting fish populations around the world. Which is important, mind. But Houseman wrote a seminal book —"

"Sinks and Sediments of the Pacific Plate."

"How —?"

"But we've been advised, sir, that Dr. Houseman stole that book. From Oskar Kisselbaum."

"My God. You're serious…. *Oskar?* Excuse me, Detective — you've just shifted the plate under me….

"All right. Then say Houseman is a hack. Oh, it makes sense….

"What you need to know is that seas around the globe are suffering biomass depletion. When's the last time you saw orange roughy, in a store or on a menu? Climate change is a factor, but an added problem is that technology has enabled fishing of the high seas to a degree that used to be impossible. Fish have nowhere left to hide now. We have management organizations to set quotas for how much of every species can be harvested each year, to keep them sustainable — but of course those numbers are decided on the basis of what a commission's scientific advisers recommend to keep the stock from collapsing."

"That sounds political."

"Oh, very. Say that Houseman goes estimating skipjack stocks in the Indian Ocean. His recommendation is that the maximum yield next year should be five thousand tons taken, instead of the thirty-five hundred tons some more alarmed conservative suggests. To most people, will that sound like a big discrepancy? To the extent they care, their reaction is, 'Good, fish will be less expensive.'"

"It's incredibly expensive."

"You think so? Let me tell you — at auction in Tokyo, one premium tuna can bring a few thousand. So imagine the financial difference to the fishing industry represented by fifteen hundred *tons* of fish. I don't know what kind of bribes governments are handing out to someone with the authority to inflate those quotas. But I'd guess ten or even twenty thousand dollars is a joke, compared to the grief their fishermen will cause them if they feel starved out. And there are many countries, many governments affected."

"Thank you for this, Professor Law. Just one more thing. Out of respect, I ought to mention — it appears that whoever murdered Allan messed up. By mistake, they killed his pregnant wife first."

"…Detective. If this is a hoax… I'll never forgive you."

"No, sir. I find it unforgivable."

A few years ago, a non-violent but rash act of Abelove's landed him in trouble with Internal Affairs. Wisely Linda declared his mistake "heaven-sent," because as penance he began accepting groups of surfing students from the barrio, offering them a group identity alternative to gang membership. This was a charitable activity he'd long hankered to initiate. The youngsters St. Rita's selected for him had to document proof of their swimming proficiency. Thus an early and oversized consequence of his surf groups was that, after the impoverished Orchardton neighborhood noticed its lack of swimming facilities, a donor from the richer end of Santa Christina endowed a public lap pool, with a wading pool for the very young or old.

Although his groups met just once every two weeks, those days did require a fair amount of Abelove's "free" time. After driving to Orchardton to pick up five boys with the boards he loaned them, he would proceed to one of Christina's surfing beaches for their lesson, then transport them home again. The long ritual made him feel like their parent. He hoped being chauffeured in this privileged way made them feel middle class. When the lessons begun in the summer months were received with enthusiasm by kids from gang areas, another donor provided Tor with winter-water wetsuits to loan the students along with his surfboards.

Since the times of Tor's volunteer surfing classes were dictated by tides, so too were his hours "off" work. After returning from

Norwald and speaking with Avery Law, he asked Smithers to phone the store where Nicola Harbison was employed and find out if she had been working on Saturday the twenty-ninth. Then he left to pick up his barrio students, in time to have two hours of daylight remaining for their fourth lesson.

His current group had begun the Sunday a week before Linda's birthday. During their first lesson, entirely in flatwater so they could learn to paddle and become familiar with the motile sea beneath, the upstart declaring, "I wanna stand on it!" had been Joey Huerta.

Sure enough, Joey scrambled to his feet on the board and immediately toppled face first into the water. Following thanks to Joey for his comic catapult came the boys' physics lecture. They must sense how gravity and the force of a wave's motion create *glide* to carry a board as far as their skill might navigate it.

By today these youths ranging in age from thirteen to sixteen were already trying to stay upright on their boards. That provided uplift to Abelove, too. After returning them to their barrio, he superstitiously forced himself to drive out of Orchardton into the historic Ocaso district, where he felt better karma. Then, his skin still smelling of the beneficent sea, he stopped to phone Officer Smithers.

Tactfully asking no questions, Tina reported, "Sir, her store says that on November twenty-ninth Mrs. Harbison clocked out at five."

"If Carl's friend wore a fake goose head over his, how could he see to play his guitar?"

"Eye holes in the shirt attached to his glasses. Worked great — the stage was so dark. Singers had spotlights on them but Ray was backlit, to show off his bird silhouette."

The young professor who attended the Adlers' party in a red shirt marked up with "X"s had been photographed by several people. Some of those arrival photos included a time of 5:22 or 5:25. Since the gentleman in red came at the same time as the Housemans, the photos of him in the Adlers' foyer with Hiram established when Allan and Lisette were present too.

Allowing twenty to thirty minutes from the valley shopping center to the Adlers' house, depending on how long it took to park, certainly Nicola might have entered that house before the Gershwin piano performance began.

If she knew about the party.

Tor kept recalling a photo of his own silhouette — atop a wave, backlit in rose by Peru's setting sun. That was a long time ago.

FORTY-SIX

BETRAYALS

After his escapist whiskey binge followed by excursions to Norwald and then a surfing beach, Abelove needed a healthy meal and eight hours' sleep. When his Wednesday morning phone call to the third academic named by Jon Doerr produced a response equivalent to Avery Law's blunt remarks, he drove alone to his last appointment with one of the Adlers' party guests, discounted owing to her age and status at the oceanography school. He did not see Claire Fields or any other secretaries, because Dr. Savage had asked to meet him in the rose garden.

When he approached Hiram Adler's lunch spot under the arbor, someone rather shapeless, of indeterminate gender, gray-haired and sixtyish was there waiting on the bench. Rebecca Savage looked vaguely familiar. Shielded from wind and weather, the bench offered a long view down the coast to downtown — maybe, on clear days, to Mexico.

The Institute's top scholar was ripping dainty shreds from a croissant when she noticed him. While a coffee mug warmed one trousered knee, her thermos waited beside it on the bench.

"Good morning, I brought out a cup for you too."

The detective politely declined coffee.

"I hope you don't mind sitting out here. It's privacy of a sort."

"We have nothing like it at Bay Street."

On the African tulip trees across the walkway, unusually late orange flowers were studded with wet drops that made the trees appear to be igniting in this bleary gray atmosphere.

"I wondered if you'd get around to me. Was a little hurt."

"No one suspects you."

"Why? Old folks don't have feelings?"

"'You don't appear to be involved at all with Houseman. Generational, not emotional."

"Oh. So wrong."

"I am intrigued."

"Tell me where it stands. At least, with poor Lisette. That made no sense at all."

"To begin, naturally we wonder about the husband. But in his unique cold way Allan insisted she was an asset. To his aspirations."

"You've no idea. Her parents own a French kitchenware store and give lessons, back in Pennsylvania. She cooked divinely. People cut Allan a lot of slack, after eating at his home."

Tor confided that after learning of Houseman's offshore accounts they'd just received an explanation of how he might have obtained so much money.

"I could have told you that too." Unsurprised, Rebecca finished her coffee.

"Okay. Let's pretend I've come to you first, then."

"Detective — this institute hired Allan Houseman while I was on sabbatical for a year in Maine — much of that time away at sea. In Antarctica, specifically. I didn't participate in the decision. Had I been here, I would have opposed it."

"He was already involved in graft?"

"Crooked, differently. In the last century I studied under a wonderful scholar named Oskar Kisselbaum. He died a long time ago. Then Allan's groundbreaking book came out. It's what landed him his position here. I knew from page one it was Oskar's prose. He had his own cadence. Not American at all." Appearing downcast, she ate the last morsel of croissant.

"I've no idea, honestly, whether Allan ever guessed I knew. That somehow he'd acquired it. But ever since he came here and I returned from Maine, I've always been a little afraid of him. As you say, of his 'unique coldness.' So, people consider *me* aloof. It is awkward, since academically we're — almost siblings, you could say. Oskar's students, decades apart."

Considering Cris's fate, Abelove decided this woman was no hysteric to have feared Houseman. But he could not tell her that.

"Did you — by chance — happen to know Cris Harbison?"

"Oh! Of course! Cris was my student, in two classes. A wonderful young man. I was so upset — many of us were — when he disappeared. He was supposed to go to Woods Hole —"

"I met him Monday."

"You must have liked him, no?"

"Very much. I did."

"I know his mother, somewhat. Not well enough to ask her, though, what happened to him. You understand — from fear of what the answer might be."

"You know her… how?"

"Some of the better stores offer a shopping service. Geared to professional women. People who need to buy something but don't have time to shop all day. So you make an appointment, and when you arrive the saleswoman has selected a few things that seem appropriate for what you've described as your event — to attend a Florida conference, say."

"You mean… like for the Adlers' party?"

"Exactly. Since Cris was a student here, Nicola knows most of us by reputation, or did. Not personally. I explained about needing something entirely black, and when — it was a novel party, Mrs. Adler has such flair. Nicola had three or four choices ready for me."

Tor felt so sad and incompetent he could scarcely speak.

"He — Cris — was seriously brain-damaged in a drowning accident."

"Oh, no. *No* —"

"But when Dr. Bradley examined him…. He has plenty of I.Q. still. His father was with us. He looked… to me, anyway — as if he recognized his son again."

"That young man did so largely love the sea!"

Driving back to Bay Street, Tor remembered again that today was Wednesday, one of the nights Linda had martial arts lessons. Since he'd been an absentee the past two evenings, he should go home early and spend some family time before her departure, even though Marjorie would be babysitting.

But writing this report was going to be difficult.

Wasn't it becoming unconscionable not to mention Nicola Harbison as a suspect?

They had no evidence against her. Still, a powerfully tantalizing set of suggestive circumstances surrounded her. While watching the road, he imagined interrogating Nicola as a ruthless murderer, and *searching the trunk of her car for Houseman's blood...?*

But by the time he'd parked and forced himself upstairs to his desk, a sudden insight had filled Detective Abelove with horror at what he was about to do.

Must do.

What if Cris — understandably! — *had never told his mom what really happened?*

What if Nicola *had no idea* that his supposed "accident" was an attempted murder?

The thought of questioning his mother on the basis of mere conjecture seemed intolerable, if she might be spared the cruelty of learning that hideous fact!

And wouldn't gratuitously informing her — just for the sake of creating scrupulously exhaustive notes about the investigation — be an unforgivable betrayal of Cristoforo Harbison, who had suffered so much and labored so hard, *trusting them when he told the truth?*

For that matter... wouldn't it also be a betrayal of the benign physician who had assisted the police with such bravura in eliciting that truth from their abject witness?

Dr. O.G. Bradley was thoroughly cold-minded. The detective understood that. But Ogy was also thoroughly warmhearted. What would he think of Tor's inflicting such maddening pain on a loving mother?

If she was completely guiltless?

No doubt, Ogy would recoil. Regard his former friend with polite revulsion.

Tor pictured the "TRAITOR!" scrawl and realized, "That will be me."

Depraved indifference, personified.

After the fiasco of pitiable Mr. Vaccari's over-hasty arrest, now he thought reflexively that he would be totally justified in never mentioning Mrs. Harbison at all!

For a long time he sat wondering whether he might describe his interview with Rebecca Savage omitting the fact that Nicola had been aware of the Adlers' party and had at least some familiarity with numerous people involved.

He knew, though, that he really must report those facts. Somehow. Figure out a way to include them… invisibly.

Instead he kept mentally humming Tina's wild goose song in the car yesterday morning. Insisting that Officer Smithers was simpatico with a waterfowl, its subversive absurdity undermined his own inner compass.

Had investigating Mrs. Harbison become a compelling law enforcement imperative?

Or would flying that wild be an inhumane breach of ethics?

Or might it possibly be both, simultaneously?

Soon he'd forgotten again that it was Wednesday.

FORTY-SEVEN

LUMPY CARGO

One of the things Ted Friedland liked about his new job designing software and video games at Sanchrist Technologies was that occasional work from home was not frowned upon. Among his fellow nerds it was understood that often when people were alone at home, creative juices flowed better in brains saturated by their own favorite music, enhanced by drinking or smoking whatever best evoked their own empyrean concepts. Other times the opposite was true, and their collective creepiness or goofiness turned out more lunatic than any individual input.

Since the Sanchrist building was downtown and the showers forecast sounded insistent, Ted decided to leave before rush hour.

During his commute he puzzled over a spam blocking application he wanted to create. Only when he noticed again what looked like red flames licking out from under his roof did he remember he'd intended to cut a box of poinsettias to take to Casa Bunya. His aunt Babby had been in the habit of delivering fruit from her orchard to the retirement home. Now that poinsettias had grown clear to the gutters on the mini-castle's only single-story side, the Christmas season did present an opportune time to prune.

He got the ladder and tossed down enough long bracts to fill the trunk of his little BMW.

Gladys Apted, Casa Bunya's manager, was taken aback when the Casa's neighbor two doors down walked in carrying a chubby armload of variously hued poinsettias.

"Are those Babby's? Goodness! She brought us fruit, but never these. Thank you. I don't know what we'll do for vases."

"Just pails would do, no?"

"Yes. Rustic. Good thought." Mrs. Apted phoned her assistant.

"Teddy —?" hailed a graveled female voice from the lounge. "Come join us."

Ted circled the desk to see Babby's old friend Ingrid Becker seated in an overstuffed chair beside Dr. Bradley in a matching chair. They were sharing her pot of tea. Ogy had been telling Ingrid about meeting Vaccari's son on Monday. He was explaining the young man's neurological problems.

"Ted, I was just about to invite Ingrid for a drink at Volpe di Sera. Please come with us, won't you?"

"Nothing I'd like better!" Ted announced with vehemence.

Leaving Ogy's two-seater in the Casa's parking lot, they drove to Volpe in Ted's car. After opening the car door for Ingrid, Ted sprang the trunk.

"I still have another big pile in here."

He removed an enormous armload of poinsettias.

Rocco the barkeep betrayed more feeling than he usually allowed himself when he saw who had entered his cocktail lounge.

"Mr. Friedland!" he exclaimed in surprise when he saw the brawny young man bearing a load of holiday decor the girth of a Christmas tree.

"For the house. — I'm Italian, you realize?"

"All the better, sir," approved the silver-haired gent. "*Grazie, buon Natale.* Dr. Bradley and Dr. Becker, too. Your usual table? Clams Casino?"

Maybe because Ted and Ogy were still engrossed by their meeting two days ago with Cris Harbison, they both chose Chianti. Ingrid, partial to the wines of her husband's native country, ordered the Weilberg riesling, with clams for three.

"Weilberg is grown in red soil. Christmasy."

Inspired by Ted's bundle of pied color, she then exclaimed, "Rocco! If you have vases, empty wine bottles? I can arrange these. Enough for every table in your bar — and the piano."

"That would present a field of cheer," agreed the barkeep.

"I've been wondering aloud how much improvement might be possible for Cris," Ogy told Ted. "Cerebral destruction can't be undone, but it leaves the question of what might be made of all the function he has left? He'll never be a gymnast again, but could he use gym equipment for therapy? To improve his gait, take stress off the pelvic joints? I can't stop thinking."

"Neither can I," said Ted. "Selfishly, I admit. You saw how Pete went ape over the guy? Ginger says he keeps pestering her, 'When can I see Cris again?' She doesn't know what to tell him. But obviously we're wondering if he'd ever be willing to babysit."

"Sounds like a happy prospect, for both of them," agreed Ingrid. She went to request two knives from Rocco, who had returned behind the bar with a box containing vases, empty bottles and half-bottles. He began filling them with water.

"I'm really pleased I ran into you," continued Ted, "Because I have another project churning now. Wanted to ask what you think. I'm realizing, I'm going to need a bigger house."

"Oh, Teddy. That makes Ogy and me both sad."

Ogy went to the bar and brought Rocco's tray with vases of water to their table.

"But — I'm also very attached to Lionel and Babby's house. And Leilia's, for that matter. Cat gets a vote. So I'm wondering if I could expand it."

"How? If you added a full second story you'd lose the high ceilings. I can't picture what you'd do. You've got lots of property, but the house sits on a narrow pad."

"Right. So what I've been thinking is — how about a sort of barbell-shaped house? Leave the original place basically as is. The big bedroom becomes a family room. The small bedroom's my office, nice and isolated. But then we run a corridor — roller-skatable — with windows all along, because it views the ocean and gardens, front and back — and there's a whole new wing, bedrooms in the same style as the original house. What do you think?"

"You're ambitious in more ways than one," teased Ingrid, as she selected and trimmed poinsettia bracts to fit the containers.

Understanding her perfectly, Ted nodded. "You bet I am."

"So this corridor crosses Babby's meadow?"

While Ingrid combined pink, striped and white poinsettias, Ogy was trimming only red ones.

One of the other waiters brought out a larger vase.

"I sacrifice only half the meadow, if this new bedroom wing has upper rooms —"

Ogy filled the large vase with the red bracts. He carried it to the back of the piano.

"— With a second fireplace, in the vaulted-ceiling part of the addition — I call that the 'good morning room.'"

The pianist shifted gaily to "It's Beginning to Look a Lot Like Christmas."

"Could serve as 'bedtime story room,' too," Ingrid hinted.

"*Oh*. Nice. And if the corridor is glass, those wild meadow flowers will come up to the windows."

"Honestly, Ted," said Ogy, "I'm touched. It sounds beautiful. And very romantic."

"*Grazie.*"

Since nothing had ever been said about Ted's actually being engaged to be married, further discussion about multiplying his bedrooms seemed cut off.

"Ogy tells me your restaurant app will debut very soon. Congratulations. Are you working on something new?"

Rocco began distributing the first tray of small bouquets to other occupied tables.

"When I saw Ogy's friend Abelove at Hwan's, we talked about some kind of surfers' app. I had no idea there are categories of waves. Not deeply into that yet."

"That reminds me, Ogy," said Ingrid. I've had another call from Linda. This time she invited me out for a coffee date. What an unusual girl she is — stratosphere above the manners of this century. Imagine, after describing the bakery and getting me eager to go — she apologized for presuming to invite me." Ingrid had to pause for a few breaths. "As if her company were unworthy of my time. And she's delightful."

"Maybe Linda worries she can't converse about archaeology?"

"No. When I squawked, she did explain. She's enjoyed meeting people at that martial arts place — especially two older women. But there's a younger one who's also a beginner — Mara. I remember, from our lunch date, Linda admires her blonde curls — but this girl has been invasively friendly. Makes her ill-at-ease. So with Mara's pushiness in mind? Surfer Linda worries — about forcing herself on elderly New Englander me."

"But that doesn't sound right." Ted looked puzzled. "I know Mara, from another dojo. She can't be a white, she was a green belt, months ago — I'm sure of it."

"Could be another girl." Ogy trimmed striped pink poinsettias and passed them to Ingrid, as their waiter approached with hot stuffed clams.

"I doubt it. Lots of people know her —" Ted accepted the clam platter.

"Lots of people know our Homeless Guy —"

"Not that many women in martial arts, though —"

"— But the police just got into a colossal mix-up about Artie. Embarrassed themselves."

The piano had modulated into "I'll Be Home for Christmas," causing Dr. Bradley to pine already for Caelan.

"Mara's a green." Ted began shifting aromatic clams onto three small plates. "Not bad, I've sparred with her."

"Hm." Engaged by his scalpel work on poinsettia stems, Ogy kept reminding himself how lucky he was to have enjoyed a visit from the poised and cheerful almost-congressman.

"Even her curly hair's the same — except, it's a wig. She told me, 'Don't get fussed if my hair falls off.' Said she'd rather wear wigs than dye her own boring hair."

Laying aside a barkeeper's blade that felt like an extension of his professional hand, the surgeon rose and circled the piano's merry vibes to the restroom hallway. When he touched the top name on his phone, his still vulnerable heart was pounding.

Last June he had tried and tried without success to reach Tor when he urgently needed to.

But now the voice he was praying for announced, "Homicide."

"*Tor.* Forgive me, but I am disturbed. Linda told Ingrid this woman 'Mara' at her dojang has been making her uncomfortable, trying to get close to her. Ted knows Mara. He's sure she's not a white, not any beginner. He insists, he knew her as a green belt.

"And Tor — Ted *knows* she wears a wig! *A blonde one. Curls.*

"You asked my hunch. I have to say — too many wigs.

"I think that 'homeless person' sighted everyplace had to be somebody strong, in a gray wig — impersonating homelessness. I think I know *what* lumpy cargo got bunged around the Strand in that cart. I could be wrong —"

Abelove's howl carried through cavernous Floor Three's Murder Room, "*HELP ME —!*"

FORTY-EIGHT

EMPTY MIND

As usual, Master Hwan resumed by reminding his students of their previous class.

"You remember on Friday we talked about Sŏn Buddhism, right? If your family's from India and you want to say Mahāyāna Buddhism, or — we got Chinese people here? Maybe Tiantan — or if you like Zen better, that's okay. Point is, if you got an 'empty mind' — not so much heavy furniture upstairs?" He pointed at his head. "Then your muscles act more free, too. You got faster reaction time, without upstairs furniture. Oak bureau, weighty on your brain.

"Sounds like a song, hey?

"Later we'll talk about 'expanded awareness.' Does everybody remember our last earthquake?

"Kind of big one? You remember *how long* it took?"

All murmured in agreement.

"You remember what you thought about during that quake?

"Did you think about where you'd go for dinner? Some car you want to buy?

"Or just the quake, huh?

"So, we'll talk about that *intense awareness*. How you learn concentration. Focus.

"Also — this comes up each session. This here is Seoul Dojang — S-*E*-O-U-L. The 'Seoul' refers to branch of martial arts. Origin, history. Looks almost the same, but it's a different word from Christian 'soul.' If anybody likes the idea of 'soul' dojang instead of 'Seoul' dojang, that's okay. Christian tao not so different. I don't care how you think about it.

"Only, if you're writing me a check, then spell it my way, okay?"

Later Hwan saw something among the white belts that he had noticed during a previous lesson. The blonde with well-developed shoulders did not pay attention. Instead she seemed to stare at the young woman to her right in the row ahead.

Inattention to the discipline displeased him. Now it occurred to him that this blonde woman might be a lesbian attracted to the dark-haired girl in front of her. But when he scanned the rows, no male students were ogling any female.

Being gay was no excuse for sloppy practice. Consulting his list, he said, "Tamara? Tamara Goodhew? Your friend tries to concentrate on her front kicks. You should, too."

Although Mara made no response, she began concentrating more on her practice.

Hwan noticed her form improve, suddenly quite superior to all the other whites.'

~ ~ ~

Detective Chuck Lianopoulos was the division's best driver. He drove Tor, while Captain Marcos and Bruno Belknap followed in the second car. Since sirens were a routine sound downtown they used them. For the benefit of both Bay Street and the car behind, Tor explained the layout of Seoul Dojang— front and back entrances, changing rooms in back likely to be in use, since the 'dobok' uniform is not considered casual streetwear.

"Claire's targeting my wife somehow. Maybe she thought we suspected her long before we did? What I'm scared about — if she's bent on vengeance. If now I'm another 'traitor.'"

In the cruiser following them, veteran Marine Tony swore over the phone.

"Ted insists she's green belt. But she pretended to be a beginner — to get near Linda.

"Class should be ending now, so going in, first I find my wife. If this curly-head blonde is anywhere near her *we do nothing* until they're far apart, okay? I'm just strolling in to say 'hi' to Hwan and pick up Linda."

"After you've secured her, if Fields is there we'll move quietly," promised the Captain.

"The nightmare is — Linda can't defend herself and would never believe she was being attacked anyway. Fields could be on her before anybody intervened. With all due respect to Master Hwan's 'empty mind,' I don't count on him reacting in time. He'd never imagine one girlfriend could attack another.

'My first impression of Fields was — strong character. Please don't underestimate this woman. Her last job was performing with a whale. She controlled the whale."

Rush hour was over. It had been dark almost two hours. Since there was no urgency except Abelove's nerves, they killed the sirens while still half a mile from Seoul Dojang. Even though there was white mist in the air, with overhead lighting Tor recognized the formerly red roof of his rusted Ford van in the dojang's parking lot while still half a block away.

"There's a little lobby inside the door, you don't walk right into the gym area from either front or back," he explained before they parked. "We'll scope it before going in. I'll take the front because I'm known. Bruno to the front too, but ten seconds later — look like a student. Tony and Chuck to the back. It's probably locked. If you're not inside a minute after us, Bruno is wandering back there to let you in. Act like a spectator, Bruno. Keep grinning."

The Captain approved this plan, then headed for the alley with Lianopoulos. When Tor and Bruno arrived in the lobby, class had ended. A few boys jostled in horseplay, and one with a mini video camera filmed a girl still practicing before the mirror. Her graceful movement suggested ballet influence. Some class members were conversing in their white uniforms, but many had already changed into street clothes. Tor spotted Linda immediately, in shorts with black tights and her hooded sweatshirt. She was standing with Jane and Nadine and a younger blonde whom he recognized even from behind as Claire Fields.

As Abelove began crossing the dojang towards Linda, Bruno started along the front wall behind milling class members, toward the back exit.

But at the back of the building already the plan was falling apart. When Chuck and Tony reached the alley door it was open. One of the assistants was taking out trash. Tony flashed his shield and the two of them slipped inside. At that point the unexpected sight of two older male strangers skirting the women's dressing room caused one emerging girl to squeal.

Suddenly three male martial artists confronted the officers, poised for combat.

"Police," the Captain whispered to them, again displaying his shield. "Step aside, please."

Chuck took advantage of that confusion to rush twenty feet farther into the room. Bruno was in the teaching area, Tor behind Bruno, and the women students clustered in the middle, with their Korean instructor reading something behind them. But as soon as Chuck recognized Tor's wife, the taller blonde behind her saw Chuck and seized Linda.

The blonde dragged Linda away from a pair of conversing black-belted women who reacted only with gasps.

Both black-belts and the hapkido master froze when from nowhere a shiny blade appeared, pressed across Linda's throat.

Chuck kept advancing until the curly-headed wielder of the knife hollered, "STOP!"

Even the youngsters still partly combative in their white tunics all became motionless.

While Claire glowered at Chuck, Tor backtracked yards toward her left. Only Bruno, with an unobstructed view across the room, did not step closer or need to. He kept his eyes locked very wide on Claire — to deter her from looking to her right, where Captain Tony Marcos crept along the mirrored back wall behind her sightline.

Dispersed across the dojang's front wall, three policemen knew that just days ago this woman had used a knife to kill. Three drawn semi-automatics, two Glocks and a Smith and Wesson, were all aimed in the same direction. But the best position in the room, with a corner behind her and the wall on her left leading unobstructed to the door, was held by Claire Fields.

The worst position was Linda Abelove's.

Staring at the Glock straight ahead of her, with a knife against her throat Linda spoke softly into the silent room.

"Bruno. Please. *Don't hurt my friend."*

FORTY-NINE

THE TAO OF GLOCK

Master Hwan understood that his loss of face was unimportant here. He dared not move. Any motion would attract the attention of this Tamara who could suddenly kick so well. If she glanced his way she'd see the policeman inching towards her along the wall.

What did the officer have in mind? Surely not to rush the woman. He himself might more easily rush her. In less than two seconds he could disarm her.

But if she had any desire to cut her hostage, being rushed would make her use the knife.

No, the stealthy policeman must be angling for a shot.

Without moving his eyes or glimpsing the P226 in the Captain's hand, Hwan watched his advance in a visible flicker of the mirror on the slightly angled wall beside him, even guessing that this officer was left-handed. That would provide a much easier aim along the wall to the woman's right. She clutched her prisoner in front of her, but the policeman was behind.

He might blow off the back of her head, and she would never even have seen him.

"As usual, my wife is right." Abelove's voice tugged Claire's attention left, away from the advancing Captain. "Nobody gets hurt. Just drop the knife. With good will, we can talk this through."

His plea produced a grin that looked more like a sneer.

"PEOPLE WHO THINK EVERYBODY ELSE IS STUPID ARE EASIEST TO FOOL! *READ ALL ABOUT IT!*"

That was not responsive. Ominously, her thoughts seemed elsewhere.

"We'd like to hear all about it!" Sounding as friendly as he had on the day when he met Ms. Fields, Tor capitalized on his obvious admiration for her, which she probably recalled.

"Tell me what you need, to release her. Maybe — have you written to Patrick about it? Toss the knife aside, and tell us, too. Why not? …It must be important?"

While Abelove commanded Claire's gaze, Officer Belknap raised his weapon by degrees.

"Bruno!" begged Linda again. "Mara doesn't mean it."

"Tell me, please, Claire," persisted the detective, in a voice that sounded almost intimate.

Some of the women and younger male witnesses looked perplexed by this semblance of conversation. Why would the pretty captive appeal to the youngest officer, when her husband appeared to be in charge?

"Please, Claire? Let me help you. Christmas is coming. *Help me — for your mother?"*

Why did the cop address his wife's assailant so familiarly?

Master Hwan could not help being moved by the scene before him. For a long time Seoul Dojang had been his business, almost his temple. But this alien situation belonged to the police. He must defer, no matter how abhorrent their intent.

He had wondered before if this young Japanese brought last month by the policeman might not be a natural. In her beginning exercises he'd thought she showed an instinct for the fluid circle. Now, with a knife at her throat, her first impulse was to try to restore harmony.

The fourth cop, to the youngest one's left but now also beyond Hwan's field of vision, was surely too far offside to be any factor, except as a distraction. No doubt his gun too was raised.

But the hapkido master guessed that, to the older men watching, the drama's psychic core was clear. Despite zen Buddhism or one's capacity for empty mind, there were only a limited number of minutes, very few, that any man could tolerate such a threat to such a wife.

Although all four officers were competent with firearms, the youngest, Bruno, was a superb marksman. Lianopoulos and Abelove both knew that Officer Belknap would favor a head shot. They also knew he would consider the added trauma to Linda that witnessing such a wound would entail, and forgo it if he could.

But Captain Marcos, moving in behind those two slender women, could not contemplate any body shot. It would be too dangerous to the innocent citizen in the suspect's tight embrace.

"I don't want anyone hurt, Claire. Professional pride! You understand all about that. And you don't want anyone hurt either. Relax. Talk to me. *Please — a knife is a danger —*"

In the near distance, a wailing siren suddenly ceased.

"Beautiful things die!"

If Abelove hated that, he maintained an even tone. "They don't have to, do they?"

"I SPEAK FOR THE SEA!"

Claire screamed the words, but the long high room absorbed the sound as if it were no more than a squeak on a plastic mat from a twisting rubber-soled shoe. The thirty-odd people watching felt more impact from the ancient rage distorting her young face.

The ambulance siren resumed, closer. In less than a minute it stopped, outside the door.

It had arrived.

In that shocking abrupt silence Claire Fields appeared to laugh. As if she were about to go greet the ambulance her body rotated to her left as her right arm jerked up, pressing the knife under Linda's chin. The reflected flash of raised steel made every witness cry out.

That ended it.

Her torso's pivot exposed Claire's chest.

No one waited.

~ ~ ~

In a millisecond of intense awareness Tor saw that the flat of Claire's blade, not the edge, was pressed to Linda's neck.

But the tao of Glock does not permit reversal of a trigger.

Three weapons' near-simultaneous report deafened the room like a bomb.

Instantly Hwan was there to catch Linda, dragged backwards, before her head could strike the floor. Blood from Tony's shot flooded Claire's blonde wig.

In a crimson pool the yellow curls floated off her normal short brown hair.

Hugging his devastated student, Master Hwan raised his head to confront the vision of a golden dragon with mouth of flames, charging across the floor at him.

He almost felt afraid.

But instead of any dragon's attacking Hwan, Mr. Abelove bowed deeply in apology.

All in the same motion he seized his wife, to carry her from the room where he had sent her to become safe.

Master Hwan bowed after them, also in apology.

With Linda clutched high against his chest Tor strode beyond the ambulance, ignoring the two black-and-whites pulled up just prior to gunfire inside Seoul Dojang. Impatient to gain distance, he trotted downhill, west, where wind not broken by large buildings bore the taste of coming rain.

Today was December tenth, two weeks before Christmas Eve. Friday would bring a full moon, but tonight the sky was hardly dark. He stopped at the intersection. Obeyed the signal.

Beneath street lights they presented an arresting sight — an officer's long legs in military gait crossed by the curved legs of the woman he was carrying, her black tights gleaming, ankles laced by basketball shoes. Somebody waiting at the red light took their photo, struck by the visual rhythm of the man's arms wrapping her back and legs, her arms around his neck, while great black swells of her billowed hair lashed a gale about his head.

Above them the crowns of palms heaved, creaking, as he angled toward the harbor. Fallen fronds twitched, skated over grass, appearing to respire like dying fish.

When they passed those quaking leaves someone in a slow car caught another photo.

But photographs would not reveal blood spray on Linda's face, clothes, hair. Tor was radiating so much heat he didn't consider that she might get chilled. They were both ocean people and he knew where he was taking her. In his mind he saw the wave ascending, more luminous than the night sky — a swayed, wind-warped parabola.

Such waves always came to him.

Rain began to splatter, but he bore ahead still, over glistening sidewalks toward the quay. Her wet face sparkled in kaleidoscopic colors, sequins of reflected neon passing Bar, Pawn, Bail Bonds. She'd begun to shiver but they were almost there. He strode faster, ignored moored boats that knocked and groaned; pictured only the approaching wave, its rising line all musical translucence thinning to the kindest blade. He would carry Linda Kimura out to meet it, let that cleansing plume cascade upon her, a white lace veil that could restore the girl she'd been that day when she was cursed to meet him.

But tonight the harbor's choppy waves were chattering like rats. Around hulking yachts and sailboats the water slunk all oil-stained. Stank of creosote. Hawked up trash.

"Please, I want my children —" Linda was shaking in his arms.

A bad detective, Tor failed to notice the vehicle following until he heard its engine cut.

When he finally turned from the bay, the car door opened.

Officer Smithers stepped out, carrying a blanket.

FIFTY

WITH GOOD WILL

On Thursday morning Tor confessed to Captain Marcos. At the moment he fired, he had seen it was only the flat of the knife pressed against his wife's neck.

"Linda was right. When she told Bruno, 'Mara doesn't mean it.'"

"You must have really good eyesight."

"I do. Comes of never reading much."

"Because Bruno didn't see that, and all I saw was her arm yanking the knife up. That's what everybody saw. Both of us, we were scared that ambulance crew couldn't make it through the door fast enough. To save Linda."

Tor could not speak.

"It was suicide. You were used. We all were. Linda, the worst."

The police killing of a twenty-five-year-old woman in her exercise class at downtown Seoul Dojang, reputed to be frequented by Orchardton gang members, was noted Thursday at the bottom of the *Sentinel*'s front page. The story was small because the reporter sent to cover it was unable to learn much. When she arrived, the shooting victim's body was being removed. Two teens remained watching outdoors. The "gorgeous" victim, White and blonde, had allegedly threatened an Asian woman with a knife. The Asian was married to a former surfing celebrity. Now a member of the SCPD and the lead shooter, he was known to frequent city beaches with young men associated with the Machia and Loberos gangs.

Short but salacious, the story mentioned Abelove by name. Within very few hours, the *Sentinel*'s city desk had received four photographs, all good ones, taken the previous night. Each showed the recognizable Russian surfer striding down South Marina Drive carrying a woman with lovely legs in short shorts and high-top shoes. Unable to decide which to print in Friday's morning edition, the editors had the inspiration of using them all. Dominating page one was the earliest and most dramatic, taken at the Santa Christina Bay Street intersection. Crested by her blowing hair, the couple's bodies crossed over his long legs suggested the shape of a crazed bird. The others appeared on page five. Each sequential locale was identified, tracing the cop's night hike after killing his wife's alleged assailant. On Friday *Sentinel* reporters staked out the route. Sure enough, curious citizens arrived throughout the day, eager to be interviewed about this shocking episode of police brutality furbished by romantic photos.

Many Bay Street Station personnel had occasionally been exasperated by Chief Margolies' political hypersensitivity. However, after the Seoul Dojang event the Chief's instinctive politicking was celebrated by all his officers and by staff personally engaged in Bill's bitterly laid plans. Officially the three who had discharged their weapons were placed on temporary paid leave. Despite public pressure, Margolies played his cards very close and granted no interviews, assuring the paper's editor that "investigations were ongoing" — which was entirely true. But while the department interviewed every witness at the dojang — including the underaged, if their parents agreed — and while they scoured the computers of both Allan Houseman and Claire Fields, they allowed the press to fulminate about a 'cover-up' of a criminal use of excess force in handling what the paper hinted was a sordid mixed-racial sex triangle.

~ ~ ~

One evening Hiroshi Kimura received an unexpected phone call from someone he feared might be a reporter. But the caller's name looked somehow familiar.

"Mr. Kimura," said a husky female voice, "I'm Linda's friend Ingrid Becker. We were supposed to visit a bakery, but she had to cancel. Your kids are being staked out by the press?"

"Oh, yeah."

"I'd appreciate it if you'd give Linda a message. I'm in assisted living now. But I have a house in El Albergue Strand. I'm inviting your daughter's family to move in — until Clematis and Andrew go back to school. No one would know where they are." Ingrid paused to breathe. "Tor could surf every day. It's peaceful."

"That's real kind of you, ma'am. I just — I don't think they could. They have a dog. At the place my wife and me live, no pets allowed. We couldn't take it."

But Mrs. Becker was laughing.

"The rest of my message, sir — my husband and I worked traveling the world. The aspect of that life I regretted was — I couldn't have dogs. I love dogs, and prefer big ones. But even if theirs is small and yippy, I'd be thrilled — if they'd bring it to my house."

~ ~ ~

When Claire Fields yelled like a street newspaper crier, "Read all about it!" she wasn't kidding. The contents of her computers and Allan Houseman's almost mirrored each other. On his home desktop police technicians found nothing incriminating. Brazenly, Houseman had "hidden" records of his illegal dealings, with payments noted and accounts documented, in old scientific data files on his work computer at the Oceanographic Institute.

By contrast, Claire's computer in the shared ocean sciences office contained only departmental business. But in her apartment, behind a huge publicity poster of herself posed straddling Lupe the whale, who appeared to be smiling, the police were ecstatic to find much of Houseman's hard drive, cached on labeled CDs in paper jackets taped to the wall. Clearly she had found his passwords and copied everything to read at home.

Claire's purse still contained a crumpled grocery receipt from Wednesday, December third — the day before Allan disappeared — for two pounds of hamburger.

The Chief allowed accusations against his department to burgeon uncontested. Lacking factual information, the *Sentinel*'s vague 'exposé' soon degenerated into documenting Claire's swimsuit styles and water show performances.

Then with every ducky component arrayed for his own ducks' water ballet, Bill Margolies held his news conference in the Beaux-Arts former bank's Christina Bay Street lobby.

Standing below a large dark television screen, he began, "A couple of minor points before we advance to major ones. First, I'm told there's a rumor of an intimate 'relationship' between Detective Abelove and Ms. Fields. Detective Abelove performed one routine interview of Ms. Fields. That is, he met her for the first and *only time:* December first, at her workplace. Accompanied by a female officer, regarding the murder of Lisette Houseman two days prior."

As Bill knew, that sex scandal by innuendo was the heart of the *Sentinel*'s fabulation.

"And let me add, on a personal note? Detective Abelove is the last man in this building I would ever accuse of having joined the force because he was gun happy. I don't believe he ever expected to use his weapon at all, during his entire police career. He's on leave now because he is so distressed by what he was forced to do in the course of duty. Same goes for my other two officers — who are not being relentlessly maligned."

For a room filled with press and media, Chief Margolies then began laying out his case, working backwards.

"The four officers who infiltrated Seoul Dojang on December tenth went there to arrest Ms. Claire Fields for the murders of both Lisette Marie Houseman and Allan Robert Houseman."

Uproar ensued. The *Sentinel* had never in any way connected Ms. Fields to the Houseman murders. But the Chief didn't bother to pause.

"They had just been tipped that, *using an alias,* Ms. Fields was stalking the wife of Detective Abelove, who was lead investigator of those murders. After what she did to the Housemans, she was regarded as highly dangerous.

"Which she then demonstrated in that martial arts academy.

"Let me emphasize — our testimony from almost three dozen witnesses in that room is unequivocally in agreement. *Every* man. *Every* woman. Every *child* in Seoul Dojang that night believed they had just seen Ms. Fields slice the throat of Mrs. Abelove when three officers felt forced to fire — *with extreme reluctance, because we all REALLY wanted to prosecute her for two barbaric murders.*

"Every witness agrees — the whole room screamed, fearing for Mrs. Abelove. Every aghast witness in that room expected to watch Fields' uncomprehending victim bleed to death —

"— Because Mrs. Abelove had no concept that her pretty *classmate* was as vicious a killer as I've come across in my career."

Margolies hefted a heavy cardboard box onto the table in front of him.

"Transcripts of all that witness testimony, right here. Since many of them are children, all witness names are blacked out.

"— Some of you want to run and make that call, before I launch details?"

While members of the press raced up to collect transcripts, the television screen mounted high on the wall above the Chief lit up, revealing video reproduced from the camera of someone too short to capture coherent images of people talking far across a room as expansive as Seoul Dojang.

First heard was Detective Abelove's voice assuring, "I don't want anyone hurt, Claire. Professional pride! You understand all about that. And you don't want anyone hurt either. Relax. Talk to me. *Please — a knife is a danger."*

The siren of an ambulance interrupted, and then a woman's voice screamed, "Beautiful things die!"

"They don't have to, do they," soothed the sorrowful reply.

The picture flipped to another scene, where the officer encouraged, "Nobody gets hurt. Just drop the knife. With good will, we can talk this through."

Then it cut again, and he entreated, "Please, Claire? Let me help you. Christmas is coming. *Help me — for your mother?"*

At the next splice suddenly all the students of every age were heard shrieking. Even the boy holding the mini camera emitted a soprano squeal, as his hand spasmodically jerked and lowered the camera eye down another student's dobok, then over his own white trouser legs before raising it again, still recording the classes' collective scream.

As members of the press audience crowded to film the overhead TV's video, it looped back to the first snippet and Detective Abelove's insistent, "I don't want anyone hurt, Claire. Professional pride! You understand all about that —"

FIFTY-ONE

STATUS AND PRIDE

The day after Chief Margolies laid out the case against Claire Fields for the murders of Lisette and Allan Houseman, a feature story about her appeared on the *Sentinel*'s front page, column left. Its headline was "I Speak for the Sea!" — Claire's valedictory cry before dying. Recalling the incident of the euthanized whale, Lupe, it pointed out that she protested that action. The next day the paper related the crimes of Allan Houseman, whose falsification of world fish stock numbers threatened the survival of critically important species.

On that same morning, sidewalk vendors downtown began offering T-shirts printed with a picture of Lupe and Claire, emblazoned *"I speak for the sea!"*

Claire Fields' journey toward sanctification had begun. After the media interviewed her family and reverently discussed her "ideas" for a few days, the SCPD's medical examiner became so incensed that he wrote a rebuttal which the *Sentinel* duly printed on its op ed page. In his essay Dr. Davies, who had autopsied both the Housemans, described what Claire's poison had done to Lisette — the terror, pain and probable blindness that pregnant young woman experienced before she tumbled one hundred feet onto rocks backing the Strand.

But Dr. Davies' tragic portrait of a sacrificed literature lecturer could not compete with the image of a bathing beauty who rode a whale bareback before being gunned down by police.

~ ~ ~

Mrs. Becker's house in the Strand proved unconventional.

Before the Abeloves moved in Ingrid assured Linda, "Since your husband is a policeman I should mention. My husband had receipts for everything you see in there. Nothing's pilfered."

They found out what she meant as soon as they opened the door, to be greeted by a life-sized marble statue of a nude male in a straw sunhat. An umbrella hung from his welcoming extended arm, and one shoulder was draped by a jacket with a garden trowel in its pocket.

Antiquities were everywhere. The living room was dominated by an enormous eighteenth century oil painting of deer in the Black Forest, shipped from Matthias Becker's ancestral Bavarian chalet.

After several days Linda was getting tired of sleeping on the sofa, even though now each morning she opened her eyes to those cute deer foraging in a shady woodland. Contrail had moved into the bed with Tor, and Tor seemed fine with that.

She tried talking to him. She said, "Mara was a life. Maybe you need to cry."

"I don't."

"I keep seeing *her* behind your eyes."

Linda really had no idea where her husband was.

"Look at *us*. The children are noticing. Your eyes are always focused inward."

But Tor shunned himself too and refused to visit the police psychologist, who could never expunge his recent interviews with four scientists. Beyond our watery selves, past the planet's final rainfall and last creatures who remembered rain, having known weather as an adjunct bodily process; after the oceans dried and Earth in forfeit sloughed its living face to emerge a pocked and socketed skull sardonically "reflective" in a place where no story remained but Time's, the surfer met his Hell.

"Marjorie? Could you keep the kids for a day and a night? Would that be all right?"

"Sure. Hiroshi just bought an electric ice-cream machine. Are you going someplace?"

"I need to spend a whole day making love to Linda."

"Oh. Well, we'll be eating ice-cream."

Was the Beckers' bedroom meant to be aphrodisiac? Its shelves were lined with artifacts and little figurines, people and animals thousands of years old. Even Matt's favorite, the fossil head of a baby dinosaur, appeared to grin despite its orbits void of eyes.

All these relics attended two golden bodies moving on the bed in living bliss.

That night Linda's choice was to lie before the fireplace. Tor noticed that after centuries the painted Black Forest's oils still glowed, though less than the firelight reflected on her hair.

Important as those hours alone cleaving together were, primal love for the sanctity of Claire's life confined him in withdrawal.

He didn't like her.

She was The Anti-Linda.

In the week before Christmas his surfing students were scheduled for their fifth of twelve classes. When the detective's faded red van arrived at St. Rita's two days before Christmas Eve, his boys were waiting solemnly with one of the nuns. Accusingly Mateo tattled, "José said you wouldn't show up."

"If I can't come, I let you know."

As they climbed in with the boards and neoprene suits, Howie complained, "My mother says, the newspaper put you down for 'associating' with us."

"I don't associate with *them.*"

The kids noticed his flat mood and were surprised by it. They sat quietly for what seemed a long ride — until they realized that today he was taking them all the way north to El Albergue Strand.

When they'd carried their boards onto the beach, a woman with long dark hair who had been sitting there with two young boys stood up. One by one they recognized her from the newspaper photos, even in jeans instead of shorts and tights. The sex-minded teens were exultant, entering an aura between this man and a woman with two boys who proved what he often did with her. Mrs. Abelove pronounced the name of each as she shook his hand, saying, "I'm very happy to meet you."

They sat with Linda, Andy and wriggly Timmy, observing while the surfer cop took them out singly for Monday's lesson. Even though Tor was a bore today and Timmy kept trying to kill his sand toys with his plastic shovel, the friendly lady surfer could explain everything about their classmate's learning exhibition on the water. She knew lots of surfing stories, and proved much more entertaining than the policeman ever was. But sixteen-year-old Howie had once pointed out that the cop never attempted to win their loyalty — only to teach them his sport.

These boys inhabited a culture where having killed someone conferred status and pride. Yet it was obvious to them that their normally energetic instructor was now acting half dead himself. They felt cheated of their usual connection to him. When it was time to start back to Orchardton, they loaded their boards and rinsed suits back into the van. While Abelove was unlocking the passengers' doors, Joey gave him a half grateful, half disappointed hug.

That had never happened before.

Tor kissed the thirteen-year-old's head. Despite their silent machismo, the other teens also hugged him before returning to whatever Christmas held in store for gangland.

~ ~ ~

When Ted Friedland's invitation arrived, at first Tor refused to go. "What's the point of 'Open House' on a Thursday?" he scowled.

"Thursday will be New Year's Day. Day One, Tor. *Aloha?* You told me this Ginger Ted's seeing is very nice too. She writes we should bring the children. Her boy wants to play with them. We're going, and we're even dressing up. *You hear me?"*

The Kimuras were happy to spend New Year's afternoon with Timmy at Ingrid's house, where Marjorie arranged Linda's hair in a traditional updo copied from a Japanese woodblock print. When Tor saw his wife in an unfamiliar dress, a silk sheath the pale yellow of Chinese porcelain, he was surprised.

"You look like a flower," he said. "I'm glad you got a new dress."

"You like it?" she chuckled. "Thirty years ago this little number looked sensational on Mom, Dad says. Maybe it got me conceived?"

Three weeks ago, photos of Linda with her hair soaring through a night storm swept a black-and-white splash in the newspaper. On January First she accompanied her pariah husband to a party where they encountered the new councilman who lived next door. The Chromstads greeted them both cordially. Last month's celebrity had been Linda Abelove, who had no idea of her fame. If people were staring, they might be inspecting her antique hairdo, or Marjorie's vintage shantung dress.

Conversation was difficult because a string quartet was playing in the dining room. Ted also came to welcome them, with a fondness for Tor that seemed almost courtly.

Linda was delighted to see Mrs. Becker across the room with a woman who had to be Ginger Guardian, of the fabled hair like pumpkin pie. Tor meanwhile was surprised to be greeted by Cris Harbison, who labored to say, "You — o' all peo'l' — *a goo - d new year!"* as he clapped Tor's weapon hand.

But almost before he recognized a familiar tall, broad back, Detective Abelove felt his heart pounding with anxiety. Cautiously he walked up behind that conversation. The woman's face he had seen sometime, although he didn't recall her name.

"— About babysitters," she was saying. "The dishwasher's computer was haywire, and right that afternoon he fixed it for me."

As Tor nodded when she craned around her companion's shoulder, the large man turned.

"How wonderful to see you!" he exclaimed. "Gloria, you must remember my dear friend, Detective Abelove?"

Ogy caught Tor in a bear hug radiating such balm that for a few seconds the younger man lacked any will to let go.

"Please," insisted Dr. Bradley, "After this, you must come to my house! Ingrid has been pining to see Linda. If you want, go collect the children's swimsuits. Gloria's husband just installed a Booster Boy on the mountain for me, so our pool is warmer now."

Meeting Ted's nerdy partners from Sanchrist Technologies, Tor expected to be regarded with subtle scorn or even open contempt. But despite the *Sentinel*'s campaign against him, these M.I.T. and Cal Tech men lit up with something closer to the wonderment of surfing circuit fans.

By now the house was sufficiently filled with people that no one noticed when Ted, Ginger and Peter all slipped away. But when the quartet began to play the *Lohengrin* march, the glow of the large downstairs chandelier lowered while another chandelier behind the second floor balcony slowly brightened.

All the downstairs guests looked up.

The first person to appear on the balcony was unfamiliar to most of the guests. Next, when Ginger in a blue silk suit and Ted in an unlikely morning coat joined the rabbi, immediately a collective sigh welcomed them, followed by applause.

The ceremony was not long. Ten-year-old Peter handed over the rings without mishap. Tor felt his eyes misting, in part because six months ago he had first entered this house to investigate a murder. Despite the photo of an alert cat on the piano, it had seemed so lifeless.

Then from the balcony Ginger was tossing her bridal bouquet. One of the young Sanchrist designers caught it, and his friends all cheered.

After the newlyweds returned downstairs, Ogy kissed the bride's cheek and exclaimed, "I don't know which of you I'm happier for!"

"Oh, Dr. Bradley, I can't believe how much I love him! When we met I thought he seemed nice but immature. But that's not true. Ted has a youthful personality, and always will. But he's a wise man."

Ogy bent to whisper in her ear, *"I know."*

He and Tor watched the circle of the Sanchrist brotherhood open to welcome their new sister and her husband. Having checked Andy and Clemma outdoors, Linda found Tor again. Her light arm wrapped his waist.

In this company, no demon interceded to spit poison on his love for her.

FIFTY-TWO

COSMIC CONFLICT

Timothy insisted on remaining at Ingrid's funny toys house with his dog, grandparents and ice cream, but Clematis and Andrew wanted to swim in Ogy's heated pool. They were excited about making underwater faces illuminated by bright lights. To accompany them, Linda changed into jeans and the basketball shoes that had been selling out across Santa Christina. (Vice officers never informed Homicide Division that recently black-wigged prostitutes had been frequenting the streets wearing high-topped black shoes with tights, shorts and a hoodie.)

~ ~ ~

While they waited for the Abeloves to arrive, Ogy continued fretting to Ingrid that he could not resist devising "plans" for Cris Harbison.

"I keep wondering if with speech therapy he couldn't become credentialed to teach biology or chemistry," he brooded. "Maybe to special-needs children? I hate myself when I think of getting their hopes up, but he just seems so promising. After solving the blocks puzzle he couldn't stop fiddling with it, trying other schemes —"

"Still a scientist then. And such merry eyes, I noticed today. Children would like him. For a gymnast? Speech therapy shouldn't be too challenging."

When the Abeloves entered his home Ogy finally noticed that Tor appeared unnaturally listless. His sense that something was amiss heightened when, before joining her children in the water, Linda cast her husband an apprehensive glance, as if worried he might misbehave.

With the gas heater keeping the patio table comfortable, Tor sat between Ingrid and Ogy, under fairy lights. For a while they chatted contentedly about Ted, Ginger, Peter and Babby's house. But after that tactful interval, Ingrid digressed to the point.

"How are you managing, Detective?"

Tor shook his head.

"I couldn't figure out Artie Vaccari. What game that man was playing. Now… I've become him. And there isn't any game. It's just dark."

"With all this nonsense making Fields a heroine, I find myself thinking — in your place, I'd feel damned wedded to her." Ogy passed him a wine glass.

Tor nodded, "Now she owns the ocean."

"There's room for you."

Ingrid poured Bordeaux, patting Tor's arm. "Was Linda very frightened?"

"No, ma'am, I was. Or, I should say — not for herself, she wasn't scared. But our junior officer who was there? He could shoot a running rat between the eyes."

Tor quickly swiveled to check behind them, where his wife's slender arms cut clefts through a liquid bar of azure light.

"She could have died right there, and never have believed what was happening...

"With every case I make mistakes. But this! It was... *risk shooting Linda... or else risk....*"

"Just tell it all... to Omar."

Like a bass viol, Ingrid's rough voice throbbed through him.

Linda's elderly friend always offered such unvarnished candor that admitting fears came more easily than thinking them. How Dr. Savage told Nicola about the Adlers' party. How he'd been all but convinced he'd have to arrest Cris's mother.

"That paralysis of will made me late contacting the parents of Claire's fiancé. They complain — he enlisted because she was too controlling. Imagine, preferring war."

"I can well imagine not wanting to arrest Cris's mother," Ogy commiserated.

"You haven't seen her. But —" Despite the tiny lights like a closer rim of stars circling the umbrella, the detective cast a shadow of malaise. "— I should have prevented this! *How?* You'd figured it out already by the time we released Artie. What was I supposed to see, to stop it?"

To Dr. Bradley it was a most welcome sign of mental health that his friend tried to focus on policing, instead of surrendering to tormented conscience. So relief made Ogy sound incongruously cheerful protesting, "You give me too much credit! I'd say, you weren't deceived, just misled by a criminal's blunders and bad luck."

"I see how bumbling it was, poisoning the wrong person," agreed Ingrid. "But one question's baffled me since you deserted Ted and me and your clams?" A gasp for breath.

"Why was Claire at that martial arts place — where Ted knew her, long before Seoul, also with an *alias* — ? Before Priscilla even dreamed up her Black Saturday?"

"Ah. But there's a corollary. Why did she later switch dojos, yes — but enroll at Seoul Dojang as a beginning student?"

"To infiltrate Linda, spying on me. Plus, her dad didn't want her involved in anything dangerous," recalled Tor.

"Presuming any of this was rational," grumbled Ingrid.

"I do. Concealing her skills could have been important."

"If she got identified as 'Claire Fields' at Seoul Dojang? She was a student who didn't want her risk-averse parents to find out," Tor repeated. "What other motive?"

"Claire seems rancorously obsessed by Allan. Maybe he belittled her somehow?"

"Oh, very plausible. He had plenty of snark to go around."

Ogy nodded. "That young woman — haughtiness would rankle her. Did anyone at the ocean school know she was a martial artist? Keeping that secret could account for the alias. It's made me wonder — could her original fantasy have been to kick Allan to death *herself?* "Improbable, but — Tor, imagine — being beaten to death by a woman? Might be the perfect crime."

"What a thought. You're right, though, even cops would never consider such a possibility, without knowing she had the skills."

"Putting that unlikelihood aside — judging by her research, from what's been revealed about the bribe-taking and so forth, Houseman's murder was meant to be an assassination. Targeting him was a 'pure' motive, idealistic?"

"I won't justify murder. That's what terrorists do. Applaud the holy motive."

"Contrary to what the *Sentinel* writes, you're more principled than most of us."

"But the surprise? Her snoop files didn't contain gossip about anyone else. Only Allan."

"So possibly she stumbled on something, overheard him on the phone, got suspicious? Maybe her motives were both 'the sea' *and* personal. I suspect her anger was stoked by more than just Allan's malfeasance. After the whale injured someone, she gave up celebrity for a zero-visibility office job. Probably surrounded all day by middle-aged women. Hard to believe she wasn't somewhat gripped by bitterness. Was that beauty content to dead-end facing the wall at a desk? How tempting was the chance… to make a big difference? Even if only she knew."

The delivery girl from Mariscos Valorosos rang the doorbell. Tor beat Ogy to the door and paid. While Linda and the children changed out of wet swimsuits, the feast of seafood tacos, salad and guacamole was spread across the table. Clemma and Andy wanted to eat indoors in front of the TV, with Ghazi. Ingrid brought candles from the dining room to celebrate the year's first dinner.

Linda's luminous skin outshone the candles as she offered a toast.

"Mr. and Mrs. Friedland! May their married life be as happy as all of ours."

After several bites of langoustine taco Ogy resumed, "*Black Saturday* — so suggestive. The coincidence of the Adlers' party falling on Mrs. Fields' birthday might even have seemed a goad — a divine intervention! Tipping Claire into a much better scheme than she'd probably fantasized about. *No martial art required.*

"But when her sneaky justice went terribly wrong she must have been frantic. So much so that the message appeared on Housemans' wall, to proclaim the rectitude of her intent."

"When Smithers and I visited the Institute, she cried about Lise. I give her that."

"No doubt. Losing Lisette ended the fantasy that she was an avenging angel of ecology. Imagine the stupefaction of learning that Houseman had *made her responsible* for Lisette's death!"

"So killing Allan mitigates sacrifice of his wife?" Ingrid crested a chip with guacamole. "She does sound like a personality disposed to act, not weigh."

"At least —" Linda rose to go check her children playing in the house" —— "I can stop feeling so guilty about not warming to her. Her eyes on me always felt… mmm… under my skin."

While Ingrid observed Tor with her bemused scholarly smile, Ogy continued, "Figuring out that Cris Harbison was born 'Vaccari' — and also learning that was the name of one party waiter— would have seemed a bonanza, casting suspicion on Artie. My guess? It's likely Claire never connected Houseman with either Vaccari or Cris Harbison. *Not at all.*

"She was Allan's contact in the office. Probably, he'd told her when to expect him back from Norwald. It was easy to plant a grocery cart in his backyard."

"Almost for sure, we collected Vaccari before Houseman got home from Norwald. I clocked the drive from Fairwaye Inn. He would have been slower at rush hour."

"So after the mistaken poisoning, that was her second piece of rotten luck — incriminating someone who was already in police custody when Allan disappeared. Creating a look-alike of a familiar person who time-wise could not have done it."

"You said, you thought she *did not* know the connection between Artie and Allan —?"

"She *didn't* know. But *you police did find out* Artie was Cris's dad!"

"So I jumped to a bum conclusion. Right."

"By chance, Claire's homeless-with-cart masquerade strongly implicated a man of interest to you. *By her bad luck,* that man had an alibi. (Imagine, if he hadn't!) So you defaulted back to your lady-angry-at-a-traitor scenario. Because, her third episode of flukey luck was that Allan's body beached in Rosarito. The knife-in-the-back attack reinforced your female killer hunch.

"— What's the chance that administrator you spoke to at the water park phoned her?"

"Awful thought." Ingrid grimaced. "She would know you must be closing in."

Ogy nodded. "But three days prior, the man with the Mercedes took his final ride — cramped in a supermarket cart, shrouded with trash bags."

Sliding back onto the bench beside Ingrid, Linda pleaded, "But why?"

"Just conceivably, dear, so this homeless gray wanderer might be remembered and suspected — *especially* if she'd learned who Vaccari was, with a motive to kill Allan. That idea is logically pleasing but extremely unlikely. As remote as the chance the police would find the abandoned cart with blood evidence and begin inquiries.

"But the third, obvious reason is overwhelming."

"Ghoulish," shuddered Linda. "Roaming so close to his dead body. For hours?"

"She even pretended to snooze beside him under the pedestrian bridge," Tor frowned.

"While his pockets were packed with shark bait? That's taking dramatics a bit far." Ingrid was a minimalist thinker.

"I bet she enjoyed acting again," Ogy grinned. "Especially, impersonating an old man?" Nostalgically he mused, "For after dark trick-or-treating, Sylvia drew in little Anthea's witch wrinkles with light eyebrow pencil. Sure scared me."

"She took an unnecessary chance," insisted Ingrid. "Wandering with a corpse in a cart!"

"Ooooooh, NO, NECESSARY!"

The surfing teacher slumped, head in hands. *"She had to wait for ebb tide!* A rough water swimmer! She would know the currents too…!"

"Exactly. *To wait,* until she could haul him out — or dump him off the pier? That was the utterly simple purpose of the disguise. Being seen all around the Strand area as *somebody the physical opposite of Claire Fields —"*

"HOW could I possibly have overlooked considering the tide? HOW! ME?"

"You've just been telling us *how.* You were worried sick that Mrs. Harbison might have invaded the Adlers' party. You stopped thinking about your stranger with a cart, that's how.

"— Because it had to be done in this ritual way. The ocean should consume Allan as callously as he disregarded it. He was meant to disappear, like all the happy fish from the acidifying sea."

"Would any of this have happened?" pondered Linda. "If her whale friend didn't die?"

"So — Ogy? Still — how did you unravel all this? What did I miss?"

"Honestly? You missed arguing with Ingrid."

"Huh. That's a first," huffed Ingrid, rising to fetch more wine.

"After Lisette's death — of course that catastrophe was total bafflement — I was wailing that it didn't make sense for someone so mild to be murdered so maliciously. And Ingrid accused me of thinking like 'an important person' — she meant 'arrogant.' She argued that murder motives tend to be crudely prosaic. She said, 'Murder doesn't usually have cosmic implications.'

"But later I wondered, *What if it does?* Because even if this killer isn't somehow powerful, it might very easily be someone messianic. With a huge message for the world."

"As our 'TRAITOR!' graffiti did hugely confirm," admitted the disgruntled detective.

"It was that scruffy gray-haired fellow with the cart, killing time on a wet night *without smoking,* that sealed it for me. An actor center stage — her favorite place! — with a corpse concealed in plain sight until the wee hours when the tide would usher him away.

"It's a terrible honor Claire conferred on you, Detective. Whether consciously or just by instinct, she chose her executioner. Claire liked you more than you guessed."

"Understatement," grimaced Ingrid, returning with a bottle of sparkling rosé. "With her 'I'm-the-star' ego, she checked out Linda — how hard would his wife be to displace? My guess, Claire fell for Tor. Like falling on a sword."

"In her mind," Ogy nodded, "Her chosen death may have been almost an act of love."

"But *why?*" pleaded Linda again. "What could make such an 'honor' necessary?"

"My dear Catholic girl — why die *a holy martyr?* For a cause she truly believed in? Instead of living as a reviled felon convicted of two such ugly murders?"

"When we mentioned Claire to Allan he just dismissed her, as not knowing ocean science."

"But she did care. Until Claire announced it, there was one unspoken presence all through this case. It's revolved about the sea — the subject of Harbison's love and Houseman's indifference.

"— There's your cosmic conflict, Ingrid.

"Think of Tor, Linda. He loves the ocean less than he loves you, but still it's fundamental in him.

"Imagine never stepping into the sea again? Not smelling it, or hearing the surf? Consider, for the rest of his life, having no hope of even seeing the ocean. Ever."

"That far," moped Tor, "I did not think."

"Your rough water swimmer had to think… finally."

Primly, Linda sat forward like a child called upon in school.

"What you explain about the end convinces me," she nodded, with a genuine smile for Dr. Bradley. "But, about the beginning…?

"Mrs. Houseman died from her fall. Not from the 'poison.' What if Mara didn't mean to *kill* Mr. Houseman, at all? Just to make him very sick, with bad home-brew potato juice?

"Throwing up — or getting violent diarrhea at an important party, with so many people? That would be awfully embarrassing.

"— I'm not being charitable, just trying to be fair.

"Imagine — the whispering about how *Dr. Houseman stunk up the Adlers' bathroom?*"

"If Allan was such a snob, he'd be remembered with ridicule, forever. But when he passed the drink to his nice wife instead, and she died accidentally — Mara had to be horrified, and furious. I can believe then she really did want to kill him."

"You keep saying "Mara'," Tor pointed out. "What about —"

"The fake name? Oh, she craved attention. And probably she wanted to keep dating, behind Patrick's back, but with no risk he'd find out — just in case he ever did come back to her. They weren't exactly engaged, you said. Could be she even suspected he was dumping her? He did disappear to Afghanistan.

"Tor, I think she was shopping around for a replacement lover. Especially in dojos — two, that you know of. Mara would only want someone strong, and super athletic. Like you."

All three were staring at Linda as if they didn't recognize her. The detective looked incredulous.

"THOSE — were two strokes of Occam's razor!" laughed Ogy. "Well done, Linda!"

Then with a hand on the detective's shoulder he added, "You've gotten too thin, Tor. You look like a defector from the Russian ballet. I've no idea how you close this wound, forgive yourself.

"But you must. You *are* important — and not replaceable from any dojo."

FIFTY-THREE

EPILOGUE

Early on January second when 'El Al' University's administrators convened in Chancellor Hughes' office, the air was already clear. From his conference room windows the "padre view" displayed gloriously. Sunlight striking Father Baroja's shoulder atop Mount Reposo was deflected north across the Strand neighborhood to the administration building's upper floors.

"Each time he starts his laser winking that way," observed the Chancellor, "I get the feeling Jacobo Baroja is headed here to filch my coffee."

"Maybe he just wants to register for a class," suggested the Ethics Officer. "In ethics, of course."

That chuckle at the expense of the reprobate priest put everyone in a mood to get through this business quickly. Provost Adler having recused himself, the Chief Counsel read aloud a letter from the Director of the Sculpture Garden. Protesting that the addition of any new sculpture was his own prerogative, he insisted that the gift under consideration should be submitted for his approval; or, in the case of a commission for a new work, that selection of the sculptor to be awarded the job also fell within his purview. After pointing out that all the administrators lacked arts background, he suggested that, in fact, the creator of the sculpture garden's beloved crustacean orator did not have pressing work at the moment and would be available to execute a provoking new interpretive project.

The administrators' problem was that the substantial gift in question was contingent upon the donors' selecting the sculptor themselves. Otherwise the offer would be rescinded.

"Why are you all so quiet?" chafed Chancellor Hughes. "I have better things to do. I recommend we reject the caviller's protest and gratefully accept the donation.

"Any discussion…?

"All in favor…?"

During the past weeks' news controversy about the Houseman murders, the Seoul Dojang shooting and its aftermath of T-shirts glorifying a murderess, the only overlooked party was the family on whose premises those controversies began. To express their own sentiments, early in January Hiram, Priscilla and Wolf Adler made a brief trip to Mexico City, where they had arranged to meet a realist sculptor whose work they admired. For his studies they brought a portfolio of photographs of Lisette Houseman. Included was one of Audrey Hepburn from the film *Sabrina*, in which the young star wore a black top and slim black pants with flat shoes, similar to Lisette's usual teaching costume.

Placed outside the Humanities Building, the life-sized bronze would appear to welcome students to Mrs. Houseman's history of the novel class. In a gesture to euthanized Lupe, the smiling lecturer would hold a dog-eared book whose engraved title would be legible as *Moby Dick.*

The End

Acknowledgements

No one has ever been a more prized friend and mentor than Rita Przybyla Rotta, whom I quickly grew to love in high school, when she made grammarians of us all. Rita also engendered my first recognition of the concept of a gifted personality: that even a familiar individual can possess powers of character and intellect able to influence and uplift others. Enthusiastically she has read all the Cop&Doc chapters as they were created. Also appreciated is the generous interest of Ken Hull, John and Helen Schoenhals Hart, Anne Pollock, Diane Petryk and Diemut Heller, who indulgently coddled messy mystery newborns. Besides much photo editing and technical drawing, with great patience talented Julie Taylor has contributed not just invaluable guidance, but also artistic inspiration in creating an often challenging book design. Knightly friend and photographer Lane Hauck performed pixel wizardly. Also, I must acknowledge the generosity of Monotype in allowing their airy "Rosella Deco" font to surf across the Cop&Docs' chapter numbers.

Long after his passing, in a world that often seems less civilized than when I knew him, I remain grateful to Princeton professor of Islamic Studies and former Christian missionary T. Cuyler Young. Professor Young's extensive experience and friendships in the Mideast contributed rare authenticity to an exceptional class that pried open our minds to the possibility of comity among the world's great religious cultures. On a similar theme, I remain grateful to my late father, whose gift to a small daughter of a large, repeatedly read tome describing ancient wonders of the world surely inspired creation of the Becker and Bradley archaeology team. — *Reader, give your children challenging books!*

For his manifestly painful candor, I must admit an obligation to — Anonymous: a Soviet-born naturalized American who years ago riveted us natives at the table with an aggrieved description of the bad citizenship practiced by members of his own expatriate social circle. As nearly as I can reproduce that litany of petty crimes and his own moral distaste, they are transcribed in Detective Abelove's confession of the humiliation he feels from association with "Soviets." (Sometimes surfing champion Abelove betrays an edgy streak of inferiority complex. At first that vulnerability appeared just sensitivity about his lack of education. But as his children grow older I attribute it more to the "un-American" conduct of their granddad's grifter circle.)

Friends who must be thanked for color contributions are Steve Bolton, who at age thirteen revealed a precocious vocation for medicine that proved saintly; and ardent animal advocate Sandra Nobile, for a most memorable introduction to the dog park. Model of graciousness Rocco Nobile is the Cop&Docs' single character cast more from life than imagination. Barbara Zirino introduced the fertile notion of oceanographic research cruises. (Also, since the '60s I am grateful to restaurant Villa d'Este for letting *Gourmet* magazine publish its veal chop recipe.)

In various ways all the California-based Cop&Docs involve immigrants. Born into Detroit's immigrant community, I must acknowledge the essential example in my own first eighteen years, the grandmother who cared for me. These novels memorialize her as the Bradleys' beloved cleaning dominatrix, Mrs. Park, who even without schooled English always makes herself understood.

About TEKLA Press

Prior to World War I, my maternal grandmother was a farmer in her early twenties when she and her small son boarded a ship in Hamburg to join her unreliable husband in the New World. With courage, intelligence and devotion, as an almost-single mother she cleaned other people's houses, raised three children and elevated our family into the lower middle class. More than a century after she left Ukraine, I discovered her baptismal record among my mother's papers, and was shocked. The name "Tillie" with which she signed documents throughout her life had been pressed upon her by immigration authorities who discarded her true given identity, *Tekla*: an ancient Scandinavian name presumably transported to Ukraine and other countries by Viking explorers. Because my mother worked, my grandmother was the household influence to whom I attribute my pleasure in flowers. She particularly loved gathering dried bouquets of orange berries from Michigan's wild bittersweet vines, a sprig of which becomes the logo of her eponymous press. With these novels, I declare the name of a woman lost many decades ago. Yet almost daily, as roses bloom and fruit ripens, my heart cries, *Nanny! How I wish I could show you my garden!*

Freya S. 2022